MOKI STEPS

A fast-paced, vividly realistic adventure story that
tests character connections, motivations, choices, and chance.
—D. Donovan, Senior Reviewer
MIDWEST BOOK REVIEW

... features captivating elements of Aztec culture.
—KIRKUS REVIEWS

MOKI STEPS

J. REED RICH

Arête Book Group
Denver, Colorado

first edition

Arête Book Group
PO Box 260722
Denver, CO 80226

LIBRARY OF CONGRESS CATALOGING-IN-PUBLICATION DATA
Rich, J. Reed
Moki Steps / J. Reed Rich
p. cm.
ISBN 978-0-9976352-4-9

[CIP DATA TO COME]

Printed in the United States of America
1 3 5 7 9 10 8 6 4 2

This is a work of fiction. Names, characters, places, and incidents are the product of the author's imagination or are used fictitiously. Any resemblance to actual persons, living or dead, is entirely coincidental. Any similarity to businesses, corporations, institutions, companies, events, or locales is also entirely coincidental.

The author has made every effort to provide accurate telephone numbers and Internet addresses at the time of publication. Neither the publisher nor the author assumes any responsibility for errors or for changes that occur after publication or for third-party websites or their content.

*I would like to thank several individuals who
provided much assistance, from spitballing in the canyons
to proofreading and critiquing in the wee hours.*

*First and foremost, thanks to my wonderful husband
for believing in me, despite the odds.*

*Thanks also, to my daughter, Amanda, for reading
numerous rounds of drafts and for always being honest.*

*My endless gratitude goes to Judy Pottle and Mike Loyd
for their excellent proofreading.*

*And to my daughters Emily and Joanna:
Thanks for being supportive and proud and encouraging.*

CHAPTER 1

A TRICKLE OF SWEAT SLID DOWN HER LEFT TEMPLE. MACKENZIE Campbell swiped at the defiant drop, glad her back was to her students. On the white board in front of her she wrote, "The boy gave her the telescope."

She turned and gazed at them, or rather, at the clock on the wall behind them. "Okay. Who wants to diagram this sentence?"

The summer sun picked its way into her classroom through streaked windows that didn't open, and dust motes floated around her.

Her hand trembled, and she forced it to her side. This is ridiculous, she thought. I've been teaching for a year now. These are freshman college kids. I should be able to call on a student without shaking.

Again she urged the class to respond, turning toward the board. "Come on. This is an interesting sentence. Really."

A few students tittered.

Mackenzie felt her ears turning red and she imagined their words, low and snarky, behind her back. Sticks and stones, she thought. Ignore them.

Swallowing, she said, "Jerry, why don't you give it a try?"

A boy with spiky black hair and hipster glasses scanned the room, eyebrows arched over thick black frames. He rose slowly.

She handed him the marker, avoiding his eyes, and walked to her desk. "You know, Gertrude Stein once said, 'I really don't know anything more exciting than diagramming sentences.' "

"Then let her do it," Jerry muttered. The class laughed in unison, like Jell-O wiggling on a plate.

"Who's Gertrude Sty?" A blonde in the front row asked, frowning.

Mackenzie clamped her mouth shut and sought out the clock again, wrapping her arms around herself in a protective embrace.

It had happened again. She had lost control of the class. Her heart seized in her chest and it took everything she had not to run. It was her, she knew. She was the problem. She just couldn't convey the importance of the fundamentals. How diagramming sentences would help them understand the intricacies of grammar.

The class was Survey of Linguistics, an interdisciplinary course she had created to fulfill one of the English Department's composition class credits. It was an experiment she had proposed to her Dean.

And it looked like the experiment was failing.

Her students had complained from the beginning. It wasn't the easy 'A' they had hoped for.

Jerry asked, "Why do we have to diagram sentences?"

"It helps you learn sentence structure."

"It seems pointless," he countered. "I'll never use this in real life."

"Think of it as the foundation. Like a skill you need for your job."

"And are there jobs like that?"

"Not many."

"Do they pay well?"

"Uh," she floundered, "no." She couldn't lie to him. That would break the student-teacher trust she wanted so desperately.

"There you go. I'm more into the flow and the bigger picture."

She tried again. "Diagramming sentences helps you understand the logic of sentences and the function of words. *That* will help you write better."

Sherry, a brunette in the back of the class said, "I doubt it. Why would I ever take the time to draw little pictures of the sentences I write?"

Mackenzie understood then that arguing would only make it worse. She just couldn't persuade them to give it a chance. It struck her that she was the one being tested, not the other way around. That trusting your teacher to be an authority was old-fashioned and naïve. There was the Internet, after all. And YouTube.

Ten minutes remained until the end of class. She walked over to the board and erased the offending words. "I'll see you all Monday." She exited, not looking at her students.

Once outside she stopped, waiting for her heart rate to slow. Why couldn't she do this? She was a professor of linguistics at a top university. She had published papers in prestigious journals—and was considered an expert in Uto-Aztec languages. Why couldn't she motivate a group of 18-year-olds?

She headed for the parking lot, skirting clumps of students who seemingly rose from the lawn like overgrown bushes. As she walked, her heels punctured the grass, forcing her into an awkward gait.

Safe in her car, she rolled the window down, letting the pungent scent of grass and asphalt and exhaust fumes seep in. She studied her eyes and nose in the visor mirror with dismay and wiped a red slash from her chin. Smudged mascara exaggerated the paleness of her skin, and rebellious strands of coppery hair frizzed about her shoulders.

She closed her eyes. It was Friday afternoon. No more classes today, but she was slated to be in her office to help the students who rarely came. She thought about the survey class and remembered how her ex-boyfriend, Charlie, had complained that she was too traditional, too rigid. That she never tried anything new.

Well, she had tried something new. She had spearheaded this survey class.

And it had bombed.

Later that afternoon, she lounged on the second-story deck outside her apartment with her friend, Hillary.

"You can't let them ruffle you." Hillary poured herself a second glass of Cabernet. "They're just kids. You have to show them you're the boss. You know, like dogs. Or is it men?"

They laughed. A soft breeze flicked aspen leaves and ruffled the tips of badly mown grass. The deck, although small, faced east and offered respite from the late afternoon heat. A wooden fence separated the tiny yard below them from the alley, providing the illusion of privacy.

The friends had developed a tradition of spending Friday evenings discussing the week over a bottle of wine. On the surface they were a mismatched set. Mackenzie, lean and angular, almost rangy, was nothing like her short, curvy, oh-so-compelling friend.

Suddenly serious, Hillary continued, "What's going on, really? I mean you know your stuff. You speak twelve languages, for Christ's sake. You know linguistics inside and out."

And I can diagram the first sentence of A Tale of Two Cities, Mackenzie added silently.

"So, what happened?" Hillary leaned in.

Mackenzie slouched on a slatted Adirondack chair, her legs hanging over the wide wooden arm. "I don't know. You're the shrink. You tell me."

"I am not a shrink," Hillary retorted. "I'm a psychology professor. There's a difference."

Mackenzie brought her knees to her chest and smiled. It was a long-running feud between them. "Right, I forgot." She shifted in her chair. "It sounds so ridiculous, Hill. I love everything about linguistics. And I'm good at it. It seems logical I should teach. But I'm not so sure anymore. I don't know what it is. I just can't seem to connect with them."

"You have to hang in there. It's the first time for a new class. Creating a curriculum is hard. It's only the second week of the session. It will get easier. You'll find your stride."

"I hope so," Mackenzie said. "All I know is I'm not getting through." She munched on a carrot stick.

Hillary traced the rim of her wine glass with a bright pink fingernail. "Well, I think it's particularly hard for you, because you look so young. And, you're introverted. The world is not easy for introverts."

"Introverted meaning 'nerdy.' I know what you mean." Mackenzie held up her wine glass. "And you're right, I must look young. I still get carded at bars sometimes. At thirty-four years old."

"You're complaining about that?"

"Well, I guess I should be grateful, but it's kind of insulting."

"Just wait till you're forty," Hillary said, raising an eyebrow. "Then you'll be glad you look young."

Mackenzie changed the subject. "You know, I'm worried about Garrison. He's been observing my classes this week. I keep freezing."

"Mac, department heads always try to intimidate new teachers. Don't let Garrison worry you. Stop being afraid and trust yourself. You just have to give it some time. How the hell did you pass public speaking in college, anyway?"

Mackenzie swirled her wine, taking a long sip before speaking. "I didn't. I traded my way out of it. Did extra credit for the department head."

"Figures. You are a nerd, Professor Campbell."

"It's hopeless," Mackenzie agreed, tipping her glass in a toast.

After Hillary left, Mackenzie sat down at her desk, feeling pleasantly drowsy. As she shuffled some papers aside to make room for her laptop, her cell phone rang. She glanced at it and vaulted out of her chair. The display read, *C.A. Peterson.*

Charlie. Her ex-boyfriend. The phone buzzed around in the papers like a dying insect. She perched on the edge of the desk, watching it.

She had met Charlie while researching ancient Mesoamerican languages at Arizona State University. He was an exchange student from the University of Utah studying art history. They had shared a few graduate seminars and ended up studying together, drifting into dating without even realizing it. After several months, it had ended badly. He had broken up with her over the phone.

She took a sip of wine and clicked on her voicemail, her heart tap-dancing in her chest.

"Mac, I think I've hit on something big. Really big. I need your help. Can you get away for a few weeks? It could mean a lot to your career. Call me as soon as you can."

She listened to the message again, realizing he hadn't even asked how she was. It was always about him. Curiosity turned to irritation. How could he call after more than a year and ask for help? After how he had left things? She rose, poured a glass of wine, and called him.

He answered immediately. "Mac. I'm so glad you called me back. What do you think? Can you come out?"

"Where are you, Charlie?" She gulped wine, dribbling it down her chin, and hoped he couldn't hear the warble in her voice.

"I'm in Page, Arizona. I've been working on my dissertation. On Navajo sand painting."

"Yes, I heard you were getting your Ph.D. Finally." A barb, she realized, too late. Oh, well.

But he didn't miss a beat. "Yup. Well, I found something while I was researching the Wetherills. You remember them?"

She searched her memory, recalling that Richard and Louisa Wetherill had operated a trading post in Utah in the 1920s. Richard had found several cliff dwellings—including Mesa Verde—and was known for exploring the Four Corners area.

"I remember a little," She said. "Didn't the Navajos call her 'Slim Woman?' And let her represent them with the government?"

"Yeah. She even adopted two little Navajo girls. Mac, this woman was awesome. She had this unbelievable collection of sand paintings, so I was looking into her, just poking around. I discovered she collected and translated Navajo legends and myths, and I got sidetracked."

No surprise there. Charlie might be adventurous, but he had a tough time staying on task.

He continued. "She was so audacious, especially for the time period. Fearless. But she never published anything, and the material she collected on her trips was lost. In fact, most all of what she translated disappeared." He paused.

"Go on."

"Well, I found some of her notes." His voice rose, cracking slightly. She held the cell phone away from her ear.

"O-kaaaaay." She was intrigued, but annoyed, by his stop-and-go storytelling.

"You won't believe it. Hear me out. I pieced some things together, and I think I've found her translation of a legend about a store of gold. Gold the Aztecs hid from Cortés back when he was wiping them out."

She laughed. "Gold? Aztecs? Charlie, I think you've been in the desert too long. This sounds like a bad movie."

"Funny. Listen, she wrote about some sort of document, a map or something, that points the way to the gold. The Navajos told her it was hidden in a cave out near Rainbow Bridge. You know, by Lake Powell."

She put her glass down and sighed.

He surged on. "You see, there's this Navajo legend about gold hidden by an ancient people.' Louisa never looked for it, probably out of respect for the Navajo. But her notes tell where to find it, or really, where to find the map."

He stopped to take a breath. "If it's really Aztec, the map's got to be written in classic Nahuatl. That's why you have to come. You're the expert."

He was right. She had written her dissertation about vowel shifts in Nahuatl. "I don't know," she said. "Tell me more."

"Come out to Arizona. I want to leave in two weeks. It's the chance of a lifetime."

She glanced at the calendar hanging above her desk. "Charlie, I'm teaching two summer sessions. I can't possibly leave." Besides, she thought, *I don't know where we stand.*

The phone was silent.

"Are you still there?" She looked at it, wondering if they'd been cut off.

"Yes." One word. She could hear the disappointment. Her heart constricted again.

Charlie, true to his nature, pressed on. "Come on, Mac. This is right up your alley. Think of how important it could be for your research. You can always get someone else to take your classes. This is momentous. It could lead to gold, for God's sake. Montezuma's legendary gold."

It would be an extraordinary find, and it *would* help her research. She felt queasy, though, and manipulated. "It sounds interesting. It does. But can't it wait? I can't leave until after the sessions."

There was another long pause. Then, "I thought this would be good for us. And good for you. It's in your field, after all."

Her thoughts collided. *Us? There was no 'us.'* Was he saying he wanted to get back together? She said, "Let me call you after finals. Maybe we could get together and talk about it."

"Never mind. I'm sure I can find someone else to go."

"It's waited this long. Can't it wait a few weeks longer? It's too last-minute. I need more info. A little more time. Why the rush?"

But the line was silent. Her ex-boyfriend, once again, had hung up on her.

That Monday, she headed back to her office and found Robert Garrison, her department head, sitting in the chair beside her desk.

He was an imposing man, even when seated. Six-foot-six and powerfully built, he had a ringing bass voice and graying hair he wore a little too long. Although he was a linguistics scholar who ranked among the best, he looked more like a thug. Or a basketball player.

Garrison stood up when she entered the room and remained standing after she sat down at her desk.

"Ms. Campbell. How are you today? And Linguistics 101?"

Mackenzie carefully placed her book bag on the floor next to her, hoping to hide her expression. "The Survey class?"

"Yes. I wondered how you felt about it. In general."

"It's all right. Not bad." She sounded like an idiot. He had to know from the website's feedback page that her students didn't think much of the class.

Pacing in front of her desk, he said, "I'm sorry to say this, but it hasn't been going very well. Your teacher approvals are low. I know you're a first-year teacher, and so we must be patient. But I want to give you a bit of advice."

She nodded, not trusting her voice. She stared at a small spider web in the corner of the ceiling.

"Standing in front of the class is not teaching. It is merely the tip of the iceberg." He paused, and she groaned inwardly. Tip-of-the-iceberg speeches were never good.

"I went out on a limb for you with this new course. It was a bold idea, but I'm afraid you're just not the one to carry it out. You simply haven't taken the time to prepare. All good teachers are relentless in their preparation and planning. They know their subject intimately and succeed because they put in the hours."

He hesitated for effect. "Their iceberg is solid because it is built on the rocks of focused hard work."

Mackenzie ignored the mangled metaphor and nodded again.

"I want you to spend more time, Campbell. I want you to focus. I don't want to worry I made the wrong decision backing you."

She hoped he wouldn't require a response and resisted the urge to argue with him.

Garrison pulled his lips back, creating the semblance of a smile, and turned, ducking slightly while walking through the doorway. He didn't say good-bye.

She jumped up and closed the door, pulling down the shade. Specks of dust fell silently to the ground.

"Spend more time," she exclaimed. "Spend more time?" Collapsing in her chair, she let her head fall on the desk. The ticking of her wall clock beat a subtle rhythm, and she found herself counting. One-uh, two-uh, three uh, four—

Rat-a-tat-tat. A tat. Startled, she raised her head, afraid Garrison had returned. But when she peeked through the narrow opening between the windowsill and shade, Hillary waved at her.

Mackenzie opened the door, and her friend sailed in.

"Hey, Hill. Don't you have a class now?"

"No, I gave a pop quiz. It was either too easy or too hard. I let them out early." She raised her eyebrows. "What's up?"

"Garrison. Not happy with my teaching. Wants me to spend more time preparing. I got an iceberg lecture."

"Iceberg? You mean, nine-tenths of it under water?"

"Right."

"Oh, Mac, shake it off. He's just that way. A bit of an arrogant ass, that one."

"I can't afford to shake it off. He's not a fan of the new class. He thinks I'm slacking off. It sounded like a warning."

Hillary tilted her head. "You're not taking him seriously, are you? No one spends more time preparing than you. I don't think you need to prepare more—I think you just need some time off. What are you doing after this session? You're not teaching the second summer session, are you? It's only a three-week mini-session. Skip it."

"I can't. I already told Garrison I would teach a basic Grammar class. It's in the catalog." She sank into the chair next to her desk. "I'd only be teaching one class, so I could get ready for fall at the same time." She studied her friend. "Hill, I need your opinion on something. Something else."

"What?" Hillary angled one hip on the edge of the desk.

"Well, Charlie called Friday. Right after you left, actually. He wanted me to check out something he's been researching. In Arizona." She recounted Charlie's request.

"Aztec gold?" Hillary's deep voice rose half an octave. "You've got to be kidding. Oh, Mac, I don't even know Charlie, and I think he's lost it."

"I know. That's what I thought, too. So, of course I said no."

Hillary cocked her head. "It's probably just Charlie's way of stringing you along. He knows you're still hung up on him."

"Me? I'm not still hung up on him. It's been more than a year."

"Please. I can see it in your face. You said he broke your heart, remember?"

Of course she remembered—how could she not? He *had* broken her heart. But he'd also made her laugh, and he'd held her, and she had loved him. And for a while he had loved her back.

"Mackenzie?"

"Sorry. Sorting it out in my head."

"Nothing to sort. Don't glorify it. From what you've told me, he was a selfish bastard."

Mackenzie nodded. She knew she should be angry with him, but at the moment all she could remember was the way his voice cracked and grew raspy when he was excited. The way he knew a little bit about everything. His brilliant blue eyes and blonde hair. And how he had pushed her to do new things.

Hillary broke the silence again. "I know you think he was fun. Of course, that's seductive. But you told me he was never there for you, that he was more of a playmate. I just don't think he could be serious long enough. Or stay in one place."

"I know," Mackenzie agreed. "But, well, some of what he said makes sense. After he called, I Googled Louisa Wetherill. Everything he told me—about her lost notes, I mean—was true. She was going to publish a book, but her health gave out."

"I'm sure there's something to it," Hillary said. "Maybe not Aztec gold, but something. But do you want to get involved with him again?"

Mackenzie let it drop. She was tired of arguing.

Hillary switched to discussing her Abnormal Psych class and the difficulty of designing a good pop quiz. Mackenzie hoped she looked like she was paying attention.

Pausing, Hillary continued in a softer voice. "Listen to me. Put this Aztec stuff out of your head. It's crazy."

Yup, Mackenzie thought, it was. "You're right, Hill. I know you're right."

CHAPTER 2

CHARLIE'S PROPOSED TRIP DATE PASSED BY UNNOTICED, and Mackenzie redoubled her efforts to impress Garrison. *She had never been called unprepared in her life.*

On the last day of the session, she returned from lunch to find a single cardboard envelope on her desk. There was no return address, and the label didn't tell her anything. She picked it up, but it appeared empty. Probably a clever ad campaign for underarm deodorant. Covering it with a pile of final exam books, she dumped everything into her canvas book bag.

After locking up her office, Mackenzie trudged across the campus green. With less than half an hour before the final exam she had to give that day, she wanted to arrive early.

The final went smoothly, and her mood lifted. She was finished with teaching until the next summer session. She thought of Charlie and the trip. She had wanted him to be the love of her life. When he told her he wanted to break up, it had crushed her.

Her steps were heavy as she slogged across campus. She headed for the library to learn more about Charlie's story.

Crossing the threshold, she inhaled the earthy smell of books and paused. Amber light filtered through leaded glass windows, and a card catalog with monitors stood in the center of the room, flanked by rows of bookshelves. Two rows of computers hummed in the alcove on her left.

After tracking down a few references, she found a cozy chair in a corner. When she looked up, it was eight-thirty. Although the library remained open until midnight, her office building shut down at nine o'clock on weeknights.

She checked out a few books on the electronic pad and jogged through the stacks. Bounding down the steps, she narrowly avoided the bronze sculpture guarding the building.

The University of Denver was small for a university. She ran into several students she knew on her way to her office and nodded at each. She must look ludicrous, with her overstuffed book bag and disheveled pile of papers. A true cliché. She slowed her pace and finger-combed her bangs before entering the building.

She headed to the garden level, a large space with a rabbit warren of cubicles and offices. Her office was in the back, and she navigated the aisles in the dim light.

Leaning against her office door to fish out her keys, she toppled backward into the dark office. What the hell? She scrambled up to flick on the light switch. And froze.

Something was wrong.

Someone had broken into her office.

Mackenzie never left the door unlocked, much less slightly ajar. Although she wasn't exactly a neatnik, the mess she encountered wasn't hers. Books were strewn on the floor, desk drawers left open. Files were scattered about, and papers carpeted the floor. Her heart rate doubled. Taking a deep breath, she steadied herself. Relax, she told herself. No one was in the office now.

The wastebasket under her desk lay on its side, with crinkled papers and a cardboard coffee cup next to it. Somehow it was too much. Tears flooded her eyes. She had to report this, but she had to get out of there first. Pulling her book bag back onto her shoulder, she turned. And screamed.

"Are you all right?" A uniformed campus security guard stood there, blocking the way.

She looked up into small button-eyes behind thick glasses. A tall man with sparse gray hair stood before her. She didn't recognize him, but she didn't know everyone on the security staff. She pressed the bag to her chest, flushing. She had bumped into him, not the other way around.

"I'm sorry," she said. "I thought…"

"Ma'am. Everything okay?"

"Uh, yes. I mean, no. Someone's been in my office. Someone's broken into my office."

"Yes, ma'am, that's why I'm here. Heard a report of someone hanging around the building earlier." He strode past her into the room, trampling books and papers alike. "Did you see anyone? Is anything missing?"

"I didn't see anyone. And I haven't checked if anything is missing." She gazed at the mess. It would take forever to go through it all.

"How long have you been here?" He stood in front of the window, which she noticed wasn't quite shut. Had she left it open?

"Ma'am?"

"I left Penrose at half-past eight to get my grade book."

"Your office was locked?"

"It should have been. But it wasn't when I got here."

"Why don't you look around to see if anything's missing. I'll be here. You'll be safe." He crossed his arms and smiled, revealing yellow teeth. A faint odor of stale garlic assaulted her, and she coughed.

She scanned the room again. Kneeling, she picked up her grade book and placed it in her bag.

"What are you taking?"

"Just my grade register."

"You didn't leave your mail here, did you? No packages or deliveries?"

Mackenzie shook her head, watching as he continued to study the room. She pressed her back against the doorway, looking over her shoulder into the outer room. "Shouldn't we call the police?"

After observing her for a moment, he shrugged and turned to leave. "Probably frisky students. I wouldn't worry."

It occurred to her then she didn't know his name. Didn't security guards wear name badges? She couldn't remember.

"Could you, I mean, would you walk me to my car?" She struggled to keep up, but her stride was no match for his.

He called back over his shoulder, "Ma'am, you have a good night. Don't you worry about a thing."

An hour later, she sat on her sofa with a peanut butter sandwich. It's nothing, she told herself. Probably a prank of some kind. Students did crazy things during finals.

She sighed. It would be better to stay busy. She sorted final exams into different piles on the cushions with one hand, holding the sandwich in the other. At the bottom of her book bag, she found the oversized envelope she had received earlier. Stuffing the rest of the sandwich into her mouth, she wiped her fingers on her robe and ripped the envelope open.

A folded sheet of smudged notebook paper, much too small for the envelope that contained it, fell to her lap. It was a pencil drawing of what seemed to be mountains connected to a large stone arch. At the top of the peak were two X's, with a dashed line drawn parallel to the sheer cliff face. The line ended with a large arrow pointing to a hole, or cave, in the rock. Another arrow pointed to a place at the bottom of the cliff with the words "Painted Rock, near Rainbow Bridge. Codex."

"This is from Charlie," she muttered to herself. She turned the sheet over, looking for a note or explanation. Nothing.

Rainbow Bridge. Charlie had mentioned the place, but she blanked on the details. Was it in Arizona or Utah? Leaning over the stack of finals, she picked up one of the books on the Wetherills and flipped through the index to the entry.

Ah, it was actually on the border, she found. She glanced at another reference over on the desk and rose awkwardly, knocking the envelope off the coffee table. It fell to the floor next to the sofa. As she bent over to pick it up, a very small camera memory card fell out.

Frowning, she blew on it. What was this? She crossed to her desk and inserted it into her laptop. A folder with fifty or more numbered image files filled the screen. Clicking on an image, she sat back to wait for it to load—and immediately sat up when the image came into focus. Squinting, she enlarged it to get a better look.

The images on the screen appeared to be photographs of pages with pictures or symbols. Most of the figures were drawn in black on a white background. Large square symbols bordered the edges of the pages—dates and page numbers, she knew. The centers of the pages were covered with drawings and smaller symbols.

She quickly scanned the remaining images. Leaning back, she stared unseeing at the ceiling. It seemed to be a complete pre-Spanish Aztec codex. If it was authentic, it would be the only one left in the world.

CHAPTER 3

"HI, THIS IS CHARLIE. I'M HERE. ARE YOU THERE? PLEASE leave a message after the beep."

Mackenzie grew more and more irritated by Charlie's voicemail message. "Charlie, this is my fourth message. I *am* here. Where the hell are you? I need to talk to you. Please, please call me back."

She rested the cell phone on the car seat beside her. Glancing at it, she checked the sound for the third time and then moved it to her lap. She wasn't going to miss his call.

Pushing her bangs back, she glanced down at the phone, then swerved to avoid hitting a median. She was tired and distracted—not a good combination—and she grew more and more worried with each tick of the clock. She would call him again when she got to school, she thought. Why wasn't he answering her calls?

She sped down Evans Avenue, passing under the glassed-in skyway that spanned the street. As she pulled into the parking lot next to Hillary's building, her tires squealed, and she glanced nervously around. No one seemed to care.

Five minutes later she sat in Hillary's office.

"Now, what's this about?" Hillary arched a perfectly tweezed eyebrow and fingered the pearl necklace resting above her ample chest.

She wore an electric blue silk blouse and black skirt that flounced when she sat down.

Mackenzie dropped her bag on the floor and paced. She wasn't sure where to begin. "Well, remember how Charlie claimed he had discovered something big?"

"Is this about Charlie again? Are you still obsessing over him?"

"Wait. Yes. No. I mean, yes, it's about Charlie. He sent me something."

Her friend leaned back in her chair, arms crossed. "What?"

"A memory card with images of the codex."

"Really?"

"Yes. I'd have to study it further, but the codex seems complete. If it's real, it would be an amazing, history-changing discovery. We have no complete records of the Aztecs written by them—just stuff the Spanish wrote, which we know was biased and probably riddled with errors and omissions. A genuine codex that showed how the Aztecs lived would be worth millions."

"Still sounds fishy to me."

"There's more. The first part of the codes is like a history of the Aztec people. But the last part seems to be a map to the ancient homeland of the Aztecs. They called it Aztlan."

She paused, gauging Hillary's expression. "I'm still working on it, but it fits the legends. Like I said, the story is that the Aztec king Montezuma hid a stash of gold there to keep it from Cortés. In a cave in Aztlan."

Hillary frowned.

"But I'm worried. I can't reach Charlie."

"He could be out of range, Mac."

"Maybe. But it feels like something's wrong."

"Give it a few days. I'm sure he'll surface."

Mackenzie nodded. That would be the logical, reasonable thing to do. She tried to ignore the feeling of dread in her gut.

The next morning Mackenzie stood by her desk, letting the sunlight warm her shoulders. Her back ached. She left another message for Charlie, again with no response.

Stuffing everything into her book bag, she left for school. She wanted to clean up her office and check her mailbox for a letter from Charlie. Maybe he had sent her something else.

When she walked out to her car, a man leaning against a black sedan glanced up and then down quickly, turning his face away from her. She quickly got into her car and locked the door. Her neighborhood, although quickly becoming gentrified, was not exactly safe yet.

As she pulled out of her parking space, her phone rang, and a number she didn't recognize appeared on the display. Thinking Charlie might be using a different phone, she answered, but the caller hung up. She slowed down to check the display, and a car behind her honked. A dark sedan slid into traffic a few cars back.

She wrinkled her nose. Her sweat stank. She glanced in her rearview mirror. Was it the same sedan that had been parked outside her house? She couldn't tell.

She pulled into the drive-through lane of her favorite coffee shop. Two cars idled in front of her, and she noticed a dark sedan parked on the street a few yards from the shop. She hit the accelerator automatically and had to brake to avoid ramming the car in front of her. Calm down, she told herself. There were probably thousands of dark cars in Denver.

When she exited the drive-through, the sedan pulled out from its spot on the street into the lane behind her, slowing down. She couldn't quite make out the license plate. It abruptly switched lanes again, and she couldn't see it.

She turned onto Evans, heading toward the faculty parking lot. Instead of turning in, she drove under the glass skyway. She turned into a narrow alley behind a frat house and coasted into a small parking space next to a large evergreen bush.

Maybe she shouldn't go into her office today. Maybe she should just turn around. She sipped her coffee, trying to sort out her thoughts.

"No, I've got to do this," she said aloud. In one jerky movement, she grabbed her things and jumped out of the car, making for a gap between the bushes and the frat house. She ducked, waiting. A moment later, the dark sedan glided slowly past her, like a shark on the prowl. The windows were deeply tinted.

Without thinking, Mackenzie dashed the opposite way down the alley and crossed the street to the community center, which provided access to the skyway.

The cool passage of mirrored aqua glass threw a blue cast on the street below. A long bench ran along one wall, and tables and chairs were scattered about randomly. A coffee kiosk stood under a mounted flat screen TV near the opposite door. A few students lingered near the kiosk, gazing up at the news on the screen.

She sat down at the first empty table and stared down at cars threading their way through groups of students. No sign of the sedan. Minutes passed and nothing disrupted the scene below. Her heart returned to its normal rhythm, and her breathing slowed.

She had almost talked herself into going to her office when she spotted a dark sedan. With a sickening fascination, Mackenzie watched as it turned into the faculty parking lot. A tall gray-haired man in a suit got out. She draped herself over her table, trying to see his features. He looked directly at her.

It was the security guard who had been in her office. Mackenzie ducked, even though she knew he couldn't see her through the glass. She slammed her shoulder on the table edge and swore loudly. Several students looked over, then went back to their conversations.

The man walked toward the skyway and gazed up for several minutes before entering the sedan. It left immediately, swerving silently through traffic and pedestrians.

Shit. She retrieved her laptop. She decided to stay put for awhile.

She searched for hotels in Page. Maybe she could find out where Charlie was staying. He usually camped out, but she wanted to be thorough.

In the search engine findings, a headline stood out: MAN LOST IN CANYONS NEAR PAGE, ARIZONA. FEARED DEAD. She clicked on the story.

Page police have been searching the area of Navajo Mountain for a missing Utah man.

Charles E. Peterson, 36-year-old graduate student attending the University of Utah, was last seen four days ago at the Holiday Inn in Page. According to hotel desk clerk Stephen Andrews, Peterson left the hotel to camp overnight near Navajo Mountain. When Peterson failed to return, Andrews notified the police.

Because Navajo Mountain is on Navajo land, Page Police and the Navajo Nation Patrol will conduct the search jointly. A command post has been set up in that area.

Peterson is described as being 5 foot 10 inches tall, 160 pounds, with blond hair and brown eyes. He was last seen wearing a red t-shirt and gray or khaki cargo pants. Police ask that anyone having information contact officer George Cardiff, who is handling the investigation.

She read the words again. They swam into one another, becoming meaningless symbols. Charlie missing? Lost in the canyons?

She should have gone with him. She should have taken the risk. It had been a simple decision with simple words: Yes or No. If she had gone with him, maybe he wouldn't have gotten lost. Now, it might be too late.

Mackenzie forced herself to drive the speed limit to the airport. She was jittery and nervous. The airport, twenty-five miles east of the city, sat alone on the plains like a clump of white circus tents. It was almost five o'clock; her flight left at seven. In the previous three hours she had purchased new clothes, a rolling duffle bag, a one-way ticket to Page, and depleted most of her savings. And had either been fired or quit. She wasn't sure which.

She trolled for a close-in parking spot. The airport itself wasn't busy; the security lines were short, and she made it to the gate in plenty of time. She let her thoughts drift back to her last conversation with Garrison.

"Had you been with me for, say, ten years or so," he had boomed, "I would consider your request to not teach the summer semester. Had we ample time to get to know one another, I would take it under advisement. As it is, you are without tenure, with a mere year's worth of teaching experience, and no research to speak of. You are still on probation and have yet to prove yourself. We are not family yet. If you refuse to teach an assigned class, I must emphasize your standing at this university would be in jeopardy." He smiled then, lips curving into a thin line. "Of course, it is entirely your decision."

She had felt like a child, and the blood had rushed to her face. Surprisingly, instead of wanting to cry, her anger had flared. She sat up straighter. "Professor Garrison, I'd only miss the mini summer-session class. I'd never ask to take time off during the regular school year. I will prove myself. I just need a few weeks."

"The length of the class or when it is scheduled is irrelevant. All classes at the University of Denver are important. I must reiterate that not teaching would place you in a precarious place. However, it is up to you." He stood in front of her, staring down his broad nose. "Remember, if you leave you may find yourself without a position when you return. And you will have lost credibility among your peers."

It was unreal. She was hot and tired. Her office had been rifled, Charlie was lost in the canyons, and someone was following her. She forced her face into an expressionless mask.

During her silence, which he took as acquiescence, Garrison sat down behind his desk, a satisfied smile on his lips.

That did it. Not looking at him, she bent down to get her things, and then unfurled to her full height. Seated, in his charcoal suit and Jerry Garcia designer tie, he was much shorter than her. She no longer felt like a twelve-year-old. "I'm sorry," she said, "but I've got to help my friend. If you decide to fire me for that, well, that's up to you. I won't be teaching the class. I'm going to Arizona."

Turbulence brought her back to the present. Tugging the window shade down, she closed her eyes and let the hum of the engines lull her. Exhaustion pinned her to her seat, and she didn't resist. In her half-sleep, Aztec symbols turned into graffiti on dirty city walls, and gray smog produced plumes of fire.

An hour later, she rolled her head from side to side, rubbing her neck. She lifted the window shade. The landscape below had changed dramatically. The earth was streaked by tans and grays, and she could see long blue fingers reaching out from a larger azure body. Lake Powell and its side canyons, she guessed. Next to it stood a dark volcanic mountain. She settled back, checking her seat belt.

Thirty minutes later, the plane bumped down the runway on a mesa near Page, Arizona.

The small airport was dilapidated and seedy. Descending a set of stairs that creaked in protest, she stepped directly onto the tarmac. An acrid odor assaulted her. In the heat, the soft asphalt sucked up the heels of her shoes, forcing her to tip-toe. It was like walking on black taffy.

Even at almost nine o'clock in the evening, the sun still shone brightly. Mackenzie lifted her bangs off her forehead and plodded after the straggling group of fellow passengers toward the terminal.

After a few minutes her mood was as dark and gummy as the surface she crossed.

But small airports, she found, had their advantages. When she entered the building, she could actually watch her bag arrive on the cart. There were fewer guards than at most airports, and even a few smiling faces. The pastel Southwestern theme calmed her.

She leaned gratefully against the information counter. "Where can I get a taxi? Or do you have a shuttle to the Holiday Inn?"

The short, tanned man behind the counter shook his head. "It's just a few blocks, ma'am. Take Sage Avenue and turn right on Navajo. Hardly worth a taxi. Most folks walk." He handed her a photocopied street map.

Muttering to herself, Mackenzie folded the map, stuffing it in her bag. *Walk. Okay. She could do that. Shit.*

In ten minutes she was out in the heat again. She trekked the half-mile to the Holiday Inn, her new red tweed duffle tottering along behind her on the narrow sidewalk. She fought to keep sweat out of her eyes and dust out of her nose. Pickup trucks crunched when they passed, flinging sand and gravel and dirt, and she had to stop every few feet to right her overturned bag. Her grimy and matted hair felt like a squirrel's nest.

She looked down, her sunglasses slipping to the tip of her nose. Her brand-new celery-green linen pants, which she had hoped would be cool, were now wrinkled like an old woman's skin. To top it off, her shoes were ruined.

Mackenzie continued down Sage Avenue. "I must be crazy," she informed a tumbleweed, kicking it savagely out of the way.

Turning on South Navajo Drive, she spotted the hotel. Surrounded by small adobe houses and shops, it stood like an oasis in the deepening sunset. The place looked unnatural: green grass covered rolling hills, bougainvillea fluttered like tethered butterflies, and palm trees waved a welcome. She hoped it was a good omen.

CHAPTER 4

AT SEVEN O'CLOCK THE NEXT MORNING, MACKENZIE RATTLED down a rutted dirt road in her rental car. The coffee in her cup holder was bitter, but she took a sip anyway, grimacing.

So this was Page. From what she could tell, the town had never quite grown into itself. Lacking the glitz of a tourist attraction and the charm of the frontier, it was neither.

The landscape, however, was entrancing. Earthy reds and coppery browns folded into layers and layers of sage greens. Tans split the colors. A cyan blue sky set off the rock walls and plains.

She was growing more and more anxious about finding Charlie. When she had last called his cell phone, the message simply said, "The number you have dialed is not in service."

She bumped along, searching. A glint of white caught her eye, and she slowed, pulling up behind a police cruiser. A bullish man with a salt-and-pepper crew cut and sunglasses faced her, legs wide apart, hands behind his back. She blinked, knowing she wouldn't get much from him. There was a reason for stereotypes.

She crossed the road to the so-called command post, which was little more than the car, some pitiful junipers, and a cooler. "Hi. I'm Mackenzie Campbell. I'm one of Charlie Peterson's friends. You must be Officer Cardiff."

Nothing.

"Charlie. You know, the man who disappeared?"

The policeman inclined his head in a quick, controlled movement, and crossed his arms over his chest.

Steeling herself, she crossed her arms, too, mirroring him. She spent several minutes trying to extract information, but he was taciturn at best, responding with single-syllable answers. She heard just the slightest accent in his words and inflection. Boston, or Baltimore, she decided.

She circled to his left, forcing him to alter his stance, and pointed at a slender, overgrown trail leading up a hill toward some swells of slickrock. "Is that the trail he followed?"

"Could be."

She tried again. "So, you're not going to check it out further?"

"Nope."

"Why not? Wasn't that where he was headed? Isn't that what the desk clerk reported?"

"Maybe."

She hoped he couldn't see her roll her eyes behind her sunglasses. They weren't mirrored, like his. "Well, what are you going to do?"

"Give it a day or so." Cardiff took his glasses off and wiped them on his shirt sleeve. He didn't meet her gaze.

"Okay, but if he did follow this trail, where would it lead?"

"Couple of places. Forbidding Canyon. Red Bud Pass. Rainbow Bridge." It was the longest sentence she'd gotten out of him.

"Rainbow Bridge? This is a trail to Rainbow Bridge?"

"Mmpf," he grunted.

She took it for a yes. "Uh, how long a hike is it?"

"Well, from here, it's about fifteen miles, hard and steep. It's the old trail. Not used much. It'd take three days, maybe four, if you don't get lost."

"Charlie might have taken this very trail. Have you looked at Rainbow Bridge for him?" She was growing irritated. "Or any other places?"

"No."

"Well, why not?" She batted a fly buzzing near her ear.

"Lady, he could have gone anywhere. Some of the trails are on Navajo land, so we can't just take over. The ball's in their court now."

She took a few steps past him up a small mound and appraised the trail, her back to him. Beyond the slickrock, a wall of jagged rocks rose. "Can I hire someone to take me on that trail? Or another trail? To the bridge?"

"Yeah. But I wouldn't recommend it."

It was difficult not to categorize his accent. Definitely Boston. "Why not?"

He sat down on the cooler, setting his glasses on his knee. He spoke to her in a clipped voice. "You gotta have a permit. From the Navajo Nation. A guide. The trails aren't maintained, and they're tricky. It would be quicker on the lake, anyways. You could hire a boat and be there in a few hours."

She spun around. "A boat. I can get to Rainbow Bridge by boat? And I don't need a permit?"

"No. Just gotta get a guide."

She scrounged in her bag for some paper. Writing her name and number on an old grocery receipt, she held it out and asked him to call if he heard anything. He stood up, glancing first at the scrap of paper and then at her. He made no move to take it; instead, he put his sunglasses on and his hands behind his back. She sighed and, grabbing a rock, secured the note to the cooler. She turned and left, not bothering to say goodbye.

The dust plumed behind her in the rearview mirror while she drove off. In the rearview mirror, she could see him watching her car long after the dust had settled on the road.

Wahweap, the largest marina on Lake Powell, stood alone in a small cove on the lake, nestled between water and slickrock. Mackenzie waitedon the dock, stretching her neck, and rocked from side to side, lifting first one cheek and then the other off the windbreaker she sat on. The planks forming the splintery dock were hot and rough, and she didn't want to touch them.

Cosmo Sullivan had come highly recommended by Stephen, the hotel desk clerk. Best guide on Lake Powell, he had told her. Apparently, Sullivan lived year-round on his houseboat, guiding and giving kayak lessons on the side.

She shook her head. Living off tourists. Probably rented his houseboat to drunken frat boys. She was sure she wouldn't like him. She couldn't like him on principle. Besides, anyone who would show up thirty minutes late for an appointment was rude and, by her definition, unlikeable. Well, she didn't have to be his best friend. He just had to take her to Rainbow Bridge.

She slapped at a gnat whirring about her, irked. A lot of things were irksome here. The heavy blanket of heat smothering her. The relentless sun. The teasing wind, which should have been cool, but which was nothing but hot, hot, hot. She had waited half an hour for this guide. She was wilted, sweaty, and hungry. Not a good combination.

They had spoken on the phone—a short, clumsy conversation— and were supposed to meet at the marina, slip eight, at noon. Her watch read 12:35. She lifted her ponytail off her neck. Although just shoulder length and fine, her hair soaked up the heat. Even that bothered her.

A small power boat zoomed toward the dock where she sat. It had to be him. As it neared, she knew she had been right—she wouldn't like Cosmo Sullivan. She stood, watching him race straight at her. Banking the boat alongside the dock, he didn't glance up. No wave or smile. Like he had dropped by to see someone else. Thirty-five minutes late.

When he drew closer, she could see he had brown hair and was tall. Tan and sinewy, he resembled a dried pecan. His faded green t-shirt stuck to his body above his khaki shorts. He might be good looking, she thought, if it weren't for the craggy furrows lining his face and the brown stubble covering his chin. And his expression.

He bounded onto the dock, and she watched with dismay as a group of men mobilized. One shook Sullivan's hand, while two others tied up the boat. A good-old-boys reunion. She progressed from irked to irritated.

After chatting with his buddies, Cosmo Sullivan turned to her, studying her. She stared back at him.

"You the one wanting a guide?"

"Yes. I'm Mackenzie. Mackenzie Campbell."

"Mackenzie? Isn't that a boy's name? Means 'son of Kenzie,' or something?"

"Yes. It's a family name." And none of your business, she added, to herself. How old was this joker? As a girl's name, 'Mackenzie,' had become distressingly trendy of late.

He shoved a hand through his hair, and she noticed his hairline was receding. He pulled a sweat-stained baseball cap out of his back pocket.

"What do you go by? Red?"

She bristled. She had fought being called 'Red' all her life. Why did people think they could call her that just because of her hair color? She didn't call brunettes, 'brownie' or blondes, 'blondie.'

"Mackenzie will be just fine," she said.

He laughed. Against his tan, his teeth were almost too white. Model white. Trim and fit, with that broad smile, he looked assured and at ease—like a confident, easy-going asshole.

She asked, "Do you go by Cosmo? Or should I call you 'Cos?' "

He stopped laughing and their eyes met. She was surprised by their vivid blue. He pulled a pair of sunglasses from another pocket and put them on.

Suddenly she was aware of her appearance. Most of her hair had escaped her ponytail and was whipping about her face. Her mascara had probably glopped around the rims of her eyes. Her damp, white camp shirt clung to her breasts and torso, and her shorts sat an inch lower than she liked. She tucked a strand of hair behind her ear and crossed her arms over her chest.

"You may call me Sullivan," he said. "Or Sulley. I really don't answer to anything else." He turned. "Come on, Slim."

"My name is Macken—." Damn. He had started without her. Obviously, the discussion was over. Snatching her windbreaker, she chased him up the stairs to the hotel's bar.

Ten minutes later she reclined in the shade of the patio cover with a glass of iced tea and found her mood changing. They hadn't spoken for several minutes. Across the table from her he sipped on a margarita, staring at the water through his sunglasses.

The lake was immense, with small islands of rock poking up like shark fins. Every few minutes, boats full of tourists putt-putted by. The rocks had a definite bathtub ring; the lake, she'd learned, was receding at an alarming rate. She relaxed, letting herself enjoy the scene. She decided to let go of her first impressions of Sullivan. How could anyone remain angry in such a place? She felt a growing bond with the man next to her, this complete stranger. And envious. He lived in paradise.

Sullivan clinked his glass down on the table, and she tried to remember why she had come to the lake. Ah, yes. To rescue Charlie.

"I'd like to hire you to take me to Rainbow Bridge," she said. "You go there, don't you?"

He waited a beat before responding. "Yes, I go there. Do you want a boat tour or to go by kayak?" He shook the glass, tipping it to dislodge the ice. "I'm guessing by boat."

"What's the difference?"

"Well, the boat ride is fast. From Wahweap, it takes about five hours. Give or take. By kayak, it's slower, more scenic. I usually run a five-day trip, with excursions down slot canyons, depending on the clientele. I offer a three-day trip, too." He crunched on a cube of ice. "I usually recommend going by kayak. That way you really see the canyons, get to know them. You can almost feel the colors change with the light as the water moves under you."

The picture he painted was surprisingly intimate. She took a drink and, out of habit, mentally placed him linguistically. His sentences were well formed and complex, his vocabulary sophisticated, his cadence almost musical. Educated. Old money. He had traveled a lot and had a slight East Coast accent, with a touch of something else. The South? She'd have to hear more.

He continued. "You're only interested in Rainbow Bridge? Nothing else?"

She lied. "Yes, just the bridge. But I'd want to stay a day or so. Can you do that?"

"Not by boat. By kayak, yes."

"Okay, kayak, then." It would be slower, but she needed time to look for Charlie. Charlie. She hadn't thought about him at all during the conversation with Sullivan. "The three-day trip. How much does that cost?"

He considered. "Just you?"

She nodded, hoping he had staff who helped on the tours. She didn't want to be alone with him; something about him rattled her.

"You over twenty-one?"

Mackenzie bit back her response, trying to remain agreeable, and nodded. She couldn't tell if he was serious or not.

"For three days and two nights, it's an even thousand."

"Dollars? A thousand dollars? For three days?"

"We provide all the equipment and meals," he said, ignoring her outburst. "Show you where to camp. Guide you to Rainbow Bridge. Keep you safe." He paused. "A thousand is a good deal."

She deliberated: Would telling this man her mission lower the price? She could try playing on his sympathy. No, she decided. She couldn't tell anyone just yet. And he didn't appear to be the sympathetic type.

"Uh, I guess that'd be fine. Can we leave tomorrow morning? And do you take travelers checks?"

He drained his margarita and licked the last flakes of salt on the rim. "Tomorrow? No can do. I'm all booked up. Taking a group on a month-long expedition. An archaeological trip. I could take you in six weeks. Give or take."

"What? You can't be serious. Why did you meet with me, then, if you knew you were busy?"

A couple next to them stared openly, and she realized she was shouting. She normally never raised her voice. She added, much more calmly, "Why couldn't you have told me that on the phone when I first called?"

"Had no idea you wanted to go so soon."

"Well, you could have asked. Instead of showing up late and then completely wasting my time. Thanks for that. I'm sure I can find someone else to take me."

"Won't find anyone this late."

"We'll just see about that. I'm sure there are other guides who aren't so, so rude."

He stood up, cap in hand. "Look. You didn't say what you wanted, or when. I'm afraid it's a busy time for me, Slim. And the month-long gig I mentioned is a good one. It's a large group—too many if you ask me—but they pay well, so I'm not complaining."

She gaped at him, speechless.

"You won't be able to book a trip with anyone else this late and on such short notice. I can take you in five or six weeks, depending on who's before you. Take it or leave it." He pulled a card from his shirt pocket and dropped it on the table. Without waiting, he sauntered out of the restaurant.

Mackenzie fumed, spending the drive to her hotel in Page coming up with too-late, but satisfying, smart-ass quips. She must have appeared angry, because the desk clerk, Stephen, raised his eyebrows as she entered. She forced a smile, willing herself to relax. He smiled back and looked her up and down.

Men. Anger swelled in her again, and she decided she would confront the little twerp. She took one step and stopped. She needed him. He was her sole friend, she thought, with a shock.

Her anger flipped to fear. What was she doing here in this little town? What the hell was she trying to prove? Her stomach tightened into a hard knot. She had no plan, no strategy, no safety net of any kind. How would she be able to find Charlie? What if the codex was a fake? She was risking her career and reputation on a whim. On Charlie, the man who had dumped her. Her situation seemed even more precarious than before.

Stephen was occupied checking in a couple and their two children, tapping at his computer behind the desk. She slid into one of the armchairs in the lobby, and to distract herself picked up *The Lake Powell Chronicle.*

On the front page, in 80-point caps, the headline read: VISITING EXPERTS TO CATALOG ANCIENT GLYPHS. Curious, she read on. Apparently, an amateur anthropologist from Kanab, Utah, and a team of researchers were about to begin an expedition into the secret nooks and crannies of Lake Powell to research some unusual stone markings or carvings.

Victor Adams, hardware store owner and amateur anthropologist, has been pursuing strange carvings in Arizona, Utah, and Nevada deserts. For ten years he has been searching for the secret behind the glyphs.

According to Adams, the petroglyphs are unique in size and location. Adams states the symbols occur only along the so-called Arizona strip, a span of more than 2,000 square miles.

He proposes the symbols are markers, or coordinates, for an ancient overland map, possibly pointing to water sources or areas of shelter.

She glanced at the desk. Stephen was still talking to the couple, pointing to a map of Lake Powell. She continued reading.

The article contained six fuzzy photographs of glyphs. They were all similar, with minor variations. She studied them. They didn't resemble symbols in any Mesoamerican languages she knew, or anything in the International Phonetic Alphabet. She traced a facsimile of one of them on the coffee table, the sweat from her fingers leaving a clear outline on the glass. The physical act of drawing it didn't mean anything, either.

"Uh, Ms. Campbell?"

She jumped up, almost upsetting the coffee table in front of her. Stephen was standing there, brows pinched together. "Oh, I'm so sorry. I didn't mean to . . . . Is everything all right? You seemed, well, upset, when you came in."

Mackenzie folded the newspaper under her arm and smiled. "Hi, Stephen. Everything's fine." She placed her hand on his forearm, and he stiffened slightly. She withdrew it. "I was just focused, I guess. Reading about the expedition. You know, the one where they're looking for those strange symbols carved in the rock?"

She took him for about twenty or twenty-one, the same age as most of her students. He shoved his hands in his pockets, and she felt her ears burning. Flirting with a young boy was new for her. God, she decided, I'm *so* not myself here. Her friend Hillary would approve.

His voice cracked. "Oh, yeah. I know the one you mean. There's a bunch of them staying at the Resort. I think it's kinda funny, though. Saying the carvings are a map for water holes or whatever. I think they're hiding something. It's gotta be gold mines or something."

Suddenly, she realized what the glyph reminded her of. A circle with a line through it. The reflection of a rainbow over water. Like Rainbow Bridge. Stephen may be right, she thought; the glyphs could be about gold.

"Ms. Campbell? You all right?"

"What? Oh, yes. Sorry. Just thinking."

"Well, like I was saying, they're hiding something. Either that, or they're on a wild goose chase."

Stephen's from around here, she thought. The rhythm of his speech and evenness of his vowels were distinctive. "I bet you're right. Interesting, don't you think? You seen any glyphs?" She slowed her speech, flattening her vowels and matching his inflection.

"Nah. Couple of people in town have seen them, but not me."

She smiled down at him. He was several inches shorter than her. "Know anything about the group looking for them?"

"Uh, not much. It was sort of short notice. Sulley's taking them out tomorrow."

She gasped. She couldn't help it. "Sulley? You mean Sullivan? Cosmo Sullivan? He's taking them out?"

"Well, him and Sam, his partner." Stephen stood still, like a cornered animal wavering between fight or flight.

She sighed. Sullivan again. Dammit. If only Stephen had told her about the trip earlier.

"They're leading the trip?"

"Yeah. Him and Sam Two Banks run Canyon Outfitters." He looked back at the desk, bouncing on the balls of his feet.

"So they're heading out in the morning? From the Wahweap Hotel?"

"Uh, yeah. I mean, no. It's called the Lake Powell Resort. You really ought to talk to Sulley." He sidled toward the desk.

"Oh, right. I will. Thanks." She grinned, and instead of heading for her room, turned around to head back out.

Twenty minutes later, she stood in the luxurious lobby of the Lake Powell Resort. Mission-style armchairs and an overstuffed leather sofa formed a cozy conversation area in one corner. Thick slate gray carpet cushioned every step. Cactus and succulents contrasted with pale pink stucco, complementing the color scheme. She wondered how much rooms cost. The Holiday Inn was nice, but nothing like this.

She bounced along the springy carpet to the front desk and, smiling, asked the woman there for the amateur anthropologist, Victor Adams. Clerks were important, she thought, remembering Stephen. Good to get on their good side. This desk clerk, however, didn't look quite so friendly.

"I'm sorry ma'am. Can't give you his room number." The woman behind the desk gazed at her with an unblinking stare.

Mackenzie froze, taking in the clerk, who had dark brown hair cut short. Choppy. Her shoulders were square and her back straight.

Former military, maybe. With such a broad accent, she could be from Alabama or Georgia. The vowels in *ma'am* changed the word to *may-em,* and *can't* became *caint.* The cadence was slow and smooth. The clerk, whose name tag read "Rebecca," was at least six feet tall.

Mackenzie instinctively mimicked her. "Oh, tha's all right. I'll just call him on my cell." She started rummaging in her bag. "So how long you been away from Georgia?" A fifty-fifty chance: Alabama or Georgia.

Rebecca tilted her head. "How'd you know I'm from Georgia?"

"Oh," Mackenzie replied, "I'm a linguistics professor. A specialist in languages of all kinds. I can usually tell where someone's from within a hundred miles or so, 'specially if they're from the South. You grew up outside Atlanta? Small town?"

The clerk's eyes widened, and she bobbed her head. "Dang. I'm from Thomaston. Sixty miles south of 'lanta. Been away, uh, 'bout a year now." Her accent was much stronger now. She was relaxing. Mackenzie smiled back at her, still fumbling in the bag for her phone.

"An' how long you been in the military?" Mackenzie cut off her word endings and emphasized diphthongs. It would be tricky to sound similar and still retain her position as an expert.

"Uh, well, I was in ROTC in high school. I'm not in the army yet. Y'all can tell that by my accent, too?"

Mackenzie hesitated. She didn't want to explain her guess. "Yeah," she replied. "But that's not my best stuff. I really know Mesoamerican languages. You know, ancient Mayan and what-not."

Rebecca nodded slightly but looked confused.

"That's why I'm here. Suppos't to be on the team cataloging the ancient stone carvings. I'm their linguistics expert. Dang-it, I can't find my phone."

Rebecca scanned the lobby and held up a finger. "Hold on. I might could help you." Tapping a few keys on her keyboard, she whispered,

"Room 348. At the end. I'd call him first from one of them lobby phones, though. He's been in and out all day."

"Thanks. I'll do that. Right nice of you."

Victor Adams was in, and he was very accommodating. A tall, athletic man, he met her at the door with a broad smile. She guessed him to be about fifty. He didn't look like an amateur anthropologist from Utah. He looked like an actor. She shook the hand he proffered.

"Hi, I'm Vic," he said. "You're interested in the expedition, are you?"

"Yes. I'm a linguistics professor at the University of Denver. My expertise is in Mesoamerican languages."

"Ah, Mesoamerican languages. All of them?"

She shook her head, laughing. "No. There are at least forty separate languages and even more dialects. I focus primarily on Nahuatl, and other Uto-Aztecan languages. A little bit of Mixtec and Zapotec. Pre-Columbian."

He gestured toward a chair next to the window and parked himself across from her on the edge of the couch. They were in the sitting room of his two-room suite. Through the picture window she could see tiered hills of red and tan and brown above the gleaming blue water. Sounds of children yelling and splashing in the pool below rose over the gentle hum of the air conditioner.

"Quite a few languages, there. Do you know much about what I'm, or rather, we, are doing?"

"Not much. Just what I read in the newspaper," she admitted. "I think I could be helpful, though. I'm on an extended vacation, and a bit at loose ends. Not used to this much leisure." That much was the truth.

He grinned. "Yes, I know what you mean."

She cleared her throat. "I know you're looking for specific glyphs, and I think it's possible they're tied to other petroglyphs or pictographs—ones that may link up to one of the languages I'm proficient in. I can get you my *c.v.* if you wish."

He leaned forward. "Let me get this straight. You really want to join the expedition?"

She hesitated. If she appeared too eager, she might scare him off. "Well, as I mentioned, I'm on vacation. Alone." She shrugged. "I was supposed to be with someone, but that, uh, fell through. Your trip sounded interesting, and I thought maybe it would be nice to explore the area with others. Especially others who had similar interests. I have all this time, you see, and I'm by myself. I'd just tag along. I wouldn't expect to be compensated, and I could pay my way."

"Hmmm. I don't know. We're being sponsored by the LW Foundation. They're footing the bill for the entire trip."

She forced herself to smile and tried to appear professional and competent. Her fears were threatening to take over. She wanted to go back, to grovel in front of Garrison. To sip wine with Hillary. At least then she knew what to expect. Here she was, on the verge of joining a group of strangers under false pretenses. In the desert, for God's sake. Part of her wished Vic would say 'no.' But Charlie's memory pushed its way into her head, and she knew she was doing the right thing. The brave thing.

He continued. "They've allowed me to build my own team. The chairman did mention he wanted to have someone who knows the Aztec language along. He seems to think the symbols are Aztec. I have my own theory, of course, but ... well, we'll see. Do you understand that language?"

"Yes. Mr. Adams—"

"Vic, please. Call me Vic."

"Okay. Vic, I'm also familiar with the symbology and languages of other cultures in that particular area." A slight exaggeration.

"Ye-e-ss," he said, cocking his head. "And another expert would lend more credibility to the expedition. Can't have too many of them, right? Not that we need credibility."

"No, but having more experts in more fields will provide more balanced findings."

"Exactly. I've devoted eleven years of my own time to this project, and any publicity or tie-in would be invaluable."

"Right," she said.

"You know," he continued, "much of the Lake Powell region is so isolated and difficult to get to that it hasn't even been completely mapped. One of the few true wildernesses left, in the States, anyway. The Navajo Nation owns quite a bit of it around here, and they've resisted exploration. There are miles and miles of canyons, some almost as deep as the Grand Canyon, that no one outside of the tribe have even seen."

"Really?"

"Absolutely. I have to warn you. If you go, it's not going to be an easy trip. We'll be roughing it in the worst sense of the word. Once we get underway, we won't have cell phone coverage or any means of communicating with the outside world. It'll be strenuous. Camping and that sort of thing. Are you up for that?"

"Yes, of course. I spend much of my time doing field work." An outright lie.

"Good. Anyway, I'll have to talk to the Foundation. And our guide. It seems our group is already too large for him. He doesn't approve of the way we've put it together."

She smiled. "I promise I won't be much trouble." God, she was flirting again.

He grinned, flashing white teeth. "Well, we may be gone as long as a month. Do you think you could manage that much time?"

"Oh, yes. I'll have my own gear, too, so no need to get any more. Is it a matter of money?"

"No, money won't be the issue. The Foundation seems to have deep pockets."

"Is there another reason, then?"

"Well, it's last-minute. For logistics. Food and such."

She smiled. "I'm sure your supply company could handle it." She paused, pretending to remember something. "Aren't you using Canyon Outfitters?"

"Yes. You know them? A man named Sullivan. He's the guide I mentioned."

Striving to sound casual, she replied, "Yes, I know him. We just met for drinks, actually."

"You did? Wonderful. I found Sullivan a bit uncommunicative and overbearing. But I guess that's what we want in a guide. Right?" He winked at her. "Assuming the Foundation is agreeable, I'd be delighted to have you on board. What a wonderful coincidence. I'm sure since he knows you, Sullivan won't mind the addition. Of course, I'll have to check with him, too."

She kept her face expressionless. She didn't want to think about Sullivan's reaction to her tagging along. If he said 'no,' it would destroy her plan. She shouldn't have lost her temper with him.

Vic stood up and held out his hand again. "I'll call them right away and let you know. You're staying at the Holiday Inn? Fine. I'll call you when I talk to the Foundation. Oh, before I forget. You're aware we're leaving tomorrow morning around seven, right? Can you be ready then?"

Mackenzie glanced at her watch. It was almost six o'clock. Less than ten hours to get everything done. Swallowing, she said, "Yes, of course. No problem."

CHAPTER 5

IT WAS ALREADY SWELTERING THE NEXT MORNING WHEN Mackenzie drove from the Holiday Inn to Wahweap Marina. Vic met her at the entrance of the resort. The expedition was leaving soon; they had minutes to spare. Thankfully, she had only a small duffel, backpack, and sleeping bag.

Vic grabbed the duffel as they headed toward the end of the marina. "You made it. Great. I'm glad you're joining us. As I said yesterday, the Foundation always wanted to have a language expert along. I figured our historian would have to do, but this is better. The Foundation actually encouraged me to include you."

His blue eyes crinkled under thick eyebrows the color of almost-burnt toast. When he smiled, which was often she realized, fine laugh lines radiated from his eyes. His wide nose was slightly crooked and his chin too prominent. Although not quite handsome, he was magnetic and compelling. Arresting.

"Will someone from the Foundation be here, too?"

"Nope. We're on our own, so to speak. Except for Sullivan, of course."

"Yes, except for Sullivan. Did you tell him I'd be tagging along?" Best to be prepared.

"Uh, I wasn't able to reach him last night. I left a message and, well, here you are."

She didn't answer. She wasn't sure what Sullivan would say about having her on board. But Charlie was still out there, and this would help her find him. She had to try.

Near the end of the marina, houseboats rocked side by side, with barely five feet between them. From a distance they had seemed identical. Up close, they varied widely. Some had two levels with an observation deck on top. Some were basic, with one level and a deck on the roof. The larger, more elaborate ones boasted tinted windows and satellite dishes and spiral water slides.

Most of the boats had their windows closed. Mackenzie couldn't see inside and was intrigued. She'd never been on a houseboat before.

Three men and a woman loitered at the end of the dock, surrounded by clumps of duffels and backpacks.

"So, Mike's on the left," Vic said. "He's a Glen Canyon Ranger."

A compact man in a khaki uniform leaned against a pole. Although his hat shaded much of his face, Mackenzie could make out his nose, which was wide and straight, and his lips, which were full. His hands were in his pockets, and under the short sleeves of his shirt she noted tanned arms with bulky muscles.

Vic grinned. "The Glen Canyon people insisted I have a ranger along, to keep us safe, I guess. The Lake's under the jurisdiction of the Glen Canyon Park Service."

"Is he Navajo? Does he speak the language?"

"I'm pretty sure he's Navajo. Not sure if he speaks it, though. I know Sam does. His family's been in this area forever."

"Sam?" She remembered Stephen mentioning Sam Two Banks. "Is he here? In the group?"

"No. He's with Sullivan. They're supposed to pick us up."

"Pick us up? Aren't we going in one of these houseboats?"

"No, Sullivan has his own houseboat in some secret cove."

Oh. A secret cove. Of course. Was he hiding? Or had he discovered his own little slice of heaven? She'd find out soon enough.

She turned her attention back to the group, feeling like a kindergartener walking into the classroom for the first time. God, she hated this. If only she could keep from blushing. Drawing a breath, she focused on what Vic was saying.

"Okay, Lucy's from the Museum. She's the only woman besides you. Don't know anything about her. She was the last to join us. Not what I expected a museum representative to be, but what do I know?"

Lucy looked like she was in her twenties and sported cropped, spiky white-blonde hair with dark roots. She wore a tank top and looked tanned and fit. Vic was right; she looked way too chic to be on a wilderness trip.

He continued. "Next to her is Sandy, an environmentalist from Boulder. The guy with longish brown hair. A bit hippy-dippy for me, but he came with good references." Sandy's chin rested on his knees, and he hunched over, withdrawing from the others. He'd probably be tall when he unfolded. Tall and skinny.

She'd never remember all this. "Right. Uh, and who's the older guy?"

The last member of the group was sitting with his back to them on a large suitcase, fanning himself with a newspaper. His bald head gleamed in the sun.

"That's Henry. Henry Whitehall. British and extremely connected. Been in the states for awhile, though. He's an archaeologist with the National Archaeological Society. Or at least he was. There was talk of his retiring, but I don't know if it happened."

"Wow," she said. "I think I've read one of his books. If he's along, you already have some credibility."

Vic's head bobbed. "I know. And now you're here. I'm excited."

He marched her straight into the middle of the group, and she fixed a smile on her face that she hoped looked genuine. Polite introductions followed. She walked over to Lucy, who was now sitting on the edge of the dock a few feet from Sandy. When Mackenzie sat down between them, Sandy jumped up, leaving the two women alone.

They chatted for a few moments about the lake and the upcoming trip. Lucy handled the heat well. Short hair was the way to go out here. Mackenzie's hair lay limp and frizzy, her neck was sticky, and her tank top clung to all the wrong places.

The women fell into a comfortable silence. Mackenzie's nose was slick from sunblock, and her sunglasses kept sliding down. Her freckles would double, she was sure. Already her sunburned shoulders stung, but she resisted changing her clothes. It was too hot to wear anything but a tank top. She would have to change into a long-sleeved shirt soon, though, to keep from frying.

Lucy told Mackenzie in a low voice that Vic had been contacted by the LW Foundation only ten days ago. They said they needed to use some grant money or they would lose it. So the Foundation offered to fund Vic's expedition to find and document the glyphs, all expenses paid. The catch was it had to begin in a week.

Vic, of course, was delighted. He had been trying for years to put an expedition together, but the finances had never worked out. He had had to scramble to assemble experts. And he had found them: historian, environmentalist, archaeologist, ranger.

Mackenzie pulled her knees up to her chest. "How did you get to be here, Lucy? Does Vic have ties to the museum?"

"No. Uh, the Foundation is one of the museum's largest donors. I had no choice. My bosses and the directors wanted someone to go. I view it as a vacation. I don't expect we'll find anything momentous."

"What do you do at the museum?"

Lucy rubbed her nose. "I'm in charge of research for museum exhibits and programs and other stuff. I recommend research projects." She coughed and clasped her knee, retying her shoe.

Mackenzie was about to ask for more details when a speed boat approached. Sullivan was at the wheel, and once again he docked the boat expertly. His mouth was set in a grim line, and her heart hopscotched despite herself. It wasn't looking good.

Vic helped tie down the boat. Once on the dock, Sullivan scanned the group. When he got to Mackenzie, his gaze lingered and he clenched his jaw. She stood a little straighter and stared back at him.

"So, she's joining the group?" He addressed Vic, but his eyes were on her. "You know five was my limit, right? My upper limit. And now we have six."

"I know, Sullivan. But the Foundation wanted her. They're paying you for your inconvenience."

"It's not an inconvenience, Adams, it's a matter of safety. Most of you don't know what the hell you're doing." He scanned the group. "How many of you have camped in the desert before? Besides you, Mike." He jerked his head at the ranger. Sandy and Vic raised their hands.

"And how many of you have been down a slot canyon?" This time, only Vic raised his hand. "Well, there you go. The rest of you are a liability. Especially you." He glared at her.

His words came out much too quickly. Had he practiced? Her jaw fell open. She was surprised by his intensity.

Vic started to reply, but she broke in first. Something about the guide brought out her defiant side. Not many people did that. "Why especially me?"

"Because you're inexperienced. Because you're too fair. You're high maintenance. And you're a pain in the ass."

She sucked in her breath, trying to think of something to say.

"I don't know how you manipulated your way into this group, Red, but I don't like it."

"I didn't manipulate my way in, *Cosmo*," she replied, narrowing her eyes. "I'm a fully qualified expert in Mesoamerican languages.

I speak a dozen languages. As a professor of linguistics, I specialize in writing and language. I'm also familiar with different styles of petroglyphs and pictographs. Just because I haven't been down a slot canyon or whatever doesn't make me inexperienced. You don't even know me." She broke off before swearing. She didn't know the group well enough yet. "I am *not* high maintenance."

The rest of the group was silent, watching the exchange. Too bad she didn't have an ally among them.

"My name is Sul-ley," he said, pronouncing each syllable distinctly. "And I don't care how many languages you speak. This country is difficult, and it can bring out the worst in people. It's not like walking in a park or even hiking. Much of the land out here is uncharted, and when we get back into the canyons, I doubt we'll see another living soul. We'll be on our own, without a cell phone or GPS. Without a bathroom. No showers, no conveniences at all. Your true nature emerges when you travel through canyon country. It's going to require more of yourself than you could even imagine. I don't have time to babysit you."

"You won't have to babysit me, Mr. Sullivan." She refused to call him by his cliché of a nickname. "I'm more capable than you think. I can take care of myself." She picked up her duffel, planning on moving to the rear of the group. Instead, she caught her toe on a strap, tripped over a backpack, and nearly fell into the water. Lucy caught her arm just in time.

Sullivan folded his arms across his chest. "Right. You're so very capable, Red."

They clambered into the boat. Mackenzie concentrated on placing one foot after the other. High maintenance, huh? She would show him she was no princess.

The speed boat was deceptively large, and the group fit with no problem, although they had to keep their bags in their laps. Vic, Lucy, and Mike braved the wind in the front, looking like hood ornaments, while she sat in the back on the bench seat with Henry and Sandy.

The motor and the relentless wind made it difficult to speak, which suited her. It was a bumpy ride. They sped through the wide channel, rising and falling with the waves, sometimes landing hard as they cut through someone's wake. Sullivan would occasionally point at side canyons and caves high on steep walls and comment. She couldn't make out a word. Most of the side canyons they passed were wide, but some were so narrow she doubted a speed boat, let alone a houseboat, could make it through them.

The sun and wind and scenery bleached out her anger. Sullivan had every right to be angry, she conceded. The trip had increased in size without his knowledge, and it was short notice. She knew he'd have to get more supplies and equipment. She bit her lip, wondering again what the hell she was doing. She was on her own with strangers in a dangerous place. She'd never done anything so impetuous before. She forced her shoulders down and breathed. She could do it; she could change. It was for Charlie. She'd show that idiot of a guide just how low maintenance she was, and she'd make herself indispensable. "Babysit me, my ass," she said aloud to the water.

They boated slowly down the main canyon for more than an hour, passing houseboats and speed boats. Jet skiers swerved around them from time to time, leaving long, thin wakes like tails in the water. Finally, Sullivan slowed, guiding them into a small side canyon. They drifted along to a low put-put. The smell of wet stone was strong, reminding her of rain on concrete. Up front, Mike, Lucy, and Vic were talking. Next to her, Henry and Sandy were busy snapping photos and didn't seem to want to converse. Fine with her.

The canyon they turned into was at most fifty feet wide. Tremendous red and white walls flanked them. The water here was a deeper green than in the main channel and smoother.

They kept their speed low as they floated. After half an hour or so, they rounded a sharp corner to the left. The channel narrowed and the walls rose even higher. Several hundred yards later, two side canyons opened up on the right. Sullivan entered the larger one.

In this canyon, the walls were more white than red and smooth as glass. The waterway curved sinuously, and she was sure only a speedboat would be able to fit through such a narrow waterway. But when they rounded the next sharp bend, a sage-green houseboat materialized like a mirage, glistening in the distance.

"Yours?" Vic asked.

"Yeah. We're going to pull up behind it. Think you can grab the rails and pull us in? Then put out the fenders." Large rubber tires hung on the back of the houseboat.

"Sure." Vic must have spent some time near boats. He tied their boat to the larger one quickly without thinking, pulling it up slightly to one side of the back deck.

The houseboat looked brand new. A full two-stories, it was top-heavy and immense. It was hard to believe it could float on the water.

Sullivan gestured toward the deck, and they climbed aboard on an aluminum ladder, single file. A large freezer and a barbecue grill were off to the left side in the shade of an awning. A spiral staircase on the right led to a smaller deck overhead, from which a water slide curved down to the water. At the top of the houseboat, above the second story, was the top deck. On it, a striped green-and-white canvas awning flapped a tattoo in the breeze.

They followed him around the perimeter walkway, passing tinted windows. Bedrooms, she assumed. On the front deck, three two-seater kayaks were stacked side by side.

How in the world were seven of them, including Sullivan, going to kayak when there were only three boats? Opening her mouth to ask, she thought better of it. She had enlarged the group and she was the reason they were short.

Sullivan told them to drop their luggage on the front deck. "Ready for the nickel tour?" Without waiting for a response, he led them through a sliding glass door.

She stopped at the door, and Lucy bumped into her. Apologizing, Mackenzie continued, stepping onto the dense brown carpet. A dining space and kitchen were separated from a lounging area by a large granite island. The three rooms were easily bigger than her entire apartment.

The interior was subtly elegant: The walls were paneled in rich oak, with built-in shelves and cabinets. In the front were two captains chairs, one with a steering wheel, panel of buttons, and digital screens.

She wasn't sure what she thought a houseboat would be like, but this wasn't it. "Definitely not what I expected," she whispered to Lucy.

"Oh, I know. Now this is what I call living. Look at the kitchen."

The kitchen sported two stainless steel refrigerators, a double oven, and a Jennaire grill. Another spiral staircase rose next to it, and she spotted a hallway beyond.

Mackenzie studied Sullivan as he pointed out amenities. The contrast was almost funny; in his tattered clothes he looked like the handyman, not the owner. But he spoke well, with an even, deep voice. She wondered how he'd been able to afford such a huge houseboat. Obviously, the guide business was doing very well. Either that, or he came from money.

They followed him through the hallway. Three bedrooms were on the right, with two sets of double bunk beds in each. Shelves and cabinets lined the left wall. They traipsed through the hallway out to the back deck, and Sullivan started up the stairs.

The upper deck had a single stateroom the width of the houseboat. It was obviously his bedroom. He opened and shut the door, without commenting. On the other side of the deck, a hot tub bubbled away, next to a curving bar. A second grill and freezer were on this deck as well. The houseboat was a private penthouse floating in the middle of paradise. What would it be like to live here?

Sullivan strutted around the deck, proud of his boat. Lucy asked its name, and he replied, "*The Amoreena.*"

"After the song?" Mackenzie blurted, without thinking. "The Elton John song?"

"Right. You know it?"

"Of course. It's one of my favorites. It was before Elton went pop. From the album *Tumbleweed Connection.*"

"Never heard of it," Lucy said. Sullivan reached a tanned hand up to his jaw, rubbing the growth of two-day-old stubble. Golden-red in the light and shot with gray, his beard didn't match his hair. In the glint of the sunset she could see the hair on the back of his hand was blonder, with just a touch of red.

He regarded her for a moment and then motioned toward the set of stairs. Their conversation was over. He continued, "This boat has a fabulous sound system. We'll put music on for dinner." His tone was clipped, and he seemed irritated.

Dammit. She'd done it again. Why did she continue to call attention to herself? The song was an early romantic ballad about an unspoiled country girl. It just didn't seem to fit him. She took a deep breath. Keep your mouth shut, she told herself.

She led the way to the stairs, descended several steps, and screamed.

Standing just below her, a naked man was pulling on jeans. He grinned as he zipped up his fly. He was thin but muscular, and her eyes rested first on his chest, then on his flat abs, then drifted lower. She turned away. Somehow she couldn't move and felt herself blushing. Above her, they were all speaking at once. She desperately wanted to head back up, but she was trapped.

"You must be Mackenzie," Half-Naked man said. "I'm Sam, Sulley's partner. Nice to meet you." He looked about forty years old. Straight hair fell to his shoulders like a gleaming black waterfall. His eyes, framed with thick black lashes, were a surprising blue and shimmered with reflected light. He held out his hand and stepped forward. She stared at him like a startled rabbit. Smiling, he took her hand and covered it with both of his, leading her down the last two steps.

Just then Sullivan yanked open the sliding glass door behind them and burst into the room, breathing hard. She quickly retrieved her hand.

Sullivan let out a breath. "What the hell were you screaming at?"

Sam grabbed a shirt off the sofa before turning his back. She caught a flicker of a smile.

"And you," he continued, turning to Sam. "Glad to know you made it, buddy."

"Thought I'd tidy up a bit." Sam smiled.

"So what's all the ruckus about? Tell me." Sullivan was red-faced, from the exertion. Or anger.

"I, well, he ... well, he was dressing," she faltered. "I mean, he didn't have pants on." She was aware of hushed whispers above.

"You've never seen a man dressing before?"

"Of course I have," she snapped. "But not here. In the wilderness. Or on the boat, I mean. I was surprised. I had no idea who he was. He could have been a robber, or worse."

"Princess, out here, everybody's a friend. Who did you think it would be in this canyon? We're hell and gone from anywhere."

"I don't know, but I didn't expect to meet a strange man dressing in your living room."

"Salon."

"Whatever. You can't blame me for being surprised by a naked man in your *salon*."

Sam looked at her, eyebrows raised, and disappeared down the hallway.

She shifted from foot to foot. "I don't mean strange. Well, hell, I do mean that. He was strange."

Sullivan ignored her, crossing to the stairs. "It's all right," he called up to the group. "Nothing to worry about. Ms. Campbell just met Sam. Come on down."

She stumbled backward, bumping into the table.

"Not high maintenance?" He walked past her, heading toward the hallway.

Several moments later, the group gathered around her, and she explained what had happened, omitting Sullivan's comments. Laughter filled the small space, and she realized it *was* pretty funny.

"Tell me, were you surprised most by the man, or the fact that he was dressing?" Mike grinned at her.

"I think I would have watched," Lucy said, with a throaty chuckle. "Nothing like that ever happens to me."

"Yeah, quite the show," Vic added.

She was pleased the group was accommodating. She still felt foolish, but it was wonderful to have some support. Her eyes filled with tears, and she blinked them back.

Sullivan returned carrying a hank of blue-and-white striped rope, with Sam behind him. "Okay, you all remember Sam, right?" He caught her eye, pausing a beat. "Sam's my partner. You won't find a better man anywhere."

Sam nodded and then without smiling turned to Mackenzie. "Nice to meet you, Ms. Campbell. Again." He offered her his hand. When she took it, he pulled her a bit closer. "I would have screamed, too, if I'd seen me."

She laughed.

Sullivan coughed, a bit too loudly. "Sam, let's tie up those kayaks. We need to get dinner started. How does salmon and asparagus with twice-baked potatoes sound?"

A few minutes later, Mackenzie flopped onto one of the sofas in the lounge, watching the two men through the window as they headed down the walkway toward the back of the boat. Sam had kayaked over, bringing extra kayaks and supplies. A splinter of guilt pierced her. Adding to the group might have affected them more than she realized. Ah, well. Too late now.

They waited on the deck for dinner. Apparently, Sam was king of the kitchen. After starting a couple pitchers of margaritas for the group, he grilled salmon and asparagus and pulled pre-stuffed, baked potatoes from the oven.

She rested on the railing, her back to the group. The houseboat was moored in a secluded nook with canyon walls on three sides. The clouds were crayon shades of yellows and oranges and reds. As the sunset deepened, the canyons became black silhouettes against the darkening sky.

She glanced over her shoulder. Sandy, the environmentalist from Colorado, was relating the history of Lake Powell; as he talked, it was obvious he thought the decision to create the lake was wrong. Loud and bombastic, with arms flying, he punctuated his sentences with sharp gestures.

"They shouldn't have dammed the river. I know they say it creates electricity for the power plant, but for what? Inexperienced people trying to farm on land that wasn't meant to be farmed. It shouldn't, no can't, be farmed." He pounded one fist into his open palm. "Lake Powell was a mistake. Even the Sierra Club calls it a great big bathtub full of silt."

Mike joined her during the monologue. He was still in his ranger uniform, although he had ditched the hat. They didn't say anything for a few moments. They watched dusk deepen to nightfall.

"You know, that group almost got the lake drained," he said. He was younger than she had thought at first, and she had to lean closer to make out his words.

"What? The Sierra Club? Really?"

He nodded.

She angled herself toward him, considering. "Where do you stand on that? I mean, you're Navajo, right? Isn't a lot of your history under the lake?"

"Well, it's complicated. Those prissy nature groups wanting to drain Lake Powell would destroy the Navajo Nation's economy. Sandy's not looking at the whole picture. The Navajo Generating Station provides more than electricity. It also provides 100 million bucks a year for the Nation. Jobs and security and such for the young. It's good for them to be able to stay near their elders, to remember their past. To live on their own land. There's nothing else on it."

She chewed on her bottom lip, not responding.

"But, it's not that simple. Violence and crime are rampant on the Res, and substance abuse is tearing the Nation apart, old and young alike."

"Why does the Sierra Club want to drain the lake?"

"Oh, lots of reasons, and some of them good, I guess. The Club isn't the only one. The dam destroyed the natural ecosystem of the river and canyons. You know, Sandy's right: Lake Powell *is* a big bathtub of water. It's an artificial reservoir, not a natural lake. But all bodies of water sit and collect silt and debris, natural or not."

Mackenzie pulled her sweater around her. It was growing cooler. The group behind them had moved on to discussing bats. She cast a quick glance upward.

Mike took a sip of his margarita. "Sandy's right on another level, too. It's not meant for farm land. It wasn't ever supposed to be. It was a tangle of canyons and slickrock, with a tiny river cutting through it. Not so great for farming. Still, my heritage lies in those canyons, which are now beneath 500 feet of water."

She glanced over at him, but it was too dark to see his face.

"More than half a million people visited Lake Powell last year. Before the lake, only a handful of people even knew about this area. That's good and bad."

"It's confusing," she agreed. "And complicated. I don't understand it all."

"We'll never get that history back," Mike said. "I know. I try not to take sides. Thing is, I like being close to my family. I could get a job at another National Park, but I'd have to move away."

She mmphed, not knowing what to say. He turned back toward the group, listening to Sandy.

Mike was intriguing. He spoke confidently, with a gentle assurance that belied his years. He had a strong profile and generous mouth. Muscular and trim, he didn't carry an ounce of fat. She wondered why he still wore his uniform.

"Your family's nearby?" She shivered.

"Most of them. And my fiancee's. They're here, too."

"You're getting married? Congratulations. When?"

"We haven't set a date yet, but we're thinking in the fall. An outdoor wedding with the canyons as a backdrop."

"Wow. That would be fabulous. What's your fiancee's name?"

"Mary. Mary Louise Nasjah." He lowered his voice. "She's actually related to Sam. Everyone's related to everyone here, in some way." His words were jagged, like the serrated edge of a knife blade. She wondered what had caused the change.

Sam was tending the grill. He stacked roasted asparagus spears on a huge platter and piled salmon on another. With his hair back, he looked younger than she had estimated, maybe mid-thirties. The group, sensing food was imminent, gathered closer around the grill on the other side of the deck.

"What's Sam's story?"

"Well, he's half Navajo. His mother was a rancher's daughter. Trying to get back at her family, I guess. She didn't stick around long, took off after having Sam. He never knew her. Probably a good thing. But I wouldn't mention all that if I were you."

"Oh, I wouldn't dream of it." She studied Sam, who was now arranging baked potatoes on another platter.

"Are you two close, Mike? I know he's older than you."

He snorted. "We're not close. And not because of age." He emptied his glass.

She didn't reply. Life on the reservation was bound to be as political and difficult as anywhere else. She motioned to him with her empty glass. "Looks like we'll be eating soon. Maybe we should go."

They joined the group. Sam ate at the kitchen island, standing up. Sullivan was nowhere to be found.

An hour and a half later, the group was lounging in and around the hot tub. Party lights flickered above the bar, and the underwater lights cast a rippling green glow.

"Here's to a new adventure," Lucy toasted, and they all clinked glasses. She and Mackenzie were sitting in the hot tub, along with Vic and Sandy. Lucy was in a floral bikini two sizes too small that showed off her hard body; Mackenzie felt like a skinny prude in her high-cut one-piece. She stayed low in the water, with only her neck and head visible. Sam and Mike were behind the bar, talking to Sullivan. Dr. Whitehall, or Henry, as he had told her to call him, had retired early, complaining of a headache.

Sullivan leaned over the bar and cut the lights. The deck went dark, and more stars than she thought possible sparkled in the blackness.

Vic pointed out the Big Dipper and Cassiopeia, as well as a few constellations she hadn't heard of. She pressed her back against the jets, letting them pound out the tension. It had been a pleasant night, and she'd enjoyed herself. As the alcohol wore off, though, guilt tinged with fear moved in. She had a hidden agenda but still had no real plan. Not even a hint of one. The jets timed off, and she rested in the water, her chin above it.

Maybe things would become clearer at Rainbow Bridge. She had pushed the thought of the codex out of her mind. Finding something of that magnitude didn't happen anymore. It had to be a hoax. Charlie was the real reason she had traveled all these miles.

Sullivan clicked the lights on, and the stars faded.

Vic leaned in. "Are you all right, Mackenzie?"

"I'm fine," she said. "I was thinking about the lake. The glyphs."

"Oh?"

"Well, there's a good chance a lot of the glyphs are under the lake now, right? So if there is some organization to them, we might not be able to see it."

Sandy sat up a bit in the water. "Yeah. If we could figure out what they mean, it might help us find them."

She took her time answering. "I've been thinking about that. I have a theory."

Vic eased back into the water. "What are you thinking?"

"Well, it's a vague idea. I haven't seen all of the photos of the glyphs. Or any of them in person. How many have catalogued?"

"More than 200."

"They all look like a circle cut in half by a horizontal line?"

"Yeah. There are variations, though. Sometimes there are two concentric circles split by a line. Sometimes the line is longer, sometimes shorter. The position of the holes varies widely. Other than that, they all look pretty similar." He paused. "What's your theory?"

Lucy floated nearer. Mackenzie reached up, drawing a glyph with a wet finger on the deck.

"Okay. I'm probably way off-base, but the glyphs look like a picture, an image, really, that I've seen." She wasn't sure she wanted to continue, but Sandy and Vic were both nodding. The group at the bar had wandered over, too, to see what was going on.

Clearing her throat, she said, "They remind me of, well, of something I saw recently. It looked like the glyph. It was a drawing of Rainbow Bridge, straight on, you know, where the bridge is reflected in the water. Like a complete circle, with the surface of the water a straight line in the middle."

She drew it once more as she talked, emphasizing the water line. Vic glanced at her and then at the drawing. Lucy raised her eyebrows but remained silent. Sandy drew a glyph on the deck, too.

Vic puffed up his cheeks, then exhaled slowly. "You think the glyphs are of Rainbow Bridge?"

Mackenzie shook her head. "I don't know. Maybe."

"You could be on to something," Sandy said.

"It could be the symbols were a map, like you thought, Vic." She gazed at him. "But they could point to Rainbow Bridge. Maybe for a religious pilgrimage. Or maybe it was a known meeting point?"

He didn't say anything. Mackenzie could tell he was running through the glyphs in his mind, checking for a variation to dispel the theory.

"Well, it's something to think about. Maybe we'll find something at Rainbow Bridge."

"Or maybe you'll find what you're looking for," Sullivan stood above them, like Paul Bunyan, arms folded across his chest. "Something that doesn't have anything to do with glyphs, I'll bet."

"What? What do you mean?" She looked up at him, feeling ill. How could he know?

"I know you wanted to go to Rainbow Bridge," Sullivan said. "In fact, you were desperate to go. Before you knew anything at all about this trip."

The group looked at her. Nobody spoke.

"Yes, er, well, I did want to see Rainbow Bridge."

Actually, she wanted to sink below the surface of the water.

"And that's why you talked your way into this trip," he said. "To see if you could get us to go to Rainbow Bridge. You don't give a damn about the glyphs. I think you made it all up."

"No!" Why did she raise her voice when around him? "I mean, no, I didn't make it up. It does look like Rainbow Bridge to me. Doesn't it look like it to you?"

Vic cut in. "Mackenzie didn't plan this, Sulley. Her credentials are impeccable. The Foundation checked her out."

She nodded. "I simply wanted to see it. A friend of mine told me about it." It was the truth. The partial truth, anyway.

Sandy asked Sullivan, "How do you know she wanted to see the bridge?"

Sullivan gestured at her with his head. "She wanted to hire me to take her there. When I told her I was busy, she started yelling at me. In a restaurant."

That was true, too. She didn't know what to say, and she couldn't tell them about Charlie yet. She'd tell them once they were underway. If she was still part of the group.

"Is Sulley right, Mackenzie?" Mike studied her.

"Yes and no," she said. "I did try to hire him, and he did tell me he was busy. After he'd wasted a couple hours of my time. I learned of the trip myself. Later." She knew she wasn't making sense, but explaining the situation wouldn't help her case.

"When did you hear about the trip?" Sullivan's words were clipped, his jaw tight. "I didn't tell you what it was about."

Before she could reply, Sam said, "Hold on. Let's sort this out. It's getting too heated. Why don't we all calm down. Okay, Mac, are you really interested in the glyphs?"

"Yes."

"And are you a linguistics expert?"

"I am. I have my doctorate in linguistics and specialize in Meso—"

He broke in. "So, you didn't try to join the team for other reasons?"

She swallowed. It was the question she had hoped to avoid. There was no option. She had to lie. Again. Going on the trip was the only way to get anywhere near Charlie. She would explain later, she thought. They would understand.

"No other reasons. I just thought it would be a win-win situation. My vacation hadn't worked out the way I'd wanted it to, so this trip sounded perfect. I'd have a guide, and be with a group of people, and I'd provide some linguistic insight. I'm interested in the glyphs. And I know I can add a lot to the team. I was curious about Rainbow Bridge, that's all. That's why I wanted to hire him."

Mackenzie couldn't see Sullivan's face. That was probably good. She added, "I think it's because I had Rainbow Bridge on my mind that I made the connection about the bridge and the glyphs."

No one said anything, but silence was good, she thought. Silence meant they were thinking about what she had said. She could almost feel the group reassessing, believing her.

"I'm probably wrong," she said. "It's only an idea. I don't claim it's right."

"But there's a possibility," Vic said.

And suddenly it was all right again.

Sullivan snorted but said nothing.

Good, she thought. Just stay out of it.

CHAPTER 6

THE NEXT MORNING, BIRDS WOKE HER WITH THEIR CHATTERING. She could smell bacon and coffee and for a few seconds had no idea where she was, until she sat up in the narrow top bunk and almost hit her head on the ceiling.

The night before, after the hot tub disaster, Mackenzie and Lucy had chosen the stateroom toward the back of the houseboat to share, with Lucy claiming the lower bunk. They used the other bunks to store their luggage.

Lucy wasn't in her bunk, and Mackenzie was surprised; she hadn't pegged her roommate for a morning person. Maybe sleeping on a swaying boat didn't work for her? The rhythm had soothed Mackenzie, and she'd slept well. Struggling into her clothes, she tiptoed out to the back deck.

Henry reclined on a deck chair, writing in a notebook of some kind. He looked up and smiled. She smiled back and dragged a chair next to him.

Birds dive-bombed insects in the early morning air. Near the shoreline, the water rippled and swelled from large catfish pushing and shoving, trying to bury themselves in the thick mud. With a start she realized the houseboat was moving: The engines chugged a constant cadence beneath her. It was starting. She swallowed, anxious and nervous at the same time. The houseboat slipped out of the cove, nose first.

"Have you been awake long?" She was just making conversation.

"No. Perhaps an hour or so. I'm afraid I'm a bit of an early bird." He had a cultivated English accent with an American Midwestern twang. A slight hint of Spanish, in the consonants.

"Me, too. What time is it?" Her watch was back in her stateroom.

He tugged out a gold pocket watch and flipped it open. "Six-thirty. I believe breakfast is nearly ready. It's a buffet, I'm told. Would you care for something to eat?"

He was quite formal but friendly. She remembered that he hadn't witnessed the spectacle last night and relaxed slightly.

Meals, she was learning, were sumptuous on *The Amoreena*. Sam was a skilled cook. The dining table was loaded with scrambled eggs, crispy bacon, a fruit salad, toast, and coffee. Home-baked cinnamon rolls were waiting for those who preferred something sweet.

Henry and Mackenzie were the first to eat. They carried plates out to the front deck, discussing Mesoamerican culture, and she learned that in his early days he had led several digs in Guatemala. He spoke very basic Q'eqchi, a Mayan dialect. She asked him why he had joined this expedition. His answer surprised her.

"I'm, er, approaching retirement. I've been working in an office for the past three decades. Feeling a bit chained to the desk, you know. Thought I might get my feet wet again with this excursion, no pun intended."

She grinned.

"Really not interested in these water glyphs." He cleared his throat. "However, it *is* all expenses paid. Hard to resist, even if it does seem, er, a bit amateurish."

"So you're just along for the ride?" She speared a strawberry with her fork.

He nodded. "Yes, you could say that. Never know what we'll find. In situations such as these, it's possible we will discover something. Possible, not probable, if you catch my drift."

Half an hour later, she sat with feet up on the rail, sipping hot coffee. The morning was flawless, with just enough breeze to render the heat welcome. The houseboat rocked hypnotically, and she enjoyed the solitude. Henry had wandered off to get more food.

The canyons were mesmerizing, but they were confusing. They seemed to blend into each other. It was beautiful, but a hint of depression nipped at her. Her task seemed foolish and insurmountable. How in the world would she find Charlie? He could be near, and she'd never know it.

A whining speed boat interrupted her thoughts. She watched as it neared. Curious, she followed the walkway to the back deck and found Sullivan standing there, his back to her.

A woman with streaming blonde hair stood in the boat, holding onto the rail while the pilot gathered rope into a loose hank. He tossed it to Sullivan and then leaped onto the deck. His passenger followed.

"You must be Sullivan," the blonde said to him. "I've heard a lot of great things about you. I'm Jennifer Brandt. This is Jim." She beamed at Sullivan, flashing perfect white teeth. Her streaked hair was the color of old gold, and she was tanned and slim.

Mackenzie couldn't hear what Sullivan was saying. After a short exchange, the man stepped back onto the smaller boat.

Jennifer turned and with one slender finger pushed her sunglasses farther up the bridge of her nose, gazing at Sullivan with a half-smile on her lips. "Thank you so for letting me join your trip, Captain."

Join the trip? Mackenzie forgot herself and stepped out, facing Sullivan. "She's joining?"

"My pleasure," Sullivan said, ignoring Mackenzie. "I think you'll find it interesting. What exactly did you say you were covering?"

"Oh, it's a piece on Lake Powell in general. You know, history and controversy. The lake's been around for more than fifty years now, and I want to get the real story." She held out her hand to Mackenzie. "Hi. I'm Jennifer. I work for *National Geographic.*"

"Mackenzie Campbell. Pleased to meet you."

Jennifer pivoted in a smooth motion like a ballet dancer, facing Sullivan again. She should be on a runway, not on a houseboat. Or a stage. A Californian by birth, Mackenzie guessed. Educated there, too. Somewhere in the valley. She detected a slight valley-girl inflection.

She turned to Sullivan. "Do we have enough kayaks? And food? I thought you said the group was too large."

He glared at her and gripped her elbow. "Excuse me for a moment, Jennifer." He forced her to walk with him. "It's Vic's trip," he said through clenched teeth. "But this is my boat. It's not up to you. I decide who's welcome and who's not." He released her arm. "This woman's doing an article on the lake, and I happen to think that we need all the good press we can get. Especially from *National Geographic.* So I told Vic it would be fine." He glanced over his shoulder. "You let me worry about kayaks and supplies. You worry about yourself."

She rubbed her elbow. "I'm just surprised, that's all. When did this happen?"

"She called Vic ship-to-shore this morning. Told him she was all ready to go and that the magazine was paying all her expenses. And then some. Vic asked me, and I figured, what the hell. I had already agreed take you." He didn't smile. Not waiting for a reply, he turned, walking back to Jennifer.

With one hand on her hip, Jennifer asked, "Okay, tell me, where do I bunk?"

"Well, let me show you around first." He handed her backpack and duffel bags to Mackenzie. "Slim, please take her things to your stateroom. Thanks. The three of you will share a room."

Jennifer flashed Mackenzie a dazzling smile and tossed her hair. "Oh, thanks. Careful with that one. There are some breakables."

Mackenzie shrugged. It wasn't the time to fight. She had to choose her battles. She picked up the bags and lumbered after them.

Two hours later, Sullivan gathered the group together for kayaking lessons. Everyone was paired up in the water, sitting in the boats. Sullivan had spent more than an hour explaining the technique for a tandem kayak. He and Sam had helped them into their kayaks, showing them how to straddle the boats and slip into the seat using their paddles. Lecturing them on safety and boat terminology, he spoke with an easy authority. He's taught before, she thought, and he's used to leading. Comfortable and confident. Memories of her own insecurities surfaced, catching her off guard.

Sullivan continued, demonstrating oar technique and basic maneuvering. The group paddled around a bit, getting the feel.

"Kayaking is an art, not a science." He turned the kayak to face them. "You've got to gauge the current, water depth, obstacles, and your partner while you paddle. In tandem kayaks, the front kayaker sets the pace and paddling rhythm. The rear paddler steers the kayak. Good communication isn't essential, it's imperative."

Lucy and Mackenzie were partners, with Mackenzie in the back seat. Although clumsy and ill at ease, they hadn't tipped their kayak yet. Mackenzie was eager to be underway. Charlie had been occupying her thoughts, and she wanted to do something.

Sullivan sat behind Jennifer in their kayak. He spoke to her and they paddled. He matched her strokes in speed and power and steered them in a wide arc, abruptly reversing directions. The kayak skimmed the surface, returning to the group. It looked easy.

"You must have kayaked before," Sullivan said to her.

"Oh, I paddled around in Baja once. Not for maybe 15 years, though."

He nodded approval. He turned to the group. "So you see," he said, "Partners have to be in sync. Sometimes, though, you have to balance your partner, too." Sullivan stuck a paddle deep in the water on his left side and pulled up hard. Jennifer responded immediately, balancing his stroke with a shallow one.

He grinned in appreciation. "I just attempted to overturn us, and Jenny knew exactly what to do. Good. Very good."

"Doesn't look that hard," Mackenzie whispered to Lucy.

"She makes it look easy," Lucy replied, chewing on a fingernail.

Mackenzie studied the blonde. She obviously loved the attention and was animated and friendly with everyone. Except with Mackenzie. For some reason, there was a coldness between them, subtle, but real.

Shaking her head, Mackenzie focused on the lesson. Sam kayaked around in a solo boat, encouraging and helping. In a few minutes, Lucy and Mackenzie were able to paddle in a circle, stop, and back up.

Sam floated up. "Okay, you two. Can you get out of your kayaks?" He smoothly exited his and stood next to them in the water.

With his help, first Mackenzie and then Lucy exited the kayak. He led them to deeper water. In a few moments the others joined them, dragging their bobbing kayaks behind them. Sam then rearranged the group, creating different couples: Mackenzie became Sandy's partner; Lucy joined Vic.

Looking around, she understood Sam's strategy for the partnerships. He had placed novices with the more experienced, the decisive with the wishy-washy. Vic was skilled with a kayak and very patient. He was a good fit for Lucy. Mike, an experienced kayaker, was Henry's partner. Age and stamina, she concluded. She and Sandy were evenly matched, at least height-wise. Sam took the single-seater, towing a loaded supply kayak behind him.

The only pairing that didn't make sense, she sniffed, was Sullivan and Jennifer, who continued to be partners. Both were competent and had the advantage over the rest of the group. Why not split them up? They paddled down river a bit, laughing at some shared joke.

Sullivan's voice carried over the water. "Okay. This is the most important part. If for some reason you flip your kayak, you've got to be able to get back into it. "Jen, would you please show us how it's done?"

She smiled and slipped out of the kayak like a mermaid. Sullivan clapped, and Mackenzie looked away. Teacher's pet, she thought.

He continued. "Now comes the hard part—getting back in. First, float next to your kayak, with your head close to the cockpit. Stay on the surface, bellybutton down."

Jennifer obediently floated next to it.

"Next reach across the boat with your far hand, holding your paddle in one hand. Keep your bellybutton near the center of the cockpit and hoist yourself up."

She flung herself over the kayak, butt toward them.

Sullivan nodded at her, adding, "Jen, after you're in, scull shallowly while your partner gets in."

Before he finished explaining, she was moving.

"You want to slowly roll over so your backside's in the seat," he said. "Keep your feet in the water until the kayak is stable."

Jennifer flipped over without problem.

Irritation washed over Mackenzie, and impatience. It couldn't be that difficult, and she resented wasting time.

Sullivan continued with a loud voice, "Slide your feet into the foot wells, gently, and keep your feet low. If you swing them in too quickly, you'll tip the kayak. Keep your paddle low, too."

In a few seconds, Jennifer was in the kayak, smiling.

"Okay, now you all try. Vic and Lucy, you go first."

Vic helped Lucy, swimming alongside the kayak, steadying it for her. After a few attempts she wriggled her way into the back seat. Vic nimbly maneuvered himself into position and dropped in.

Mike and Henry had a bit more trouble. Mike took his time with the older man, though, and after several tries, Henry made it. He was deceptively spry and looked around myopically smiling. Mike got into the back seat like he'd lived in a kayak all his life.

"Here we go," Mackenzie muttered. She hadn't paid attention to Sandy during the training and wasn't sure he could handle the kayak. His quietness worried her. Sullivan and Jennifer were already floating down the river, and she hated being the last kayak. Sandy didn't move, though, and appeared to be reluctant to go first. She took the lead.

"I'll go first, Sandy." She took hold of the kayak, not waiting for confirmation. They had drifted farther out, and Sandy was treading water a few yards from the kayak, not helping. She heaved her torso over the center of the seat.

Entering a tandem kayak from deep water was trickier than it looked. The moment she swung her feet around into the cockpit, before she could right herself, she capsized. Upside down in the water, both legs stuck, she thrashed wildly. The water was murky, and she had no idea where her paddle was. She couldn't see Sandy's legs, or anything for that matter. Where the hell was he?

Although a strong swimmer, her mind went blank, and she couldn't remember her lifesaving rules. She willed herself to calm down, the words coming back to her: "Be like seaweed. Don't fight the water, float with it." She relaxed as much as possible, and still couldn't extract her legs. She wouldn't be able hold her breath for much longer. She shut her eyes.

Suddenly someone grasped her by the armpits, and in one rapid movement she was breathing again, out of the kayak. Her hair, loose and slimy, was plastered to her face, and she gasped, sucking in air. For a second she couldn't think.

"There you go. That's okay. You're fine." Sam had righted her and was still holding onto her. She spluttered for a few moments, coughing.

"It's okay. It's okay," he said, sing-song. "You're fine, no worries. Just a little water. We all do it the first time." He droned in the saccharine tone reserved for young children or the very old. Somehow she didn't care.

The kayak was in front of her floating low, heavy with water. She strove to wrench herself free, but he drew her back in. "Not yet. Wait a bit."

Mackenzie heard Sullivan and Jennifer laughing in the distance. She couldn't discern what they were saying, but she blushed crimson anyway, and took a deep breath. If it weren't for Charlie, she'd be out of there.

"I was going to have us do the capsize drills next," Sullivan chuckled. He and Jennifer paddled over to her. "But you've got to be able to sit in the kayak first."

She ignored him and motioned to Sam. He tipped the water out and leveled the kayak. With effort, she hauled herself up and settled into the seat. "Sandy, get in. I'll stabilize." She couldn't tell if she was angrier with Sandy or Sullivan. She sculled briskly, waiting for the cowed man to get in. It took several tries, and Sam's practiced help, before Sandy was in place.

She was glad that was over. And she then groaned, because once settled, Sandy's silence and timidity ended: He instructed her to match his stroke. She sighed. It was going to be a long trip.

After the lesson, Sullivan and Sam loaded the kayaks. An hour later, they left the safety of the houseboat.

Out on the side channel, the water sparkled like cut glass in the afternoon sun. Much to Mackenzie's dismay, Sullivan instructed them to keep their last partners. They headed back to the main channel.

They paddled single-file. Sam brought up the rear behind Sandy and Mackenzie. He occasionally paddled up to each of the kayaks, pointing out ruins and caves and rock formations.

Sandy talked nonstop, not requiring her input. He must be embarrassed, she thought. Maybe the episode had affected him as much as her. His constant babbling must be a way to regain face. Deciding it would be best to let it drop, she let his words roll over her, and enjoyed the sun and water.

After a while, Sam approached them and they stopped, side by side. She smiled, stretching her neck and arms. "How long till we rest?"

"Once we get into the main channel, we'll paddle two or three hours. We'll make camp early."

"I'm starving. I can't believe how hungry I am," Sandy complained.

"There are energy bars in the front storage compartment," Sam said. "It's hard work kayaking. Good to keep your energy up. Make sure you drink a lot of water, too."

A few moments later they rounded a prominent buttress, and their side canyon merged with the larger main channel. A few houseboats floated down the center, and speed boats zoomed by. The kayakers stuck together, forming a loose group.

"Tighten up," Sullivan commanded. "Crossing the channel alone is risky. It's better to be in formation. Sometimes speed boats and jet skiers don't pay attention. They can mow down a kayaker in seconds."

But they crossed without incident, and she enjoyed riding the larger, darker green swells. Sullivan guided them toward the right side of the canyon. Once there, the water was much calmer. They continued paddling in the shade, which was an unexpected respite from the heat.

But after another hour or so, she hit a wall. Her arms and shoulders ached; her butt was numb. Sandy must be tired, too, because they were barely moving through the water.

Sullivan and Jennifer were out of sight, beyond a curve. Sam must have picked up on Mackenzie's condition. He appeared next to them and suggested alternating paddlers to give each other a break. To her delight, Sandy was too exhausted to complain. They took turns paddling, making steady progress. Sam seemed bionic. He pulled a fully loaded kayak behind his own stocked one, and yet he showed no sign of slowing down.

The light was golden and the canyons dark when Sullivan and Jennifer appeared up ahead. "We're heading down this side canyon," he called out, "And we'll make camp for the night. Follow us." They turned and headed down a narrow, curving canyon.

"We'll camp here," he said, and pointed to a campsite in a sandy cove under an immense rock overhang. The overhang formed a cave of sorts, and with its high ceiling looked like an amphitheater. Black streaks stained the walls, and at the very top she detected green fringe clinging to cracks. Water trickled down the walls in tiny rivulets.

Sullivan dragged each of the kayaks onto the beach. After awkwardly emerging, Mackenzie flopped down on the sand, stretching her legs and rolling her shoulders.

Sam spoke up. "You all rest. It's been a long day. We'll set up camp."

She found a flat rock that protruded out over the water. She sat down, letting the cool breeze revive her. The canyon wall on the other side was about two hundred yards away. She could see a niche or cave cut into the wall just above the water level across from her. The channel was swimmable, she thought. The water would feel marvelous on her shoulders and back. A leisurely swim to check it out couldn't hurt.

Looking over her shoulder at the group, she evaluated them. Sam, Jennifer, and Sullivan were removing wet-bags. The rest were lolling about, quietly resting or sleeping.

Jennifer's voice penetrated the stillness. She and Sullivan were laughing and talking, working side by side. Obviously they'd bonded. Let them, she thought; they look good together. She pressed her lips together and faced the water. Why did their growing connection bother her? Then she knew why: Jennifer was a predator and all about men. Mackenzie had known women like her, and she usually avoided them. She frowned. Instead of worrying about Jennifer, she should be focusing on Charlie. She should make a plan. She forced the pair out of her mind.

She studied the small dark opening in the opposite wall. Stepping off the rock, she waded into the water, washing sand off her legs and clothes. The bottom was shallow for a few feet and then it fell off sharply. Behind her, the fire hissed and popped, and she smelled the sweet, smoky scent of burning wood.

She splashed a bit. No one looked up. She slid into the water up to her neck, letting herself drift. Far away, a speed boat hummed, echoing through the canyon.

Loneliness sucker-punched her then, and memories of Charlie overwhelmed her. She had to find him. She couldn't let that telephone call be their last conversation, no matter what their relationship turned out to be.

She breaststroked toward the wall. Her arms were tired, so she took it slowly, gliding with minimal effort. It was farther to the other side than she had calculated. Reaching the middle of the channel, she flipped over on her back, enjoying the contrast of the deepening shadows. It was cooler here, almost too cold. Wispy clouds tinged with reds and pinks floated above her as she floated below.

The sound of an engine interrupted her thoughts. Treading water, she searched for the source up and down canyon. Nothing. But someone was swimming toward her from the beach. She rolled to her back again, ignoring whoever it was.

The humming grew louder, sounding like the high-pitched whine of a jet engine. She tread water again. The noise bounced off the canyon walls, and she couldn't tell where it came from. All she knew was that it was getting louder.

Seconds later, two jet skiers raced around the corner, and she realized they were just yards away—almost on top of her. The pair cleaved the water, faster than she thought possible. She stared, her thoughts clear and simple. *I'm going to die. I'm going to drown in a canyon in Lake Powell.* She closed her eyes, waiting for the impact.

But it didn't come. Instead, something clutched her ankle and dragged her down, deep into the cold water.

"What, the—goddammit, what the hell were you doing?" Sullivan glared at her. The jet skiers were ten feet beyond them, and Mackenzie could barely hear him. She coughed and splashed about, glaring at him, trying to breathe normally.

"Didn't you hear those jet skis? Didn't I say they don't see kayaks in the water, much less a lone swimmer? Don't you ever think?"

He had swum out to save her, she realized. Rescued her. That made her angrier, for some reason. What right did he have to be there? She knew her anger was irrational and inappropriate. It was probably best that she couldn't speak. He remained a few feet away, treading water, staring at her.

After a long moment, Mackenzie said, "You were swimming, too. You were out here in the middle of the channel. It wasn't just me."

"No, I was coming for you. In case something happened. Shit. You could have been killed."

He was right. They would have rammed her. She pictured the collision and couldn't breathe again, this time from fear.

He looked like he was going to say something, but he quickly shut his mouth. Swimming around her, he pushed her in the direction of the shore. "Come on, let's get back. You're not hurt, are you?" His voice was quieter.

She shook her head and began breaststroking again. She pulled hard, head down, taking a breath every few strokes. Sullivan stayed with her.

Near the edge she faded, and Mike and Vic waded out, half dragging her to the beach. She felt a warm towel on her shoulders and shivered uncontrollably. Someone lowered her to the ground. For some reason everyone seemed to be speaking a foreign language.

She curled into a fetal position on her side, her head resting on a pillow. It was Lucy's lap, she realized. Mackenzie wanted to thank her, but she didn't have the strength. Another set of hands piled a sleeping bag on her, and the warmth drugged her. She slept.

"Mackenzie? Look at me."

She opened her eyes to find Sullivan squatting on the sand in front of her. She had no idea how long she'd been out. Someone had placed a sleeping bag under her head. When?

"We need to get you out of your wet things. Jenn and Lucy will help you, okay?"

Nodding, she struggled to sit up. He supported her, and she shuffled toward the overhang.

After changing, she made her way back to the sleeping bag and fell into a torpid sleep.

The odors of smoke and onion and something sweet woke her at last, and her stomach informed her that she hadn't eaten for quite awhile. She sat up.

"Feeling peckish?" Henry sat on a folding canvas chair on her left.

"Mmm-hmm."

"I believe your dinner's prepared and waiting for you. Sam's culinary talents, in such a primitive place no less, are magnificent. Roast chicken, baked potatoes, green beans: just like home. The man's a genius."

Mackenzie was warm in her sleeping bag cocoon. She didn't want to leave. But her hunger was growing.

"Look who's up." Mike and Lucy walked up.

He sat on a rock on the other side of her. "Feeling better? That was quite a scare."

Lucy squatted, studying her. "Are you okay? I was worried."

She heard Sullivan's voice coming from behind her somewhere. "Yeah. Haven't had that much excitement in years."

"Give her some room," Vic demanded.

Once again she was the center of attention, and she wanted to hide or run away. *This wasn't her. She was never the drama queen. She hated this.*

She mumbled some incoherent words, and Sandy handed her a plate and utensils. She took a tentative bite of greasy-moist chicken. Hunger eclipsed everything, then, and she quickly forked food into her mouth, keeping her head down. After a few moments, the crowd dispersed into the darkness. Except for Sullivan.

"So. Tell me what you were thinking. Why were you out in the middle of the lane?" His voice was gentle.

"I wanted to get away for a bit. Everyone was busy." She swallowed. Might as well be honest. "I had to get away. I saw a cave on the other side. A niche of some sort."

He handed her a bottle of water. "Sure. I know that one. I've actually swum out to it, myself."

She waited for him to make fun of her; instead, he poked the fire. It occurred to her then that she hadn't thanked him. "I, uh, wanted to thank you for dragging me under. I mean, for saving me." He had actually risked his life to swim out to her. She felt self-conscious.

"No problem. I'm sorry for grabbing you that way. There wasn't a lot of time."

"Oh my God, I know. They were right there. I couldn't move."

"A common reaction. The fight or flight instinct sometimes backfires."

"It was surreal. Like time expanded. Or slowed down. Something like that."

He prodded a stick in the ashes. "Time's an interesting phenomenon. In the city, it's marked out precisely. Little tics on a watch face. Alarm clocks. In the canyon, or in the desert, it moves in waves, like water, ebbing and flowing."

His answer surprised her. "Well, I don't know, but it was odd out there when it happened. Especially when they came around the bend."

"Those goddamn boys on their ski jets." He stabbed at a half-burned chunk of wood. "They think they own the place. One of these days we'll shut them down here." He nudged the log farther onto the flames. "I hope."

"Well, I shouldn't have been out there." She was grateful to him. They were actually having a decent conversation. She felt a stirring, a subtle quickening. He wasn't that bad. He had risked his life for her.

"Yeah. That's for certain," he said. "It was damned stupid of you."

For a moment she was so shocked she couldn't answer. So much for getting along. "I'm a strong swimmer," she said through clenched teeth. "I was a lifeguard for several years."

"So you definitely should've known better. A lifeguard?" He looked at her, and she cringed. Even though she had clothes on, she felt naked. "You'd think a lifeguard would be more cautious."

"I am cautious. I'm too cautious," Mackenzie replied. "I'm normally sensible and reserved, and, well, cautious. In fact, it's my worst fault."

He grunted.

"It's true. I always do the safe thing. Here in the canyon, on the lake, it's different for some reason. It's all new to me. I've never done anything like this before. And you don't even, uh, I can't even tell you ..."

"Tell me what? It's obvious you've never done anything like this before. What I want to know is why you're here. You might have them all fooled," he said, gesturing toward the others. "Maybe you've convinced them you're interested in Meso-whatever."

"Mesoamerican languages," she said, in a clipped tone.

"Right. I know you're here for some other reason."

Mackenzie searched his face. His expression was level and steady, but not angry. Disconcerted, she debated telling him about Charlie. She wanted to share her quest with someone.

"So," he said. "What is it? Why are you really here?"

"Nothing. No reason." She dropped her eyes, hoping he couldn't see her blushing again.

He stood up. "I think you'll find, Slim, that it's best to be honest out here. It's only us and the wilderness at the edge of nothing. Despite our differences, we have to depend on each other. Think about that."

When she looked up, he was striding away into the darkness.

CHAPTER 7

THEY REACHED RAINBOW BRIDGE EARLY THE NEXT AFTERNOON. The water was a deep turquoise, and the turnoff running up to the bridge wide. Continuing down the waterway, which twisted this way and that, they paddled until the full bridge emerged, spanning the water. Although she had seen photos of it, she wasn't prepared for just how astonishing it was. It looked exactly like a massive rock rainbow.

Voices rose as her fellow kayakers appreciated the bridge. The reflection in the water of the huge arch formed a circle bisected by the river: a complete circle. Mackenzie whistled to get Vic's attention. He tipped his hat at her and smiled.

A large floating dock just before the bridge marred the fairy-tale setting. What must it have been like before the river was dammed to create Lake Powell? They pulled over, and Sullivan demonstrated a dock exit. Her departure was not quite as graceful as before, but she managed to avoid falling into the water.

Mackenzie studied the landscape, but it didn't quite match the sketch Charlie had mailed her. They were on the wrong side of the arch, she realized. He must have been behind it. She could see a path along the water that led around the bridge.

She turned to Sam, who was busy tying off the kayaks. "So, can we wander around here? I mean, what about that path over there?"

"Yup, wander all you want. Just be careful. There are rattlesnakes and other varmints all about. Some pretty steep slopes. All sorts of trouble. There are signs that'll let you know if you're trespassing." He looked up and smiled, his teeth very white against his skin. "Knock yourself out. There's some beautiful scenery out here, so don't forget your camera." He stood up, standing so close she automatically stepped back. She felt suddenly nervous around him, and turned quickly back to the group.

She found Lucy and Jennifer and persuaded them to go with her. Sullivan and Sam were busy hauling out the gear, and for a second her gut tightened with guilt. She hadn't helped at all so far. It occurred to her that she just might be high maintenance. That would have to change.

After a few minutes, the trio reached the base of the left leg of the bridge. The circumference of the leg itself was prodigious, easily the size of a small building. The other leg of the bridge was even larger and seemed to grow directly out of a large, sheer butte.

Water flowed gently under the structure. It looked deep and was a clear cerulean blue. Off to the side was a small flat area, almost completely encircled by ancient cottonwoods. A campground, she figured.

She led the way, veering off the main path to a narrower one. Detouring around an imposing boulder, they climbed gradually and had to scramble over low sandstone ledges and skirt boulders.

"Seems like we ran out of path," Lucy gasped, sitting on a small ledge. "Are you sure we should be here?"

Mackenzie nodded. "Sam said it was fine. Just watch out for snakes."

"Snakes?" Jennifer leaped up, brushing the seat of her pants. "What kind of snakes? Rattlesnakes?"

"Shh. Don't worry, they'll stay away from us."

"Look, Mac. It's just like the glyph." Lucy stood on her tip-toes.

"I know. It looks even more like it from this side. I can't believe it, really. Funny how it just struck me."

Jennifer paused, eyeing her. "Yes, funny. What made you think of it?"

She deliberated. She still didn't want to let anyone in on Charlie's secret. "Um, I really don't know. Something just reminded me of it."

Jennifer wouldn't let it go. "What reminded you of it?"

Feeling trapped, Mackenzie resisted answering Jennifer's question. "Oh, probably just a photo in a book somewhere." She turned and ran lightly down a slickrock mound. Conversation over, she muttered.

They hiked farther. Much of the land around them was fenced off and labeled off-limits. She wanted to ignore the signs and explore. The Painted Rock that Charlie had drawn should be nearby. Jennifer, however, was eager to go back, and Mackenzie reluctantly gave in. They found the rest of the group at the campground, setting up tents on the sandy ground.

She had never set up a tent on her own before and surreptitiously watched Mike. Her brand-new, ultra-cheap knock-off tent was different from his. She set her jaw and fumbled along until it looked right. Finally, she stood back, admiring her work.

"Pretty tent," Sam said, walking up behind her. "But where's your ground cloth?"

She stared at him. Ground cloth? Of course. Shit. She turned back to the tent, shoulders sagging.

He cleared his throat, smiling. Holding up a finger, he walked off. She collapsed onto a nearby log, staring at her little tent. She hoped she wouldn't be singled out again, the focus of curious eyes. She could just hear Sullivan complain about her lack of knowledge. How in the world was she ever going to get the hang of this, much less find Charlie?

Sam returned with some folded-up plastic. "Come on. Let's get this under it. No problem."

They unstaked the tent and lifted it as a whole, sliding the cloth under it. He helped her restake the tent, showing her how to angle the stakes into the sand to better anchor them. He placed large rocks over the stake ends.

"There you go. You never know when we'll get rain out here. The cloth keeps, um, other things away, too."

She chose to ignore the last part of his statement. Insects? What he had called varmints? God. "Thanks," she replied.

He was in a sleeveless t-shirt and cargo shorts that rode low. She studied him, appreciating his trim, muscled body.

He caught her at it and said, "Something on your mind?"

"Uh, no," Mackenzie replied, backpedalling quickly. "Well, yes, really. Do you know anything about the bridge? I mean, more than the basic stuff?" She slung her backpack and sleeping bag into the tent and zipped it tight.

He motioned for her to follow him. "Sure. Let me show you."

They headed up toward the path she had just traversed.

"The Navajo call it Nonnoshoshi, which means 'rainbow turned to stone.' My ancestors considered it the symbol of the gods who give life to the desert. A gift from them.

"That's why the Navajo won't walk under it," He led her up a faint path to their right. "It's sacred. But we can walk around it. That is, if you don't mind crossing this little bridge." A rope bridge was before them. He ducked under, and she followed. She warily made her way across the swinging walkway that spanned the river.

She told him they'd already checked out the bridge from the back.

"Yes, well, we're going to see it from another angle. If you're game." He winked at her and increased the pace.

They climbed steadily, switching back and forth, taking their time. They were circling a-fifty-foot-tall mound next to the cliff.

"Painted Rock is just above us," he said. "There are some very well-preserved, unusual pictographs there. Have you heard of them?"

Her heart thudded in her chest, and she tried to keep her face noncommittal. Out of breath, she wiped the back of her neck with her hand. "Uh, no."

He grinned at her. "Well, we're very close." In one sure movement, he slipped through a narrow slit in the rock barely two feet wide and disappeared.

"Dammit." She took a deep breath and squeezed through the opening in the rock.

It was a narrow alcove with bowed walls that almost met at the top, creating a cave-like feeling. She followed a sandy path that twisted back on itself, like an elongated U. Turning the corner, she saw that Sam was waiting for her ten feet up the side of one of the curved walls. He was straddling a rock saddle that formed the bottom of a hole in the rock. She saw blue sky beyond it.

"How'd you get up there?"

He shrugged, a Cheshire cat smile on his face. "Moki steps."

Mackenzie surveyed the wall. Small holes pockmarked the rock and could probably be used for hand- and footholds. That must be what he meant by Moki steps. She looked up. Sam was gone again, damn him. She hurriedly climbed up, using the holes and ledges. They'd better not have to leave the same way, she groused.

A moment later she sat on the saddle. They were next to the arch, about a third of the way up. Sam sat next to a boulder, gazing up, waiting for her. She crab-walked down, sliding on her butt the last few feet.

The wall of rock before her was almost completely black and slightly concave. It was shiny, like it had been shellacked. A panel, at least twenty by forty feet long, maybe fifteen feet above the ground, covered much of the black rock. She stared, fascinated, at the painted pictographs that were extremely well-preserved and vivid. There were several human-like figures with spears that she knew dated from 200 A.D. She noticed symbols from even earlier times.

On the far right side, toward the bottom, were a set of petroglyphs carved into the rock. Aztec figures and symbols. Her heart raced. There weren't many figures, but they were large and untarnished. Wishing she had a notebook or camera with her, she sat down and endeavored to interpret the panel.

"Know what it means?" Sam was standing behind her, shielding his eyes with his hands.

"Well," she replied thoughtfully, "the ones over there are Aztec. The Aztecs didn't write sentences as we know them. They didn't write in a linear fashion."

Sam grunted. "Huh?"

"They didn't write like us, using a line of text. It was much more complex than that. Symbols usually just floated around. Not in order, more like a comic book or something. The reader had to decipher them, and from context, fill in the timeline and story."

He nodded and sat down against a rock. She knew he had reached his saturation point. She was used to glazed eyes and vague nods whenever she went into details. Almost everyone changed the subject, leaving her words hanging in the air like smoke. This time, however, she was glad, because she had no desire to teach him the intricacies of Aztec symbology.

Turning back to the panel, she saw symbols that meant a mountain or cliff, hiding, and a cave. There was also a symbol that could mean the sun god or the direction up. There was no date that she could see, but there were number symbols. She spotted the glyph for an Aztec ruler.

She suspected that Charlie's story had influenced her. As she stood there, assessing the pane, she theorized that the symbols described something of value hidden in a cave on a hillside. If Charlie was right, the petroglyphs provided the location of the codex. Gazing up at the wall, she saw a small rock ledge breaking the otherwise smooth surface of the cliff face. She tried to remember if Charlie's drawing had shown a ledge.

Searching in her pockets for a scrap of paper, she found nothing. Shit. She'd have to commit some of the larger symbols to memory and swore again under her breath.

Mackenzie stared at the panel and blinked. At the bottom, right edge, someone had recently written in white chalk or marker: *v.i.*

Vide infere. A scholarly, little-used Latin term for see below. Although rare in literary citation, she and Charlie had used it frequently when collaborating on notes. In references and citations, it meant, 'see after' or, 'go under.' She blinked. It had to be a clue.

She looked back, expecting to find Sam watching her. Instead, he was at the base of the saddle, several yards from her. He appeared to be napping, leaning against the rock with his hat over his eyes, crossed legs stretched out in front of him. She turned back to the panel and knelt, running her hands down the rough wall, searching. Nothing.

Leaning back on her heels in frustration, she studied the marks. What did 'below' mean? There didn't seem to be anything directly below the panel. *Vide infere ...*

Suddenly, it made sense. It wasn't on the panel. It was on the ground. She pitched forward, stopping herself with her hands. Directly beneath the panel she found a small boulder with crumbly dirt surrounding it. When she rocked it, it moved.

"Can't take rocks that size."

Shit. Sam was up. "Uh, yeah, I know. I was going to sit on it, but it didn't seem steady." She stood up, wiping her hands off on her shorts, and smiled, hoping he'd buy her lame excuse.

"We gotta get back, so no sitting. Ready?"

Mackenzie sucked in some air, letting it out slowly. It was better to appear calm, bored almost. "Sure," she said. "Let's go."

Later that evening, moonlight painted the landscape with grays, changing it. Everything looked strange and unfamiliar. After a few false turns, she found the path and made her way up to the cleft in the rock they had entered earlier that day. In broad daylight it had simply looked like an opening in the rocks; tonight it seemed more sinister. She pulled out her pencil-sized flashlight and took a deep breath. She didn't want to go in, but she had to see if anything was under that boulder, and she wanted to photograph the panel, as well.

Leaning into it, she splashed light over the walls. No sign of critters or bugs. Good.

The passageway doubled back on itself, she remembered, before it reached the Swiss-cheese wall that led to the saddle. She shuffled slowly, cautiously. At the wall, she paused, searching for the depressions in the rock, and then started up, using both hands in the darkness, flashlight in her teeth. She knew she'd have to descend the same way, which somehow made it seem even harder.

It was slow going. She mounted it steadily, until she could sit on the saddle. The small, sandy area below was brightly lit by moonlight, and she had no trouble sliding down to the path. She stood there for a long moment.

The displaced boulder was still there. For some reason, she had been afraid it would be gone. She rolled it away, holding her breath.

There was something there.

A small plastic sandwich bag lay half-buried in the moist sand. Inside was a folded scrap of paper. She read, *Follow the map on the codex. Heading there now. CP.*

Mackenzie sat back heavily. It was a message. She didn't know which was more unlikely: him trusting her to find it, or her actually recovering it.

The reality of her situation pressed on her then. It was actually happening. He was still alive. At least he had been when he had written the note. Her instincts had been right. She had found a clue to where he was, and he had known she'd look for him.

Stuffing the slip in the bag again, she flattened it until it fit in her back pocket and turned back to the wall. I have to get photos, she thought. I have to document this.

She took nearly fifty photos of the entire panel, focusing on the smaller Aztec inset. She climbed a few yards up the hill opposite the face to get some good shots of the cliff above her.

Time escaped her; she had no idea how long she had been there. After filling the camera's memory card, she paused, looking at the surrounding landscape for the first time. Nothing looked familiar. It was definitely time to get out of there.

Fortunately, descending the wall in the dark wasn't as difficult as she had anticipated. Either that, or her muscle memory had taken over. She downclimbed the wall a few feet, beginning to gloat, but then her lizard-like ability abandoned her. When she jumped the final few feet, her ankle twisted beneath her.

"Shit," she said, sinking to the ground.

"No shit," she heard in reply.

She stifled a scream. Someone was there.

A dark figure leaned against the interior canyon wall.

"Sam showed you this?"

It was Sullivan. She let out a breath, then shook her head. Incredible. Was this man everywhere?

"Yeah," she said. "We came up this afternoon. I wanted to get some, er photos." She rotated her ankle, receiving a sharp pain in response. She began unlacing her shoe.

"Stop. Don't do that."

"What?"

He was next to her now, kneeling on one knee, batting her hands away. "You need to leave it on." He tightened the laces. "It'll keep the swelling down. If you take your shoe off now, your ankle will blow up like a balloon, and you won't be able to get the shoe back on." He secured the laces with a double knot, and she winced.

"Why are you here?" She rubbed her calf, avoiding the ankle.

He rose above her, holding out his hands, and she reluctantly took them, almost colliding with him as she pulled herself onto her good leg. He was taller than he had seemed earlier, and stronger.

"How does it feel?" He ignored her question, keeping her hands in his.

She felt a warmth spreading through her and was suddenly tongue-tied.

"Can you put your weight on it?"

She tested the foot. She could limp along with just a little bit of pain and told him so.

"Good. Now, tell me why you were taking photos in the middle of the night." He placed her hand over his arm, and she let him. "Alone, no less."

Mackenzie concentrated, limping along. She decided to play his game and ignored the question, asking instead, "First, tell me why you're here."

"I heard you unzip your tent. And you weren't exactly quiet as you crashed about in the bushes. So I followed you and climbed that damned wall. I can't believe you're out here. It's foolhardy to go out in the desert alone at night. You never know what you might find."

"Hmmph," she retorted. He was right about that.

They were on the side of the hill; the moon had fallen lower in the sky, making it difficult to see. He led her down the path, supporting most of her weight.

When they reached the rope fence, he picked her up and stepped over it. It happened so quickly she couldn't react. He held her for a moment on the other side, looking down at her. Mouth open, she lay stunned in his arms. Then he set her gently down, holding out his arm again to help her across the little bridge.

"I'll try it on my own," she told him, twisting away.

"Suit yourself." He crossed the bridge in front of her.

She waited until he was out of sight before hobbling after him. Her ankle throbbed and was probably swollen. But she would be damned if she'd let that man see her cry. She swore under her breath as she crashed along, wiping her tears away with the back of a grimy hand. It took her thirty minutes to cover what she'd done earlier in ten.

He stood by the gravel entrance to the campground for her. "You have tape and a bandage, right?"

She shook her head, knowing her voice would betray her. She was confused and on the verge of crying again. Probably from the pain.

His voice was mild. "I'll get some. Go to your tent."

Mackenzie clamped her lips together and continued limping slowly. He met her at her tent with a first-aid kit and an ice pack.

"Come on, I'll help you in," he whispered. This time she didn't decline. The effort to get back had exhausted her, and she was emotionally spent. He grasped her elbows, lowering her to the ground. She wriggled through the opening, aware of him just behind her.

He followed her into the tent and turned his flash light on low beam, propping it up next to them. "Now, we can take your shoe off."

She flinched when he pulled it off, inhaling. Her ankle looked puffy, but not as much as she would have thought. Of course, she couldn't see much in the dim light.

"You'll have to ice it first," he said. "Then wrap it."

He peered at her. "Can you do that, or do you want me to?"

"I can do it. Thanks."

"No problem. But make sure you ice it. Don't skip that part. Twenty minutes if you can handle it." He retrieved his flashlight, and with a quick nod, left her in the dark.

Thankfully, he'd forgotten that she hadn't answered his questions.

She attached her flashlight to a tent pole and centered herself under the swath of light. Thrashing about, she tried to get comfortable. Finally, she propped her ankle on a pile of clothes, draping the ice pack around it. Twenty minutes. It takes twenty minutes to really ice an injury. Of course it does. He thought she didn't know that?

She shook her head, forcing herself to think about Charlie. Turning on one side, she dragged out the folder containing Charlie's photographed panels. She flipped through page by page, until she found an empty sleeve. She pulled the note from her back pocket, slipping it into place, and smiled in the darkness, despite her pain.

One more piece of the puzzle. One more piece.

CHAPTER 8

WHEN THEY STARTED OUT THE NEXT MORNING, MACKENZIE WAS glad to be in kayaks. Although her shoulders burned, her ankle hurt worse. She told the group she had twisted it searching for a place to pee. She could feel Sullivan's eyes on her, but he didn't give her away.

Sullivan had insisted they be on the water by seven o'clock to beat the motorized boat traffic. At first, she wasn't thrilled about having to get up that early, but the smell of bacon and eggs rejuvenated her, and she found she was in good spirits, even with her pain and lack of sleep. But every time she thought of Charlie, her thoughts returned to Sullivan, to the seconds she had spent in his arms. He'd been surprisingly tender and kind, contrasting sharply with his general behavior toward her. Maybe he was a sucker for someone in pain. Maybe he was just difficult to get to know.

The sky was clear and free of clouds, the only sound the rhythmic splashing of paddles in the water. Sam rearranged the group again, and she found herself partnered with Jennifer. She opted for the front seat, letting Jennifer steer.

Sullivan and Sandy led the way back to the main channel. They set a brisk pace. The canyon looked very different in the morning sun, almost unrecognizable. They followed Sullivan, staying close, so they could hear his comments.

"At the main channel, we'll hang a right and head down to Oak Canyon for lunch. Assuming we're all not too sore."

Several groans rose from the group, and then laughter.

He continued. "We'll have time to explore, as there are quite a few petroglyphs, if anyone's up for hiking. Then we'll float by Register Rock on the right and Hole in the Wall on our left. Anyone know the history there?"

He filled the better part of an hour describing the Mormon's obsession to get their wagons through the solid rock. They had dynamited a hole large enough to lower horses and wagons down to the river. The actual trail was now mostly below the water, with floating buoy marking the actual hole in the rock wall.

"Not much to see," Jennifer said, squinting.

"No. Hard to imagine, too, what it looked like before they created Lake Powell." Mackenzie sighed.

Suddenly, Sullivan's voice rang out, startling her. "Oak Canyon's here on the right."

She was silent while she stroked. Jennifer guided them into the large bay. The water was about five feet deep and much clearer than any they had seen earlier. Near the right edge of the beach, a shelf of rock a few feet wide broke the surface of the water. They floated close enough to touch it with their paddles. Underwater trees scratched the kayak's bottom, fondling it like eery skeleton fingers.

"Stay close to the shoreline," Sullivan said, "And be careful. The beach is wide, but the bushes are thick in some areas. Don't get stuck. Take it slowly."

Jennifer was the only one to answer. "Okay, boss. I'll do that."

We'll do that, Mackenzie muttered, driving her paddle deep for a long pull. And felt it pull back.

Shit. Her paddle was caught on something. She leaned over the side of the kayak, trying to pull it out. She was almost horizontal, extended out over the water.

"Let go." Jennifer yelled at her. "Let it go!"

Mackenzie released it, and the kayak righted itself. Jennifer sculled to keep it level. They drifted out to deeper water.

What an idiot she was. And in front of Jennifer, no less. She couldn't see any trace of the paddle. She furtively scanned the beach. Everyone else was focused on getting to shore. Jennifer continued paddling, turning them back toward the beach, and in a moment they glided onto it.

"Didn't you hear him?" Jennifer spat. "Don't you ever listen?"

"What? Of course, I listen. It just got stuck, that's all." Once again she was on the defensive.

"Well, you've got to go get it. Can't just call home for another paddle." Jennifer leaped out to pull them farther up the shore and then stalked off.

Damn it, Jennifer was right. After securing the kayak, Mackenzie pulled her shoes off and waded back into the water, gripping the sand with her toes. Her ankle throbbed but held her weight. The cool water felt therapeutic.

Several feet out, the shore rapidly gave way, and she was soon chest-deep in water. She continued on, avoiding the taller weedy bushes until she was almost to the rock shelf. She prodded the vegetation under the surface gently with her foot until she felt the paddle. Evidently, it was wedged in the muck. She dipped lower, up to her mouth, and tugged until she could free it. A moment later she held it above her head like a prize, insanely proud that she had found it by herself.

Without her hands for balance, returning was arduous. She bashed her way through tangled bushes, struggling to move. Her arms and shoulders were so tired she feared she'd drop the paddle again. She was anxious to get back to the beach before Sullivan knew what happened. Instead of retracing her steps, she headed for the rock shelf. It would be easy enough to climb over it, and faster.

She was in thigh-deep water when she felt it. Something moving under around her ankle. Something slimy and slippery—and alive.

Letting out a scream, she reflexively kicked out with her good foot. Still holding onto the paddle with both hands, she lost her balance and fell, face-first into the water.

Coughing and spluttering, she flailed, clawing at rotting branches. What the hell was that? A snake? Was it following her? Finally upright, she sloshed through the shallow water as rapidly as she could.

"Going swimming again?" Sullivan stood in front of her, water lapping at his ankles.

"I, uh, there's something out there." Mackenzie skirted him and climbed onto the shelf. "I stepped on something. Something moving and slick. There's some kind of creature out there. A snake, I think. A big one."

The rest of the group gathered just beyond her. She pointed toward the rock shelf. "Right there."

Sullivan waded deeper and retrieved her paddle. He stopped in mid-thigh water, arms crossed over his chest. "Here?"

She was afraid to look. What if it was dangerous? She didn't want him to get bitten. "Yes, Come back."

"Um, yeah, there is something out here. Something pretty scary." He paused, then shoved a hand deep into the water.

She gasped, then clamped her mouth shut.

He held up a black rubber inner tube, covered with weeds and algae.

"They sell these at the marina," he said, after he stopped laughing. "You're supposed to float on them. They're usually not that dangerous." He pulled some of the weeds off the rubber tube and headed back to the beach, still chuckling.

Mortified, she limped up the beach after him, nursing her ankle. An inner tube. God. She was grateful when Lucy joined her.

"Let's eat, Mac. You've got to be hungry." Lucy's voice was warm and encouraging. She took Mackenzie's arm.

A few moments later, they were eating lunch on a large, flat rock at the water's edge. "It didn't feel like an inner tube." Mackenzie couldn't get the incident off her mind. "It felt alive." She massaged her ankle.

Lucy handed her an orange. "You must have been terrified. I would have freaked."

Mackenzie smiled. It was comforting to have someone understand and not make fun of her. The rest of the group, except for Lucy, had laughed with Sullivan when he held the inner tube up for inspection.

"You know, I'm not really like this in real life." She tried to keep the whininess out of her voice. "I mean, in my life back in Denver. I'm usually the quiet one who sits on the side observing. I'm never the village idiot."

"It's just a new experience altogether, Mac. You need to relax. You'll get the hang of it. Think about the history buried beneath 500 feet of water. Nothing left of the people who lived there. Just a few ruins. Don't you think that's a shame?"

Mackenzie took her time answering. "Yes. But it's complicated. I'm not sure how I feel about it."

"It's a pretty controversial thing. I love the lake. Amazes me there are priceless items under it."

"Mmm-hmm. Don't know much about that," Mackenzie said, drowsily.

"You don't? I would have thought you'd know all about what was lost. From written records and all. Isn't that your specialty?"

Her friend's words were sharp, almost sarcastic. Mackenzie ignored the tone. Lucy must be tired. "Well, my field is Mesoamerican languages. There are quite a few of them, in various areas. Hard to decipher them all." She didn't want to get into details.

"But you agree that important things were lost. That someone with language skills could decipher?"

"I'm sure there were, Lucy." She added, silently: *Yes. Some of them in a cave on a cliffside.*

"But you don't know any of them. That's what you're saying?"

Why was this feeling like an interrogation? "Like I said, I haven't studied this area. I'm sure quite a bit was lost. There are always things—priceless things, as you say—lost to time. Sometimes it's vandals. Sometimes it's a newer civilization. Or treasure hunters." She paused. "Most of the time it's weather. Being a historian, you know that."

"Right. It's just so sad the lake covered it all up. Guess I'm a bit frustrated. Sorry."

"No problem." They slipped into silence, which was fine with her.

Her thoughts turned to Charlie. She'd been so caught up in the immediacy of kayaking and Lake Powell that she hadn't thought of him the entire day. She tried to visualize his smile, conjure his laugh, but instead she heard Sullivan laughing at her. What an ass. So irritating. To force herself to regroup, she said, "Have you done this much? Roughing it, I mean?"

Lucy shook her head, fighting with a potato chip bag. Her white blonde hair sparkled in the sunlight, contrasting with her dark roots. "No. But I backpack and hike a lot. And bike. Keeps me in shape, although right now my arms and shoulders are killing me." Locking her fingers, she stretched both arms overhead.

Mackenzie yawned. "I know. I can barely lift this brownie."

"But you will," Lucy laughed.

"Yes, I will. I most definitely will."

"Mac. Wake up."

Startled, she bolted up. She must have fallen asleep after lunch.

Sam was kneeling next to her. He was so close she could feel his breath on her. He held a finger to his lips. "Shh. Lucy's napping. Want to hike up to some ruins? They're worth seeing."

She blinked, trying to shake the muddle-headedness, then nodded, rolling off the rock onto the sand.

"It takes about an hour to get there. Henry's going, too."

She yawned again, fighting off sleep. "Is it difficult? I'm not sure my ankle can take much climbing."

"Walking is good for it," he replied. "We'll take it slow. No rush. Henry's going to take awhile anyway, I'm thinking."

"Where's Vic?"

"He went down the other path. Thought there would be a better chance of finding one of his glyphs. I told him we'd be on the lookout."

"Well, I hope he finds one," she said. "Or that we do. So far, we haven't had much to do with the glyphs."

"It's early yet. I figure that deeper in the canyon, farther from the lake, we'll find more."

They set off an hour later. Sam had applied some kind of salve that smelled like geraniums to her ankle and taped it up. It helped.

The shadows were absent on the rock and the colors flat. Sam stayed out in front, setting an even pace. She followed just behind, placing her feet where he did, imitating him when possible. She admired the easy and graceful way he almost danced over the slickrock.

A few minutes later, the trail curved, revealing a large, terraced mound. He pointed to the top. "That's where we're going to first. Then we'll circle around to see the ruins. Try to keep as much of your foot as possible on the slickrock. Not just your toes. And keep your weight forward. Really commit to your step. The rock's rough, which makes it easier, but you can't get careless. Let me know how your ankle holds up." He led the way up the rock.

Out of breath, she managed a grunt, fighting back a surge of fear that sucked her mouth dry. She put a tentative foot on the sloped rock, testing her ankle. It seemed to be all right.

"We'll rest right over the next ridge. It's not far." He was already halfway to the top.

She glanced up at the ridge and thought, I can't climb that. It's impossible. But with each step she gained confidence. He was right—the rock appeared smooth, but it was more like crusty sandpaper, covered with minuscule ledges and knobs that somehow provided a purchase. Although scared, she enjoyed puzzling out the next move. Edging to the right, she followed a narrow ledge that curved around the slickrock mound.

"No. Don't take the ledge." A voice rose from somewhere below her. Hazarding a quick look, she saw Sullivan close behind her. Her thoughts tumbled about. When had he appeared?

"That ledge runs out to nothing on the other side, and it's a steep drop to the bottom. It's difficult at best, even for experienced climbers, to go back. Best to go straight up."

She swallowed, searching for a way back to her left.

He was beside her now. He motioned for her to follow, and she chose her steps carefully as she followed him. He was as sure-footed as Sam, if not as graceful.

Finally, after what seemed to be hours, she was on the flat ridge. Sam was sitting a few yards away. He patted the rock next to him, and she dropped down gratefully, hugging her knees.

"That's the worst of it. Easy going from here on out. How's your ankle?"

Mackenzie realized that once she'd begun climbing she hadn't given it any thought. "Fine. Better, I think. Thanks."

Easing down beside her, Sullivan said, "It's like a puzzle of sorts, finding the best route up the slickrock. Sometimes you get into a rhythm. Sometimes it's just trial and error."

She nodded, surprised that he had echoed her thoughts almost verbatim.

Sam flashed an eyebrow at Sullivan. "Why're you here?"

"I thought you might need a hand. Henry is off taking notes or something."

"Think one of us should go back for him?"

"Let's give him a while. He might turn back." Sullivan grinned and then gestured ahead. "I'd like to scout the trail. It's been awhile since I've been to the ruins."

"How far is it?" She squinted in the general direction.

"Not far. Maybe fifteen minutes," Sam answered. He handed her a water bottle. "Here. You stay put and wait for Henry. We'll be right back. We're just going to make sure it's passable."

After wiping her lips with her sleeve, she drank, enjoying the mix of sweet water and salty sweat. The two men disappeared down the slope.

The view was spectacular, and she was grateful to just sit and take it in. Layers of rock, with jagged cliffs, rounded swells, and sandy slopes lay straight ahead. On her left, colored ribbons of slickrock heaved like waves on the sea. But on her right, the rock dropped off sharply. She debated standing up and checking out the edge, but decided she was too tired. "I think I'll just rest," she informed the landscape.

Reaching into her pack, she dragged out her camera and snapped several shots. The sky was deep blue against the reds and oranges and tans of the canyon, and she hoped she could capture the hue. As she was replacing it, she thought she heard something. She cocked her head.

"Hallooo-oo."

It was coming from her right, below the edge of the cliff. Were Sullivan and Sam coming back another way?

"Halloooo. Help me. Someone help me! Is anyone there?"

She bolted up, looking around. It wasn't them. Making her way toward the edge, she got to her knees and peered down.

Twenty feet below her, face to the rock, she saw Henry's bald head. He was clinging to the rock.

"Help. I'm stranded."

She sucked in a breath, looking around. "Henry. It's me, Mackenzie. Hold on. Just hold on." She peered down. Henry had followed the path Sullivan had warned her about. "Can you retrace your steps?"

"Nooo. I can't move. I'm stuck."

"I'm going to get help," she yelled. "Just hang on." She scuttled backward, trying to think.

"Don't leave me. ..."

It was a pitiful, drawn-out whine, but she had to ignore him, had to think.

Mackenzie gazed back to where she'd last seen Sullivan and Sam. Where the hell were they? What was she supposed to do?

She ran to the packs leaning against a low wall, hoping to find something. Sam's held only a rain jacket, energy bars, and water.

"Mackenzie?" Henry's voice was faint, growing fainter, she noted. "Are you there?"

"I'm coming," she called.

Sullivan's backpack was stained and dirty. It was larger and heavier than Sam's. Please, she prayed. Please, please, please. Reaching in, she shoved her hand through to the bottom and found a coil of rope. She tried to free it from the pack, but her hands were slick with sweat and clumsy. *Slow down; stay calm,* she told herself.

Using her feet to trap the leather straps, she yanked the hank of rope out. It was red and blue and might be long enough to reach the edge. She untied the neat knot securing the bundle and looped one end of the rope around a weathered juniper that grew straight out of the rock. She knotted the rope over and over and tested it. She then tied several knots down its length, about four feet apart. She hoped they would help.

"Henry? Henry, I'm going to send some rope down. Don't move."

Crawling to the edge, she gathered a wad of rope in one hand, still retaining her grip on the end that was secured by the rock with her other. "Okay. Rope coming down." She heaved it up, as high as she could, knowing that if it got stuck in a crack she wouldn't be able to retrieve it. With a resounding *thwap*, it hit the side of the cliff.

"I see it. I see it!"

Pressing her belly to the rock, she edged out over the rim. The rope hung straight down and was long enough to reach Henry, but several yards away from him.

"I can't get it."

Mackenzie wormed her way farther out, spreading her legs and digging her toes into the sand. She swung the end of the rope back and forth, in wider and wider arcs, until it was nearer and let it go, hoping the momentum would be enough.

"Henry, don't. …" Her words died in her throat as she watched him lean out, reaching for the rope with both hands. For a second he was still, between rock and air. And then he lost his footing.

Time stalled, then slowed. He caught the rope and scraped and bumped against the rock face. But he held on, bouncing like a rag doll on a string.

"Are you okay? Can you find a foothold?" Her voice was raspy, not hers.

He had spun about on the rope and was facing away from the wall. He leaned his body to the left and grabbed at some scrub on the cliff. "I seem to be steady here. Brilliant. Thanks."

"Okay. Good." *Now what?*

Sweat dripped into her eyes, and she wiped it away impatiently with her sleeve. She searched the distance for Sam and Sullivan. Shit. What should she do? Wait for them to return, or try to do something on her own?

It was just her, she knew. She had to decide.

"Henry, I'm going to pull you up. But you'll have to help."

She backed away from the edge. The rope was taut, snugged to the ground. She swept sand away under part of it, making a small depression in the ground that she could just fit her hands into.

Leaning back, she wedged a foot against a rock and pulled with all her strength. Nothing.

Wedging both feet against the rock, she tried again. Still, nothing. She blinked back the sweat, keeping her hands on the rope.

Suddenly, a pair of tanned hands pried hers away.

"No," she croaked. "Henry's down there."

Sullivan took hold of the rope, and Sam dragged her aside, propping her up against the outcrop of rock.

Sam yelled down to Henry and joined Sullivan. They worked together, pulling hand over hand. Moments later, Henry appeared at the edge. Sullivan and Sam's eyes met in silent communication, and Sam knelt. He lugged Henry up by the armpits. The older man flopped face down on the ground, wheezing and sucking air like a beached whale.

"I … can't … breathe," he gasped.

Sullivan turned him over and sat him up. "It's all right. You're all right. Just relax."

As Henry's composure returned, hers left. She began shaking. The full awareness of what might have happened struck her, and she fought against sobs. Anyone could fall and die in these canyons. They weren't safe. What was she doing here?

"Sam," Sullivan hissed. Sam nodded and knelt beside Henry, placing a steady hand on the other man's shoulder.

Sullivan tugged her up by her arms. She met his gaze, tears still streaming down her cheeks.

"He could've … I couldn't … Oh my God."

He just nodded, murmuring, "It's okay now. Everything's okay." He brushed her bangs out of her eyes and put his hands on her shoulders.

She closed her eyes, giving into the drowsiness. She must be in shock, she thought. She couldn't focus.

CHAPTER 9

THEY RETURNED TO THE CAMPSITE AROUND FIVE O'CLOCK. Sullivan and Sam flanked her like trained Dobermans.

Henry was enjoying his audience. He was unaccountably energized, not drained. "There I was, alone on the ledge. Everyone had gone ahead, you see. I stopped to examine a small find of pot sherds. Sketched them." He proudly displayed the pocket-sized notebook.

"Then I simply began climbing, following the trail, when I happened on a small ledge. I was sure the trail continued that way. Very shortly, I found the ledge petered out. Rather abruptly." He pantomimed his stance, hands above his head.

Sullivan let out a low sigh.

"Situated there, on barely six inches of ledge, I couldn't return the way I'd come." He paused. "Too treacherous, you see."

Sullivan sighed again, louder.

Henry continued, unaware of, or ignoring, Sullivan's censure. "I shouted out at that point, with little hope of being heard. I knew I had to hang on, however, and I kept calling out. Just as I was losing hope, my lifeline arrived." He beamed at Mackenzie.

Sandy asked, "Weren't you frightened?"

"Well, no, really, I wasn't. Until I slipped."

Someone said, "Oh, no."

"Indeed. I slipped while I was taking hold of the rope. But I was able to regain my footing, and it wasn't long before my compadres were able to assist me." He gestured toward Sullivan, Mackenzie, and Sam.

"And now we have another happy ending in the desert." Sullivan crossed to stand in front of Henry. "Okay, folks. We were going to camp at Ribbon Canyon, but in light of the time, we'll camp here. Get your gear." Signaling Sam, he strode off.

Mackenzie didn't move. Just standing and thinking was all she could manage.

"You okay?" Sam asked in a whisper.

"Yes, I'm, uh, I'm fine." She attempted a smile.

He placed an arm around her. "Stay and rest a bit. It's traumatic being forced to confront the possibility of death. Even if it's not your own."

She nodded. "Why is Sullivan so angry?"

He gazed down at her in the fading light. "Well, like I said, it's traumatic. Everyone reacts differently. Sullivan gets angry. It's just his way. And," he said in a low voice, "he blames himself."

"What? He wasn't even going to go with us," she protested.

"Yes, but he did. And someone almost died on his watch."

"It wasn't his fault. I almost took that ledge, too."

He shook his head. "I think you would have realized right away that it wasn't the way to go. It really did take some doing for Henry to follow it. A few feet in, the path is blocked off with stones. To get where he did, he had to have stepped over them."

"Oh," she replied.

"Um-hmm. That's part of Sulley's anger, too. It's a lot of responsibility taking inexperienced fools down the river."

"You mean me."

"Sorry. That was unkind. I wasn't talking about you, though. You might've been inexperienced when you first started, but you're picking up experience right and left." He smiled at her, and again she realized how close he was. He smelled wonderful, of sun and suntan lotion and sweat. She was drawn to him, and she wanted to move closer, to be comforted. She forced herself to concentrate.

He let his arm fall. "Seriously, that was good work out there. You did exactly the right thing. Henry, on the other hand, well, he did a stupid thing. And he's boasting about it. I'm sure Sulley's not too happy about that, either. He hates braggarts."

The beach was wide and level. They camped away from the water, at the junction where peach-colored sand met scrub oak. Sam tossed sweet potatoes wrapped in foil on the fire and set thick steaks out on the portable grill. In a large pan he dumped fresh vegetables, sprinkling them liberally with salt. In the canyons, salt was friend, not foe.

Mackenzie dragged her gear to a secluded spot somewhat removed from the others. She needed time to think, to realign herself. She was here to find Charlie, she told herself. To validate his discovery. She couldn't let all this other stuff get in the way. Images of Sullivan flooded in, unbidden, and she shook her head. Why the hell was she so conflicted?

Struggling with wayward poles, she managed to pitch her tent, ground cloth and all, by herself. By the time she was all set up, it was dark. Steaks on the grill dripped grease, releasing their scent, and her stomach growled in answer. She felt Sullivan glancing in her direction several times, but she ignored him, escaping into her tent until it was time to eat.

She tied her flashlight to the one of the tent poles, creating a soft, skittering light. Leaning against her pack, she pulled out her notebook, determined to keep Charlie in the forefront of her thoughts.

"Knock, knock." Sullivan was outside her tent.

So much for Charlie. She didn't answer, but she unzipped the tent flap, leaving the mosquito netting down.

He was partly backlit, with one side of his face completely dark. A smile played at the corners of his mouth. "I wanted to say, I mean, well, that was good thinking out there."

Mackenzie sat up straighter. "Thanks. Couldn't pull him up, though. Good thing you guys came back when you did."

"Well, I imagine you would have figured out a way. You seem to be pretty persistent."

This time she smiled. "I don't know. I wasn't thinking. It's like I shifted into another gear." She casually tucked the opened notebook under her sleeping bag.

"Anyway, it was good. You were good." He was kneeling on one knee, runner-style. "Henry thank you yet?"

"No. But I don't expect him to. I didn't do anything, really. Just threw him a rope. You and Sam pulled him up."

"What you did was damned important. Getting a rope to him was key. With a rope he could have lasted hours. You didn't even need to try to pull him up."

"Now you tell me."

"Yeah, well, if you'd been thinking about pulling him up, it would have been better to—"

She broke in. "So I didn't do a good job. Right?"

He pushed his cap up. "No, I didn't mean that. Let's start over. I always seem to say the wrong thing to you. I just meant, well, I came to say that you were good out there. If you'd rigged it differently—if you had tried to pull him up yourself, it might not have held him so well."

She grunted. "Okay. I'm sorry, too. It sounded like you were criticizing me. I guess I'm a bit sensitive. I know I'm inexperienced. There were probably hundreds of ways better than mine."

"Don't sell yourself short. Yes, it's all new to you, but you haven't quit. You've got good instincts."

"Thanks." His words meant a lot to her, she realized. She could trust them. Sullivan always said exactly what he was thinking. No qualifying or white lies.

He rose, brushing the sand off one knee. "We're going to be eating soon. Don't fall asleep."

"I won't. I'm starving." She paused a beat, then added, "I wanted to say, too, that it wasn't your fault."

"What?"

"Sam told me about how the ledge was blocked off. I mean, how Henry got himself into trouble. You couldn't have known."

He squatted again, peering in at her. A long moment passed before he said, "Listen, Slim. I'm responsible for everyone here. No matter what stupid thing they do. Whether I'm there or not when they do it."

"You can't take that on," she objected. "You're not some all-powerful god who's responsible for each one of his subjects." He couldn't possibly believe that everything that happened was a reflection on him.

"When I agreed to take on this group, I pledged to keep everyone safe. I'm the leader. And the leader is always responsible. Don't you feel that way about your students?"

"Yes, but—"

He interrupted her. "That's why I didn't want you, or Jennifer, to come along. It wasn't because we'd run out of food or not have enough kayaks. You see, I know my limits, and I take this job seriously. There are only so many people I can handle at a time. Although Jennifer doesn't need much looking out for."

It was a blow. He still thought she was high maintenance. As hard as she had tried. "Well, I'll do my best to keep out of your way. Don't worry about me." It was arrogance, she decided. Plain and simple. He was just an arrogant ass. No wonder he always said the wrong thing.

And he'd called her 'Slim' again, dammit.

The next morning they left early. Their goal was Iceberg Canyon, which Sam told them was named for the bright white rock that formed it.

When they turned into the canyon an hour later, Mackenzie thought it was the most beautiful canyon she'd seen so far. Great slabs of chalky rock dwarfed the narrow waterway. The canyon walls were steep but rounded, and the water was so clear that it was difficult to tell where the rock ended and the reflection began.

Her shoulders were on fire. She sat in the back of the kayak, guiding it. Vic was in the front. He was an entertaining partner and pointed out small features on the canyon walls she would have missed: ruins, bird nests, arches, caves. He was also a strong paddler, and she let him take most of the load. He didn't seem to mind.

After awhile, they reached the end of the main channel of Iceberg. Three smaller channels split off, like gnarled fingers. If she was reading the map right, the canyon farthest left was where she wanted to be, and she hoped they would just naturally end up there. If not, she thought, I'll have to convince them to go that way. Or go alone.

They stopped at the junction. Sullivan led the group to a beach bordered with scrub oak on either side.

"There's an impressive waterfall at the end of the middle fork," he told them as they floated up to him. "It's an easy, brief hike to get there."

"Will it be there tomorrow morning?" Sandy asked.

"Yeah, but it'll be in the shade then. In the late afternoon, the waterfall sparkles in the sun. And," he paused for effect, "There's a cave behind it. With a little effort—"

Someone groaned, but he pressed on, smiling. "With a little effort, you can get to the cave. You can even jump from it. The pool's deep and safe."

"You going to check it out?" Mackenzie asked Vic.

"The waterfall? Definitely. It's places like these the symbols often show up."

"Did you find any glyphs yesterday? With all the ruckus, I forgot to ask."

"No. I wish I'd gone with you to the ruins. Maybe things with Henry would have turned out differently."

She shook her head. "I don't think so. Henry, well, he's not only slow, but he's seems to like to be on his own. Always holding everyone up at the end. Kind of a prima donna."

"Yup." He looked around. "He doesn't deign to talk to me, you know. Thinks I'm not qualified. An amateur. And apparently, amateurs have no place in archaeology." He laughed, but there was a hint of something hard under it. Something she hadn't heard before.

Mackenzie chose her words carefully. "He's British. I think there are a lot of cultural things at play."

"Maybe. Anyway, I'm going to check out the waterfall."

"I'll tag along with you, if that's okay."

"Of course. Please do. Let's try jumping from the waterfall. What do you say?"

"Uh, I'll see what it's like when I get there. Maybe." She doubted it, though. She'd had enough cliffs for a while.

Before they could play, they had to set up camp. It was becoming easier and easier. Once the tents were ready, each member of the group took on a small job, falling into a natural rhythm. Sam and Lucy prepped for dinner. Vic and Mike scouted a bit, gathering firewood. Sandy started the fire, and Sullivan secured the kayaks. Jennifer often tagged along with Sullivan, although she sometimes wandered around taking photos and jotting down notes. Mackenzie carried water bottles up, helping Lucy and Sam with dinner. Henry was the only exception; he generally pottered about alone. He wasn't much help, anyway, so nobody mentioned it.

After setting up, a small contingent tramped through the brush and sand, heading for the waterfall. They could hear it long before they reached it. At the end of the middle canyon, a fifty-foot wall of water glistening like diamonds as it cascaded over rocks, falling into a deep blue pool. Mike, Sandy, Mackenzie, and Vic scrambled up the rocks to the side. They didn't find an actual path, but the rocks were solid and almost steplike next to the falls.

It was louder than she would have imagined, and the air was heavier. Although tired, she was curious about the cave.

Mike led the way. He was in better shape than the rest of the party. Sandy struggled after him, slowly picking his way up. She followed Sandy, keeping her distance.

Mike easily outdistanced them, and after several minutes, he shouted, "Hey! It's wonderful. Come on, you guys, the sun's perfect right now."

Sandy set a slow pace, but Mackenzie was glad. Slow and steady was all she could manage. Vic, below her, was patient and gave her plenty of room. Her ankle was still a bit sore, and she wished she'd taped it. She'd have to ask Sam about the salve.

Suddenly, something caught her eye—something flashing by, falling. Her heart skipped, and she went rigid. A long moment later, she heard a splash, and Mike popped out of the water below, laughing. He shook his head like a dog, treading water.

Mackenzie shook her head. What was she doing up here?

Vic yelled something down, and Mike laughed again. Sure she wasn't going to jump, she continued, focused on her climbing. Several minutes later she reached the top of the rocks, about ten feet below the cliff top.

"Can we all fit?" Sandy stood on a ledge under the waterfall.

Beads of water floated in the sunlight around her. "I don't know. I would be careful. I'm sure it will be slick. Looks like we'll get soaked, regardless."

He placed one foot in front of the other, testing each step. She didn't look down but continued following him, aware that Vic was right below her. The ledge was almost two feet wide and level. To reach the cave, they had to pass through a thin stream of water that had been diverted by a cleft in the rocks next to the bigger waterfall. Getting wet was a given.

The waterfall itself was wider than it had looked from the ground. Behind it, they found a small, clammy space seeping earth and roots. The space was just tall enough for her to stand and treacherous. It was narrower than the waterfall, but deep. Fuzzy plants lined a crack on the ceiling, and water dripped down the back wall.

"Not much room for glyphs up here," she shouted when Vic joined them. The crashing water was deafening, and they had to huddle together to hear each other.

"Amazing," he hollered back. "This is amazing. I've never been behind a waterfall. Magical."

She smiled. "Like being in a fairytale."

"Think I'm going to jump." He gestured toward the water. "Otherwise, we'll have to downclimb those blasted rocks."

Sandy yelled, "Well, I'm not. Who knows how deep the water really is. Mike might've been lucky. Besides, I'm cold and tired. I'm going to climb down."

"It'll be faster jumping," Vic said. "We'll be warm and dry before you're halfway there."

"I doubt it. You'll probably fall and break your neck, and Mackenzie will land right on top of you."

Vic winked and nudged her. "You're coming, right?"

She didn't know what to say. She certainly didn't want to be lumped in with Sandy, who was becoming whinier and whinier—but jumping terrified her.

Vic leaned closer to her. "Come on, I'll go first. Nothing will happen. Jump right after me. Just give me enough time to get out of your way. See, it's easy." And he was gone, hurtling through the water, howling, "Geronimo!"

Shit. Sandy edged closer, and she stiffened. Closing her eyes, she took a deep breath, and before she could turn back, launched herself through the waterfall.

In the empty seconds of the fall, she realized she should have waited. She *was* going to land on Vic. But there was no time to do anything.

She hit feet first, with knees bent and arms close to her body. Plunging into the cold water, she went under, relieved that she had obviously missed Vic. The pool was deep and murky. She breast-stroked toward the surface.

"Well done," Vic called to her, five feet away. "Could have waited a bit, though." He grinned at her.

Mackenzie coughed, shoving a clump of hair out of her eyes. "I know. I'm sorry. I'm so sorry. I don't know what I was thinking." They tread water next to each other.

"No worries. Just giving you a hard time. Fun, wasn't it?"

She nodded. It *was* fun. She felt like a kid. "I can't believe I jumped. I've never done anything like that. I'm glad I did, though. It's incredible."

"Wonder how Sandy's doing?" He squinted up at the rocks. "Oh, there he is, about a third of the way down." Gliding effortlessly to the side, Vic hauled himself onto a flat rock near the edge. "Looks like Mike's already left."

She drifted behind him and let him help her up, holding onto her shorts so they wouldn't fall off. The skimpy tank top she had worn was thin, and she crossed her arms in front of her.

Vic turned, removing his shirt. He was athletic, with wide shoulders, a narrow waist, and sturdy legs. A bit younger than fifty, she figured. He was attractive, and she felt her face turning red, surprised at her train of thought.

He glanced back over his shoulder. "Something wrong? I have leeches or mud or something on my back?"

She sat down, crossing her legs. "No, sorry. Thought I saw something, but it was nothing." She untied her shoe lace to hide her face.

"Good. Hate those leeches." He raised an eyebrow, smiling.

Recovering, she laughed. "Yeah, me too. Any kind of bug, really. I'm kind of bug-phobic."

"Afraid of insects? You don't strike me as the type."

"Oh, yeah. Scared to death. It's a true phobia. But, strangely, it's only when they're inside. It's like they're not supposed to be there. When I see them out in the wilds," she gestured toward the canyon, "I'm okay with them." She brushed sand off the sole of her sandal. "Well, unless they're big or something."

The rock they sat on hung over the edge of the water a few feet. Behind it was a small strip of sand, dotted with scrub oak, cactus, and weeds. She wanted to lie down, but knew she'd fall asleep in the sun. Instead, she stretched her legs out in front of her.

Vic removed a grayish tennis shoe. Standing on one foot, he shook it saying. "I know what you mean. I'm not too fond—ahhhh!"

He lost his balance and sat down hard in the sand behind him. She chuckled, ready to tease him, but stopped abruptly. He was writhing on the sand, twisting and shrieking. "Oh, God. Shit, Oh, my God. Shit."

She crouched, ready to jump to his side, but at the last moment hesitated: He had landed butt-first on an enormous barrel cactus.

She circled to the other side, threading her way through the brush. "Vic, stay still."

He had flipped over onto his stomach and was moaning softly. Thousands of little needles covered his shorts.

"Okay. I'm going to help you up. Don't worry, I'll keep you from falling back. Can you stand?" She reached down, grasping his wrist and forearm, and pulled him up.

"No. I can't stand up straight. I can't move. Fuck."

She placed his arm around her shoulders and pulled him up. They walked slowly back to the safety of the rock, tears welling up in his eyes.

"What's going on? What happened?" Sandy stood at the bottom of the waterfall, twenty feet away.

"Run and get Sam and Sullivan," she said. "Vic's fallen into some cactus."

Sandy stood stock still, his mouth open.

"Now. Get them *now*. Tell them Vic fell into a big cactus. Hurry." He took off at a trot.

Somewhere in the recesses of her mind, she recalled that removing cactus spines could be tricky. Vic leaned heavily against her, and she assured him that Sullivan would know what to do.

A long ten minutes later, Sandy arrived with the rest of the group in tow. Sullivan knelt, digging in his bag. Someone sniggered, and he looked up, glaring. "If anyone laughs again, or so much as smiles, I'll make sure you have the opportunity to see how it feels."

No one moved.

Stepping in, Sam removed Vic's arm from Mackenzie's shoulders and motioned for her to move off. She gladly obeyed; her shoulders and neck ached.

Sullivan opened a med kit and set down two towels. "It's just on his backside, right?"

"Yes," she replied.

"Thanks." Sullivan spread a towel next to Vic. "Okay, Vic, I want you to lay face down on this."

Sam lowered him gently and laid on the ground next to him.

"Everyone take off," Sullivan insisted. "Go back to camp. We'll be there soon. Don't wander away."

He pulled out rubbing alcohol, a tube of antibiotic ointment, Elmer's glue, and tweezers.

Sandy asked, "What's the glue for?"

"After we tweeze out the big ones, we pour glue over the area and let it partially dry. Then we rip it off his skin. You can get the smaller spines that way. Usually about ninety-five percent successful using the tweezers and glue. The sooner we get them, the less toxin penetrates." He paused, then said gruffly, "Now, get back to camp."

Handing Vic two tablets from a plastic prescription bottle, Sam said, "Here you go, Vic. Good stuff. Need water?"

Vic didn't reply. Mackenzie tossed Sam a water bottle and backed away, ready to join the others. Sullivan looked up. "Not you, Princess. I want you to stay with Vic. Hold his hand. Sam, I need you to hold the magnifying glass." He pulled scissors and the magnifying glass out of the med kit, handing them to his friend. "We've got to cut him out of these shorts. Thank God he wasn't bare-ass naked."

An hour later, Sullivan and Sam arrived back in camp, with Vic between them, wearing a towel. He walked awkwardly, even with their help, and his usual smiling face looked gaunt and gray. He didn't look up.

The two men led him to Sullivan's tent. Sullivan followed him in, zipping the tent flap closed. A moment later he opened it, asking Mackenzie to bring him the med kit.

The group gathered around Sam, who filled them in. "I think we got most of them out, but if he's sensitive to the toxin, it's going to be rough couple days. Most of those spines are barbed, and they're a strong irritant."

"What if you don't get them all out?" Lucy asked.

"It doesn't look like he's allergic to them. That's a good sign. We're going to try for them all." Sam rubbed his neck. "It's up to you all to make dinner tonight. Lucy, can you handle organizing everyone?"

She nodded. "I'll get started right away." She marched over to the gear. Mike and Sandy followed, after she beckoned to them. Mackenzie hung back with Jennifer and Henry.

Sullivan emerged from the tent. He rubbed his forehead with the back of his hand. "Let's give him an hour or so to rest. We should wait until the drugs have really kicked in."

"Is he in any danger?" Henry asked.

Sullivan settled onto a thick piece of driftwood, stretching his legs. "Well, cactus spines are nasty," he replied. "The bigger ones are actually not as bad as the tiny, hairlike ones that are called glochidia. Those are wickedly barbed. If they're not removed, vesicles and pustules and even focal ulceration can occur."

He looked up at the trio. "Lesions. Little sacs of pus. If we don't get them out, it could result in a dangerous skin inflammation. The fragments can become embedded and infected. So we've got to get as many as we can."

"How can you get them all?" Jennifer asked.

"We got all the ones we could see. We'll try the Elmer's glue again." He described the procedure.

"Wow. It sounds like you really know what you're doing," she said.

He compressed his lips slightly before answering. "Yeah, when you've lived in the desert as long as I have, you pick up things."

"But all that medical jargon," she said.

Sandy added, "Yeah. Didn't understand half of it."

"Knew a doctor once," Sullivan replied, tersely.

Sam took over. "Out here on our own we learn a lot about how to deal with these things. Of course, we've also taken wilderness and desert first aid courses."

"Oh," Sandy, said. "Sure."

"Will we have to stay her awhile?" Lucy asked.

"Yup. Once we get them out, and numb it, he will be exhausted. We'll have to camp here at least an extra night." Sam shrugged.

Another delay. Mackenzie sighed, rolling her head around to loosen her neck muscles. It couldn't be helped. She didn't mind waiting for Vic.

Sullivan lifted his chin at her and smiled. She took it as thanks and returned his smile.

CHAPTER 10

BY THE NEXT MORNING, VIC WAS WALKING AROUND CAMP, looking like a herky-jerky heron. Sam fixed the group sausage, eggs, and hash browns for breakfast. Everyone ate but Sullivan, who had apparently taken a kayak out earlier.

Resigned to staying put for the day, Mackenzie relaxed with the group, chatting with Lucy. They sat in the shade, backs against a smooth sandstone rock. Vic lay on his stomach a few feet from them, apparently sleeping.

"He seems to be doing well," Lucy observed.

"I heard that." He propped himself up on his elbows. "I am doing well. Not going to show you the progress, though."

Mackenzie laughed. "Thank God. Sam says you're a fast healer."

He shifted to lay on his side, head propped up on one hand. "Yeah. Sulley tells me it's because they got to me so quickly. Thanks to you."

She shook her head. "No, thanks to Sandy. He ran to get them. I didn't do anything."

Lucy put in, "That's not what I heard. Sullivan told me you helped, and that you uh, what were his words?" She broke off for a moment, staring to her left. "Oh, that's right. You were a good assistant."

Assistant? She knew Sullivan was complimenting her, and that he thought assisting him was a good thing, but she resented the label all the same. She let Lucy and Vic talk while she sopped up egg with her hash browns.

Henry meandered over with an overloaded plate. "Brilliant. The food is absolutely brilliant."

She nodded, mouth full.

"At least we have that going for us," he said.

"What do you mean?" She was aware that Lucy and Vic were listening.

"Well, on a trip like this, it's surprising to have such a good support team."

"A trip like this?" Vic's voice was low, almost a growl.

"Yes. You know, an amateur trip. Wanna-be, so to speak. On a professional trip, one can always rely on good food and intelligent conversation. At least we have excellent food on this one." He sat down on a boulder.

Mackenzie said, "This trip—"

Vic cut her off. "Amateur? With a linguistics professor, museum specialist, environmentalist, anthropologist, and uh, someone from *National Geographic?* Oh, yeah, and you. I wouldn't call that amateur."

"Oh, there is considerable talent here, no doubt. However, the thesis is, well, a bit vague, and the funding questionable." Henry shoved a fork into his mouth, oblivious to the rising temperature of the small group sitting near him.

Lucy offered, "I'm sure that you mean it's amateur in the sense that it's not affiliated with a university."

Henry rested his plate on his knees. "Yes, of course. Without the backing of a university, it's definitely an amateur trip." He wiped his glasses with a handkerchief, staring myopically into the distance. "Not a true scientific expedition."

Getting awkwardly to his feet, Vic glowered at the older man, who had resumed eating. "I've spent more years researching these glyphs than you can even remember, old man."

Mackenzie watched, enthralled.

Vic sneered at Henry. "Although I might not have a degree in anthropology, I'm sure I've spent more time in the field than you. Your knowledge is all theoretical. Mine is real." He crossed his arms over his chest, stood with his legs apart. Classic warrior stance.

Henry's eyes grew wide, and he finally understood he'd thrown down the gauntlet. "Oh, my dear man. I simply meant that this expedition wasn't based on research."

Vic fumed, his face crimson.

Henry added quickly, "University research. Most trips of this nature are funded by a University. Wouldn't you agree, Professor Campbell?"

Surprised that Henry would drag her into the argument, Mackenzie stammered, "I, well, uh, no, I think many scientific expeditions are put together just like this one." She hoped no one would ask her for an example.

"Hmm. I daresay." Henry placed his empty plate on the rock next to him, flicking some ants away. "I'm sure your quest is valid and will shed considerable insight on your topic. And I'm delighted to be along. I meant no offense."

"Thanks for that," Vic muttered. "We'll just see how this trip turns out, won't we?" He nodded at Mackenzie and Lucy, and headed stiffly for the water.

Lucy leaned forward, preparing to follow him, but Mackenzie held her back. "Let him be alone for a moment. I'm sure he'll be fine. We're all a bit tense."

"Yeah, you're probably right." Lucy closed her eyes, pressing a hand to her forehead.

Mackenzie leaned back, too. She let her eyes drift over the shimmering water. Sullivan floated into their little cove, and Jennifer ran out to meet him, helping him drag the boat up the beach. Her blonde hair glittered when she flipped it. She leaned in close, and he laughed. Then she added something, and he laughed again. They strolled to the folding table that held breakfast. Jennifer took a plate, serving Sullivan first. She stood close, and at one point offered him a taste off her fork.

Mackenzie turned away. Hadn't Jennifer already had breakfast? She couldn't remember.

Lucy looked up, blinking. "What's up?"

"Nothing. Was just watching them." She jerked her head at the pair.

Sullivan and Jennifer sat down together on a flat stretch of sand. They talked, sitting close together, and Jennifer threw her head back, laughing. She pushed him gently on the shoulder. Even from a distance, Mackenzie could see that Sullivan was grinning at her.

"I'm tired of watching her do that flirting thing," Lucy said.

"Yeah. That kind of woman disgusts me. You'd think he'd see through it."

Sandy wandered over. "See through what?"

Without thinking, Mackenzie pointed at the couple on the sand. "That. Her. Men are always bamboozled by women like that. Males just can't see their true nature."

Lucy added, "Because they're always thinking with their penises."

Sandy crossed his arms. "She's friendly. Nothing wrong with that. You girls are being a bit catty, don't you think?"

"Yes," Henry added. "No need for the green-eyed monster."

Mackenzie rolled her eyes. "We're not jealous. You don't get it. Let me try to explain." She paused, trying to frame her words. "Some women are so utterly focused on men they don't bond at all with other women. It's like they're not the same species."

Sandy attempted to break in, but she held up a finger. "I'm not done. These women are very good at what they do, which is figuring out what a man needs and being exactly that. And, of course, it feeds the ego of the man receiving all this attention, so he doesn't see what's happening. The rest of us do, though. Normal women do. They get it. But if we say anything," Mackenzie said, "We're called catty. Or jealous."

"Well, aren't you?" Sandy curled his lip in a sneer.

Lucy shook her head. "No. Most women won't stoop to playing a man like that. Being that false."

Sandy mmphed. "That's not true."

"Of course it is," Mackenzie retorted. "There's nothing wrong with flirting—when you're interested. But women like that flirt with anything male. And purposely undermine other women. They're deceptive, and it's always a competition with them."

"You're just miffed because they play the game better than you," Henry countered.

"They certainly play the game," she agreed. "But it's a game I don't care for." She rose, brushing crumbs off her shorts. "Oh, yeah, that's right, I forgot. You're a man. You're genetically unable to understand."

She angled toward the breakfast table to put her plate down, skirting Sullivan and Jennifer. No need to ruin their tea party. They could have sex on the beach for all she cared.

Sam stacked plastic dishes on one end of the table. "How's it going, Mac?"

Skipping past the greeting, she asked, "Have you seen Vic?"

"Thought I saw him heading toward the waterfall." He didn't look at her and began filling a basin with water. The pile of dishes was immense, and she immediately felt guilty. How could she be so insensitive? She offered to help.

He waved her off. "It's my turn to clean up. Why don't you go check on him? Just make sure you don't get stuck." He chuckled at his own joke.

"Well, okay. I guess someone has to needle him." She made a face. "Oh, we'd better stop. This could get sticky."

"Yeah. Enough with the barbs," he replied.

Smiling to herself, she headed toward the waterfall. A small spur canyon branched off to the left, and she noticed a water bottle and backpack by the side of the path. She climbed for a few moments until reaching a steep barricade of large rocks.

"Hey, Vic. You up there?"

"Mac? That you? Come see what I found." His voice almost crackled with excitement.

She tested the first rock. Solid. Climbing cautiously, she crested the top. A sandy path studded with shrubs snaked to the left.

"Over here. Behind the triangular boulder." He was on his knees in front of a flat, smooth stone. He was obviously doing better.

"How're you feeling? I can't believe you're already hiking like this." She squatted next to him.

"Forget how I feel. Look at this."

"What? Did you find one?"

"See for yourself." He dusted loose sand off a stone, grinning. "It's a beaut."

A large, flat stone was partially under an overhanging rock, protected from the elements. A circle two feet in diameter was bisected by a three-foot long grooved line carved into it. A deep hole more than an inch in diameter sat near the outside of the circle, a foot to the left.

She scrutinized the carving, brushing away fine dust. "I wish we really knew what they were. Even if our theory is right about Rainbow Bridge, what are the holes for?"

"Don't know. All the glyphs have one, maybe two holes. Sometimes they're in the circle, sometimes off a bit. Always thought they marked a direction. Maybe like a kind of sun dial. What do you think?"

Mackenzie tilted her head to view it from another angle. She stood, her eyes traveling over the area around them.

He returned to the glyph. In his excitement, he seemed to have forgotten about the cactus incident.

She rotated her ankle to stretch it and walked back to the path. After a few moments, she found a thin driftwood branch. He raised his eyebrows and stood up when she returned, watching as she laid it on the glyph, one end at the center of the circle, one end touching the hole, like the hand of a clock.

"Let's see. If it's a direction, it's got to be pointing to something." She stood and gazed toward the horizon in the direction the stick pointed. Nothing stood out. "Maybe what it pointed to isn't there anymore."

"Possibly," he said. "But things change slowly out here. I think that's the left fork of Iceberg. Don't see anything else."

Her heart thudded. The left branch. The one she wanted. "Are we heading that way? To that part of the canyon?"

"Not sure. I may lobby to explore it, though. We can ask Sullivan what's down that way."

"Okay. But let's try the sun dial theory, too." She poked the branch into the hole, arranging it until it was almost vertical. It created a small shadow on the smooth rock face. "I don't know."

"Yeah, doesn't mean much. The shadow changes, of course, with the hour and season. It may have required a specific time." He handed the stick to her. "This is a great example, though. Dammit, my camera's down with my pack. I'm going to get Jennifer up here, too, to get some professional photos." He straightened up. "That is, if I can move. I think I need some more Ibuprofen. My ass is feeling pretty tender."

"I imagine. Here, I have my camera with me. Okay if I take a few informal shots?" She laid the stick back on the circle. "Could you put a hand or foot near it so we can get an idea of scale?"

She shot a few close-ups with and without the stick and a few from a distance. Next, she took several photos in the general direction of the left fork of Iceberg Canyon.

CHAPTER 11

AFTER PHOTOGRAPHING THE GLYPH, MACKENZIE HEADED BACK to camp. Lucy intercepted her, motioning toward the side of the path.

"So, when you left," Lucy said, "Sandy, uh..." She broke off, eyes flitting to her left.

"Sandy what?"

"Well, Sandy sort of told Jennifer what you said. You know, about her being 'that type of woman,' and all."

Mackenzie's gut contracted. Shit. "What did he say?" She led Lucy to a small clearing in the brush. "Tell me exactly what he said."

"He said that you—"

"Both of us," she corrected.

"Right. Well, he said that we thought she was false and just playing Sullivan. That she viewed us as competition. How she tries to undermine other women."

"I should have known Sandy would do something like this. He simply can't keep his mouth shut." Mackenzie kept her back to the camp. She felt physically ill.

"And, Henry, well, he said we were jealous and petty." Lucy watched Mackenzie intently.

"Anything more?" She bit her lip.

"Yeah." Lucy paused.

"And?"

"Well, she played the hurt female. Claimed she wanted to be friends, but you snubbed her. That she felt left out and, um, ignored by you."

"You mean 'us.' "

"No, she pretty much just said you."

Damn. Mackenzie shoved her hands into her pockets. She couldn't be angry; she hadn't told Sandy or Henry to keep it to themselves. They'd merely repeated what she'd said.

What was wrong with her? How could she have said those things to them? She usually wasn't so loose with her tongue. Now, if she acted defensively, no one would believe her. She should have kept quiet. She really didn't like this new aspect of herself. "What did the others do?" Maybe they wouldn't believe Jennifer.

"Vic and Sam didn't say anything, and I don't know if Mike was there. I don't remember seeing him."

"What did Sullivan do?" Mackenzie asked.

"He didn't say anything either. He walked away. To his tent."

Mackenzie swallowed hard. She wanted to vanish, and she realized just how dependent on this group she was. How vulnerable and alone she was. She couldn't run or hide. She had to work it out with them. They were a family—dysfunctional, like all families—but still a family.

At the campsite, Sandy was talking to Mike, throwing his arms around like a hell-fire-and-damnation preacher. So much for Mike not knowing.

She patted Lucy on the shoulder. "I'm sorry, Luce. It was my fault. I pulled you into it."

"I hate this," Lucy said. "But it's not your fault. You're right about Jennifer. Acting like she's the poor thing."

"It is my fault, Lucy. I started it. And I'm going to fix it. You'll see. I'll make this right somehow." She took a deep breath and headed for the camp. Sandy and Henry stood off to the side facing her: twin guardians of brotherhood. She didn't look at them. She wasn't quite sure what to say yet, and she wanted to think carefully before speaking this time.

She cleared her throat and Mike turned. He didn't smile. For a moment her resolve threatened to crumble, like brittle dirt clods.

"Mackenzie. Uh, hi." His eyes darted around, seemingly looking for an escape route. He didn't meet her eyes.

"Hey, Mike. Look, I know what Sandy told you."

"Oh, we don't believe him," he said. "We—"

She cut him off. "No, he's right. What he told you is right." She finally got him to look at her and pinned him with her eyes. "I have no excuse. I'm sorry I said it."

"Well, you know, I think there's probably some truth in what you said. There's something a little, uh, off, about Jennifer. All that stuff about you not befriending her. I mean, that's a bunch of crap." He kept his voice low, his eyes on Sandy and Henry.

She let out a breath. "Thanks. But if I hadn't said anything, she wouldn't have had to defend herself against me. I was in the wrong."

"Sandy and Henry were just as wrong," Mike replied. "Even more so, I think. They didn't have to stir things up. Petty, if you ask me."

He was right. Sandy and Henry did have a part in it: They knew it would start a war if they told the others. She hesitated, knowing that poorly chosen words could threaten their fragile reconciliation. "Well, all I know is that I was in the wrong."

"You sure were," Sullivan said.

She looked up, startled. She ought to be getting used to him sneaking up on her. What was he, part cat?

He continued. "We're a team out here. Right now it's like we're playing, having fun in the wilderness." He gestured for the others to join them, waiting to speak until they'd assembled. "And it could stay that way. But if anything happens—if someone gets hurt, or the weather turns, or we take a wrong step and get lost—well, we're in trouble. We have only each other to depend on. This is serious business, and the consequences are deadly. Mistakes in the canyon can cost lives. I'm not going to sugar-coat it: We could die out here." He looked at each one of them in turn. "We have to be adults."

Mackenzie looked down, feeling her ears go red.

"So, let's put this behind us. We don't have to like each other, we don't even have to talk to each other. But we have to be on the same side. We have to be a team. Think you can all do that?" Again he scanned their faces. "Mackenzie?"

A quick flash of anger spread through her. Yes, it was her fault, and yes, she had been stupid, but he didn't have to call attention to her in front of the group. Others were just as culpable. She looked up at him. He smiled back, brows lifted, and she wavered, her anger fading. Was he making fun of her? Or of the situation? His smile was almost kind.

Before she could say anything, he continued, "Fine. Now, it's a beautiful day. Relax a bit. Go for a swim, jump from the waterfall. Hike or sleep or read. I don't care what you do. But play nice and be careful."

The man had a god complex. That was his problem. But he was right. Again. That made it worse. She shook her head. She'd been acting childishly, and so had Sandy, Henry, and Jennifer. Even Lucy. Determined to take the high road, she nodded at Sandy and Henry.

Just then, Vic walked up, unaware of what had transpired. He told the others about his find. "I want to hike the left fork of the canyon," he said, looking around. "Anyone want to scout around?" He raised his brows when no one answered.

"Oh, yeah. I almost forgot." He outlined the assorted theories he and Mackenzie had talked about. "So you see, I need to catalogue this new glyph, and then check out the fork."

"It's your trip," Sullivan said, after a short pause.

"Great. I'll photograph it and the surrounding area. Maybe hike up a bit to get a birds-eye view."

"And head down the left fork?" She looked expectantly at him.

"Yes, see if the glyph is really pointing to something."

"Pointing to the left fork," she clarified.

Sullivan pursed his lips before addressing Vic. "You probably wouldn't be able to use the kayaks. That fork doesn't always have water the whole way. You'd have to hike, up past the head of the waterfall to the mesa and around the rocks. It's not like taking a walk in the park." He rubbed his chin. "Seems to me I remember a slot canyon that leads to a great view of that fork, though."

"Sounds like you've been down that way," Mike said.

Sullivan shrugged. "Don't know it all that well, but I was down there a while ago. Lately, I've been in the general area, but not as far as the fork. How about you?"

Mike shook his head. "Nope. Been on the ridge above it, though."

"It's decided then," she said. "We'll explore the left fork."

"I'm up for it. I'm feeling much better." Vic looked at her, ignoring Sullivan.

"Nothing doing," Sullivan said abruptly. "You're still mending. Trust me, you'd regret it. You've got to give it a little more time."

"But, I feel okay."

"Nope. I won't take you out there."

She smiled. "I'll scout it for you, Vic. You stay and get better. I'll be back before you know it."

"Slim, you aren't going, either, at least not right now. It looks like there are a few clouds on the horizon."

Irritated, Mackenzie surveyed the sky, spotting one lone cloud miles away. "Seems fine to me. I think I'll explore a bit by myself. See what it looks like."

"The weather changes quickly out here," Mike cautioned, frowning.

"I won't go far. I'll just check it out."

Sullivan's voice was like gravel. "You can't go by yourself. Weren't you listening? Nobody goes anywhere alone. You'd have to go with someone. Especially since ..." He broke off, looking away.

"Especially since I'm a woman? That what you were going to say?"

"No. Especially since, uh, you're not that experienced." He rubbed the back of his neck, not meeting her eyes.

She took advantage of his discomfort. "Well, the only way to get experience is to get out there. Right?" She paused. "Sandy? Henry? Sure you don't want to go?"

"Not me," Sandy said. Henry nodded in agreement.

"I've got to get more firewood for tonight," Mike replied. "And I promised I'd help Sam cook dinner."

She regarded Sullivan. "Like I said, I won't go far. I promise. I'll be back in a few hours. I don't need to go with anyone. I'll be careful." She turned toward her tent. "I'll take my backpack, too." She turned without waiting for an answer.

"Shit." Sullivan said. "I guess I've got to go with her. Someone who knows what they're doing has to go, dammit."

When she emerged from her tent, he was a hundred yards ahead, hiking toward the waterfall.

"Come on," he yelled over his shoulder. He didn't look back.

She ran after him, feeling like an obedient puppy. He stayed far enough ahead they couldn't talk. Good thing, she thought.

They climbed up next to the waterfall and scaled a slickrock formation to a plateau. They circled a pinnacle, staying close to its base.

It was becoming obvious that Sullivan wasn't going to wait for her. She struggled to keep up. Suddenly, he halted, pointing at the rock.

She scrambled until she stood next to him, panting. The cliff split, forming a vee of sorts, with a cascade of fallen rock on either side.

"This way, through that pass over there. Take it easy, though. It can be tricky." He leapt effortlessly from one small boulder to the other without hesitation.

Her pace was slower, cautious. When she reached the top, the view wasn't what she expected. Sand stretched out before them. A narrow ridge was on their left.

"I thought we were heading for the left fork."

He removed his cap, fanning himself. "Well, we're heading in the general direction of the fork. There's a spur off the side—that slot canyon I mentioned—that leads to the fork. This is the easiest, safest, way. Still tough going, though."

"Where are we?"

"We're pretty close to the other arm of the river. It goosenecks, and the two arms are close here, because the river winds around so much. We're in between them, kind of like on an island." He replaced his cap, turning the bill backward. "You okay? You still want to go on?"

"Of course. I'm a little out of breath, but I'll be fine."

"We'll be doing some up-and-down hiking over slickrock."

"Can't wait."

He laughed, and once again she found herself distracted by his disarming smile. When he laughed, she thought, he was actually handsome.

"Once we get to the slot canyon," he said, "It'll be downhill."

Mackenzie nodded. A slot canyon. From what she'd heard, slot canyons could be so narrow that even a thin person could barely get through them. Great.

They tramped across the mesa side by side, not talking. When they reached what looked to be an old stream bed, Sullivan stopped to get his bearings. "Over this way a bit," he said. "By that straggly pine in the arroyo. We'll follow it."

The arroyo was like an uneven, sunken path, and they returned to single file. She kept her eyes on the ground and filled the time by thinking about Charlie, wondering when she was going to tell the group her real mission and how she would persuade them to help her. Various scenarios paraded through her mind's eye, each one worse than the previous one. She was so involved in her daydreaming that she bumped into Sullivan, who had turned, waiting for her.

"Whoa. You'd better watch where you're going." He had both hands on her shoulders, holding her away from him.

She looked up, dazed. "Oh, sorry. I guess I was looking down, not around."

He smiled, keeping his hands on her shoulders. For a moment, she imagined him sliding his hands down her back, pulling her to him. She turned red. Where had that come from?

He let go, spinning on his heel. "We're here," he said.

"Here? Where?"

Sullivan squatted, and she followed suit, keeping her distance. At their feet, a narrow trench cut through the rock like a tunnel.

"We slide down here to get to the canyon." He didn't wait for a response, but sat at the edge and dropped from sight.

She swallowed, wanting to turn back, but she'd be damned if she'd tell him that. With her sleeve she wiped the sweat from her eyes. What the hell. She pushed off.

Sliding down the tunnel wasn't too bad. It spiraled to the right like a corkscrew slide, and she could control her slide by wedging her hands and feet against the other wall. It continued for ten feet and then widened.

"Take it slowly," he called out in a booming voice. She couldn't see him, but he sounded close.

Using her feet, she pushed against the rock on the opposite wall. Alternately moving her feet, then her torso and hands, she descended another five feet. To her left was a small ledge. She braced herself securely with her hands. With her good foot, she tentatively reached for the ledge and found it was solid. Although she felt ungainly and clumsy, she made it. Below her, Sullivan smiled up, and she felt ridiculously proud of herself.

"Sit down and then turn," he said, "Facing the wall. Good. There's a good handhold above you, and a deep foothold below your right knee. Right, you've got it. Now hold onto that edge and let yourself down. I'll be here." He sounded confident and sure, like he believed she could do it.

She dropped down lightly.

He pulled out a bottle, smiling. "Good job. Did you bring water?"

"Yeah." She dug for it in her backpack.

"We're in the slot canyon now." He took a swig from his water. "It'll be narrow, but after fifty yards or so, I think it opens up. For a while."

Mackenzie nodded and looked around. It was more than narrow, it was tight. The air was cool, and the rock smelled stale. Walls on either side rose fifty feet above them.

They plodded single-file through sand in an easy silence. Now and then a lizard would gaze heavy-lidded at them. The walls were riddled with holes and moonscape formations carved by time and water and wind. It wasn't easy going. They had to work their way past several obstacles. Occasionally, they met small potholes of scummy water and had to find a way over them. All the while, they descended deeper and deeper.

A few more clouds had formed, and the sun dipped in and out. She was grateful the canyon was cool. Keeping pace with Sullivan was hard work, and she was sweating in her long-sleeved t-shirt. But, she realized with surprise, she was having fun.

He walked rapidly, automatically choosing the best way. She kept her eyes on the canyon floor—and him—trying to imitate his gracefulness. Her legs were tired, her back ached, and she could feel a blister forming under her little toe. But she'd die before falling behind.

After half an hour or so, they reached a small flat area and he pulled a granola bar from his backpack. "Hungry?"

"I'm fine." She paused. "Uh, Sullivan, I wanted to explain—"

He didn't let her finish. "No need."

"You don't even know what I wanted to say," she said, letting out a breath.

"Oh, I think I do. You wanted to go into all the gory details about your little feud with Jennifer."

Shit. He had her. "Well, yes," she admitted. "But please hear me out."

"Should I sit down?" He did so, not waiting for her answer.

Mackenzie fiddled with the strap to her backpack. "I'm sorry I acted so childishly. I shouldn't have been talking about her."

"Yup. Those thoughts are best kept to yourself. Even if you're right. In a small group like this, everyone has to step up."

Right? He thought she was right? She went on. "I wanted you to know that I haven't been snubbing her. Or ignoring her, or whatever. It's been the opposite, actually." She closed her mouth. Don't get into defending yourself, she thought.

"I know. I also know Jennifer has some kind of game she's playing. Not sure what it is yet."

"You do?"

"Yeah. Maybe she's just that way. I don't know. But I'm curious. So I've let her play it out." He flung a stone down the canyon, and it echoed as it bounced.

"You're letting her?"

"Yes, Slim, I'm letting her. You might think you women are the only ones to see the truth, but some of us aren't quite so easily fooled. I've known quite a few women like her. Too well." He picked up another stone, but this time just rubbed this thumb on it.

"I, well, I'm not sure what to say."

"Don't say anything. Learn from this fiasco."

Mackenzie opened her mouth to argue, but he was grinning, not challenging her. She smiled back, and he surprised her by looking away first. "You don't have to justify yourself to me. I'm a pretty good judge of character, and I go by actions, not words. Generally." He stood up, offering her a hand. "Come on, we'd better get a move on." He tugged her gently up. "Unless you want to turn back?"

She grimaced. "Not on your life. Let's get going." She started out ahead of him. "And don't call me 'Slim,' " she said, not looking back. "My name is Mackenzie."

They didn't talk for awhile. After a few minutes, Sullivan passed her. Like a little kid running after an older brother, she trotted to keep up. This time he was a bit more considerate, though—occasionally he would look back and nod.

The canyon twisted and turned. It grew narrower and the walls taller. Slashes of reds and browns and blacks ran through the sandstone.

They hiked a while. Suddenly, the cloying, heavy scent of water filled the air. Mackenzie paused, raising her nose to the sky. Above the walls, billowy clouds blocked the sun. The canyon colors, too, were changing: reds and greens were now almost black, tans almost brown. Errant strands of hair whipped her face, and she tightened her ponytail.

When had all those clouds formed? She jogged up to him, her brow furrowed, but he just shook his head and set off again, faster this time. She adjusted her backpack, stumbling over a rock as she hurried to keep up with him. The walls of the canyon were so close she could touch them on either side—and had to do so often to keep from falling.

Several minutes later he stopped to tie a shoe lace. "Looks like rain," she said, realizing it was a stupid comment. God, she hated it when she stated the obvious. She avoided his gaze.

"Do you have a rain jacket?" He shrugged his pack off and started digging around.

"Uh, I have this." She pulled out a light jacket that might or might not keep the rain out.

"Put it on. We've got to get moving. We need to get out of here before the rain. These canyons fill up quickly, and we don't want to get caught." He turned and once again left her behind.

"Wait," she yelled, after several minutes. She stopped, chest aching and breath ragged. A large boulder blocked the canyon like a chockstone. She'd have to climb over it to continue.

"Give me your pack." He stood on the other side of the rock.

"No, I can do it. I just can't go as fast as you." She straddled the rock, one leg over, ready to jump. Damn. It was a little farther to the ground than she'd thought. He offered his hand, and she took it. When she hopped down, his eyes met hers, but she couldn't read his expression. He turned away.

Suddenly, she truly understood what they meant by a slot canyon. The walls were so close her shoulders almost touched. It was dark and chilly, and the smell of water strong. The walls undulated, and the space between them varied. Sometimes the only way to pass was to climb higher to a wider place; other times, they had to turn sideway and just squeeze through. She fought her panic, trying to keep her thoughts focused on moving forward. At times, the canyon floor dropped, sloping down to a vee, and they'd have to wedge themselves with their shoulders and hips to scrape through. It was unnerving when the floor was far below them, nothing more than a narrow slit in the earth. To slip meant becoming stuck in the rock, which could mean spraining or breaking something. She cursed her almost-healed ankle, hoping it would make it.

Finally, a small side canyon opened up on the right. She slowed, hoping they would take it, but Sullivan continued resolutely down the main canyon. Canyons walls curved up to the sky, which was now a narrow gray strip a hundred or so feet above them.

At one point, she had to scuttle for several yards, back against one wall and feet on the other, to avoid a pothole twenty feet below. Making it across, she looked for him, hoping he had seen her prowess. But the canyon twisted ahead of her, and he wasn't in sight. Dammit, she should be worried about getting through safely, not looking for praise.

Mackenzie adjusted her cap. What were the others doing now that the weather was changing? Sam and Mike would take care of the less experienced members of the party. They would most likely break camp and get to high ground.

A coarse rumble of thunder echoed above. The light in the canyon was growing dim. Eyes on the canyon walls, she tripped over a piece of driftwood as she turned a corner, almost colliding with Sullivan. A piercing flash of light split the sky above them.

She yelled, "Shouldn't we turn back?"

"Can't turn back now. We've come too far. We've got to keep going, and fast."

They rounded a corner, and the canyon opened up a bit. He snagged her forearm, pulling her along behind him, and then stopped. They were standing on the edge of a deep fissure in the rock. It was so dark the bottom could have been twenty feet below them—or two hundred. Reclaiming her arm, she rubbed it and scowled at him. But his attention was on the canyon, not her.

"I think I know a place where we can wait out the rain," he said. "We have to get there before it floods, though."

"Floods? Floods? Oh my God." She had been deluding herself. A flash flood was death in slot canyons. Hearing him say it aloud was like being punched in the gut. She backed away from him.

"Yes, floods," he replied, eyeing her like she was a feral cat. "But if we hurry, I think we can make it. We're going to full-body stem across this section to get to safety. Now, watch me and do exactly what I do. Wait until I'm at least a few feet ahead. Then you're on your own. I can't go back to help you, do you understand?"

He didn't delay. He tightened the waistband to his pack and placed his hands on one side of the canyon. Leaning against the wall at a forty-five-degree angle, he jammed one foot against the opposite wall, and brought the other foot to meet it. Bent in the middle, he looked like a boomerang wedged between the walls. By pressing on both sides of the canyon, he kept himself in place.

"Starting is the hardest part," he said through gritted teeth. "But it's like stemming with your back and feet. You have to trust that the pressure of your hands and feet will support you." He inched along horizontally over the chasm.

Her throat was syrup-thick, and she couldn't swallow.

"Be sure to keep three points of contact on the walls," he called out.

She looked back, and then up at the threatening sky, knowing she had no choice. She could either follow him or take her chances with the flood.

"Come on. Get started. I'm waiting here for you, and I'm tired."

Mackenzie tentatively placed a hand on the cool rock, and then another. Leaning in, she felt her backpack slip to one side. It was distracting, but she had to keep going.

"That's right," she heard him say, "You're doing fine. Put all your weight on your hands and then stick a foot out there."

She did as he said and felt her foot start to slip.

"Higher. Keep your feet as high as you can. Stay horizontal if possible. And keep your feet flat on the rock. There's a tiny ledge that you can use, but don't use your toes." In a kinder voice, he said, "Trust me, it will work."

Trust him? Shit. Every muscle and nerve resisted, and her mind rebelled. After a long moment, she placed her left foot higher, finding the small ledge in the rock. It felt a little bit more secure, but she couldn't bring herself to let go with her other foot. The rock was cutting into both palms now, and she was splayed out precariously. She had to do something soon.

"Don't look down. Just listen to my voice."

Of course, as soon as he said that, Mackenzie glanced below her and felt her already-queasy stomach lurch even more. She understood then with great clarity that she had to be absolutely committed. Or die. She flexed her thigh, ready to bring the right foot up.

"Good. That's the way. Just match that other foot, baby."

Baby? Did he call her 'baby'? Even in her panic she bristled. Oddly, her annoyance spurred her on. Damn that man. Why couldn't he use her name? She gave herself to the rock, fueled by her anger. Sticking her other foot on the wall, she hung there, suspended in space over the darkness below.

CHAPTER 12

MACKENZIE PRESSED AGAINST ONE WALL WITH HER HANDS AND the other with her feet, moving surely but slowly toward the light on the other side. Once she believed the balance of the full-body stem, and allowed herself to trust it, she had no trouble. She kept on, moving smoothly, with a purpose that felt instinctive. Her hands were raw, her ankle ached, and her thighs burned, but she kept on.

A slight break in the clouds permitted a single ray of sunlight to illuminate them for a moment, and she peered below her. The canyon narrowed to what looked like an inch-wide strip at the bottom, fifty feet or so below. She quickly focused on her hands. As she neared the end, the walls gradually widened, but unevenly so; she had to find the right height on both walls to make any progress. Her arms and shoulders were beginning to shake, and her backpack swung wildly with every move.

Sullivan waited for her on a wide ledge, three feet below her. She knew she'd have to jump to it. She risked a glance. He was on a path in front of the canyon wall, both hands up, ready to catch her. Bracing herself, she transferred most of her weight to her legss and pushed off, twisting in the air like a cat. She landed on the fine dust next to him, but she couldn't stop her momentum and slammed into the rock, her knee striking a sharp edge. Warm, tacky blood dripped down her shin, and she closed her eyes in pain.

He took her hands, steadying her. "You okay?"

She nodded, opening her eyes but not trusting her voice. She didn't want to let go of his hands, and he didn't seem to be in any rush to relinquish them.

He looked up, and she did the same. The sky was a flat steel blue, the edges of the canyon outlined against the darkness. Brackish clouds hovered low overhead, growing thicker and darker.

Dropping her hands, he said, "Come on." He was already off the ledge, working his way up a rocky slope. Mackenzie scurried after him, trying to find hand- and footholds. She was exhausted and clumsy, her thoughts as confused and jumbled as the canyon itself. Nothing seemed to make sense, and she wondered vaguely why they were in such a hurry. Her thoughts were like wisps of smoke that swirled about and then vanished. She stopped, trying to clear her head, and it hit her again: They were deep in a slot canyon in the middle of nowhere, and it was beginning to rain.

She took in a few uneven breaths. Looking up, she saw the sky was an even darker charcoal gray now. As she stared, a bolt of lightning sliced through it, cleaving it in two. Thunder sounded immediately. The lightning was almost on top of them.

In an instant, it turned graveyard still and for a second she thought the storm might have passed. But the next moment rain pelted her, and the wind swirled, rising and falling. It howled and swooned like a keening lover. She tugged her cap down, hard, and tackled the slope.

Where was he? She felt isolated and alone. He was ahead somewhere, but she couldn't see him, and she climbed alone, grappling with the rock. She called out, but her words were sucked up by the rain and wind.

The wind oscillated, and a new sound emerged during a lull—the crashing of water. She groped blindly at rock and scrub alike. Damn him. How could he get so far ahead of her? He knew she didn't know what what she was doing. She bumped into a thigh-high boulder and hauled herself over it, skidding to the ledge behind it.

She could see in spurts only. The rain was slapping her in undulating sheets, one after the other. During a break, she could just make out something red moving fifteen feet above her. She squinted. On what appeared to be a sheer vertical wall of sandstone, Sullivan was climbing. She stared. He had left her. She couldn't climb that without him. She couldn't go back, and he was up there. She was going to die here, and nobody would ever find her body. She watched him appear and disappear in the rain.

Mackenzie glanced down. The narrow canyon was filling with water and rising perceptibly. She forced herself to turn back to the wall, searching for a hold. Nothing. She pounded and clawed at it.

Sobbing, she leaned against the wall. She was stranded in this hellish slot canyon, alone and cold, lost forever. Would she die from exposure? No, she decided, she would drown. Even Hillary, her best friend, wouldn't know what had happened to her.

Suddenly, something landed on her shoulder, and she jumped. Rope. It was a red-and-green climbing rope, with a loop at the end, dangling in front of her. She looked up and found Sullivan's face peering down. He was yelling at her, but she couldn't hear anything. He looks like a crazed mime, she thought, smiling despite herself. Shit. She was losing it. Stretching for the loop, she wriggled into it, backpack and all, and jerked it twice. It tightened under her armpits, and she braced her feet against the wall, trying to walk up it while she was being hoisted. Instead, she spun this way and that, hitting the rock with her shoulders and hips and knees. She covered her head with her arms and fought an irrational urge to laugh. She was like a sack of flour being lugged up a cliff.

After what seemed like hours, her progress halted, and she stared at a large boulder a foot above her. She couldn't see behind it and couldn't imagine what to do. Her thoughts just wouldn't come.

"Grab on," She thought she heard him yelling. "Grab the rock." Without thinking, she wedged her toe into a foothold and pulled herself up a few inches. Her hands slid over the wet surface, hunting. She found a deep pocket and grasped it with her right hand. She forced herself to let go of the rope that held her. Wrestling with the rock, she scrambled over it, landing in a heap on the other side.

Blinking, she looked around. She was in a deep cavern with a large overhang. It was damp and cold and smelled of mildew. She scuttled farther in to avoid the rain. Crying and laughing, she searched for him. A second later, he was there, tugging the looped rope over her head. She pressed herself to him, fighting back sobs, and he held her, not moving, his arms tight.

After several minutes she managed, "W-we're safe?" She shivered in waves.

Mackenzie felt him nod, and he tightened his hold on her. "Listen to me. We have to get dry." He gently pushed her away, and she hugged herself. He produced a gray duffel bag from behind a boulder. She was baffled. How had it gotten there?

"Here, wear these." He tossed a fleece jacket and pants to her.

"Wh-what will you wear? D-do you have more c-clothes in there?" She could barely get the words out over her trembling. Her jaw was stiff, her teeth like cold stones in her mouth. Without waiting for an answer, she turned her back to him, and struggled to free herself from her drenched clothes.

"My shirt's dry, and I have a blanket and the bag," he said. "I'll be fine."

She ditched her shorts and donned the fleece pants, all modesty gone. The jacket and pants hung on her, but they were soft and dry. Kicking her sodden clothes out of the way, she collapsed to the ground.

Sullivan, wrapped in a woolen blanket, spread his pants on the floor next to him. She couldn't make herself move.

"Let's see what we have here." His voice was loud and cheerful. He retrieved a bag from a side pocket in the duffel.

"I've used this cave before," he explained before she could ask. "I keep emergency supplies here. Christ. The, er, most of it's gone. We have a few energy bars and water. Here, eat." He threw a bar at her, but it bounced off her chest, landing next to her lump of clothes. She didn't try to retrieve it.

He frowned, cocking his head. Then he grabbed the empty duffel and sat down beside her. "Put your feet in here," he ordered, holding it open. She obediently stuck her feet in the sack, and he smoothed it around her legs, tucking her in like she was a child.

Tugging her cap off, he replaced it with something soft. A hat? She had no idea, but it was warm. He shoved bits of hair under it and threw the blanket around them. She could feel the steamy heat they created as they huddled together. Warmth flowed through her slowly. It drugged her, and she felt herself slipping into an almost narcotic sleep.

"You have to eat," he said, startling her. Had she been asleep? He retrieved and unwrapped the bar that lay on her wet clothes and held it up to her. She dutifully ate a bite of the stale, mock-food.

"Now, drink." He held the water bottle, and she drank. Water dribbled down her chin, and he wiped it with a corner of the blanket.

"Well, at least we're here, now," he said gently. She instinctively moved closer, and he wrapped his arm around her, cradling her in the hollow of his chest and shoulder. She relaxed against him, so close she could hear his heartbeat. So close that when he inhaled, it moved them both. She wondered vaguely at their closeness. The bonds of danger, she supposed, and drifted off.

It was dark when she woke. At first she had no idea where she was and began to panic, but the heavy smells of wet wool and mildew brought her back. Another odor filled her senses—smoke? She was swaddled like a baby in a blanket. A mountain of assorted clothing was piled on her. A cave. She was in a cave.

She had little memory of climbing there. The rain she remembered—and the fear. How had she ended up here? And where was Sullivan? A sudden panic rose in her, until she spotted him crouched over a small fire in an alcove a dozen feet away. He remained motionless, while the wind threatened to extinguish the flames. He moved to the other side, his back to her, to protect it. After a few moments it caught and grew, and the sharp edges of flames skipped and danced.

She coughed. Smoke was everywhere, causing her eyes to water and her chest to constrict.

He turned and stood, hands under his armpits for warmth. "Up already? How'd you sleep?"

Mackenzie ignored his perkiness. "What time is it? Has it quit raining?"

"Um, it's about eight o'clock, and yes, the rain has let up. It's just misting right now."

She struggled against her wrappings, kicking the duffel away. The cold surprised her, and she drew the bag back over her feet.

"When you're ready," he said, "Come by the fire. We don't have enough wood for all night, but it'll last awhile."

"We're staying here tonight." It was a statement, not a question. Her voice cracked, and she cleared her throat.

"Yeah, we'll stay until the water recedes." He prodded the fire with a stick. "These canyons hold a lot of water, but they drain quickly, too."

She remembered that he had been here before. "When were you here?"

"Not sure. I got to it a different way. I think I came down that side canyon we passed. On the right?"

She nodded, then shook her head no. "You were caught in a flash flood here, too?"

"Nope, when I found it, I thought it would be a good base if I was ever exploring this way. I've cached supplies in several places around here. God knows if I can remember how to get to them, but I figured someone else might need them someday, too. You never know."

"Do we have any food?" She cut him off before he could say more. Hunger pressed upon her, driving all other thoughts away.

He nodded. "Good. You're hungry. We've got energy bars and a few bags of dried fruit. The rodents got most of the other stuff." He motioned to a few bars and a baggie.

Her heart scudded when he mentioned rodents. She wasn't afraid of them, exactly, but she didn't want to run into them either. She unwrapped her legs and stood up, testing. They were stiff and creaky, and she shuddered involuntarily.

"Fortunately, we do have this." He winked, holding up a bottle of tequila. "No limes or salt, I'm afraid. But it'll take the edge off."

Mackenzie sat down next to him, shoulders high and tight. She held her hands as close to the flames as she dared. "I'm not a fan of tequila. Got a little too drunk on it once."

"More for me," he chuckled, taking a long swallow.

Was he really that cheerful, or was he pretending? She suspected he had already started without her.

He handed her another bar. It was so hard she thought she'd break a tooth, but she was hungry enough not to care. She sipped on tepid water while he rubbed his hands together in front of the blaze. He took another drink of tequila, offering it to her again.

She shook her head. It was difficult to chew, much less talk.

"No? It really warms you up." He held the bottle aloft.

"Well, I guess I could have a sip."

He was right. The alcohol burned a path down her gullet, and the heat thawed her from the inside out, like a flame spreading through her. Spluttering, she held it up to him. "Here you go." The tequila sloshed about.

He gestured for her to continue. "Have some more. The second swallow is always better."

She took another sample and followed it with a longer one. "You're right. It's not so bad."

He nodded, grinning.

They drank companionably for a while, not talking. The fire kicked and crackled, creating long shadows on the uneven wall. They passed the dried fruit back and forth. It was much better than the bars.

"You know, I don't like you very much," Mackenzie said suddenly. Her words surprised her. What was she saying? Speaking that honestly was something she never did. Not that she was dishonest. She just usually kept her thoughts to herself. It was safer that way. She took another swallow and held the bottle up. They'd finished more than half of it.

"Oh, really?" His voice was mild, and he held out his hand for the bottle. She took a quick swig before handing it over.

"No. Really. I think you're arrogant, and rude, and impolite, and, uh arrogant." The shadows on the walls captured her attention.

"Me?"

"Yes. And teshty, too." Oh, this wasn't good. She was slurring her words. She realized she was drunk. Somehow, it didn't bother her that much.

"Testy, huh? Well, you're not such a treat yourself."

She took the bottle from him. "I am too, a treat." Who did he think he was? "I'm smart and intelligent, and did you know I teach at a University? Linguishtics." *Take that, Houseboat Guide.*

"Yeah, I know. How could I not know? It's all you talk about."

She took a pull and, coughing, put the bottle down. "No, it's not all I talk about. Well, okay, maybe it is. But I have to. I have to work harder."

"Why?"

"Why?" She hesitated. "Uh, well, because I'm not very good." She shrugged. "Don't get me wrong. I'm a hell of a linguisht. But, uh, I'm not a good professhor. Or teacher, or girlfriend." There, she'd said it.

"Girlfriend? Where did that come from?" He leaned against her, snagging the bottle. She relaxed against him.

"What? Never mind. Anyway, I'm good with languages. And words."

He didn't say anything, but he put the bottle down on the other side of him, away from her.

"What about you? You live on a houseboat and teach kikaking. I mean, kayaking. Have you always done that?"

"No. But I bet you couldn't guess in a million years what I used to do. What I used to be."

He must be drunk, too, she thought. Leaning away, she tilted her head to study him, and almost fell backward. He seized her arm, pulling her up. She laughed, but it sounded like a crow's wild cawing, not her. Staring openly at him, she searched for signs of his former life. He grinned at her, showing off his straight, white teeth. His eyes were black in the glow of the fire.

Mackenzie stooped forward a bit for a closer look. There were laughter lines. Other lines, too. She wasn't sure if it was the tequila or the fire, but she decided he wasn't that bad.

He raised his eyebrows slightly, waiting, and she was aware of his hand on her arm. She didn't protest.

"So what am I, Slim?" He was very near, now, and she could smell tequila and smoke and something else. Something good.

The moment passed quickly. "See. I was right. You call me Slim," she accused. "And Baby and Princess and uh, Red. I hate being called Red. In fact, I hate them all." She reached around him for the bottle, but he blocked it.

"Linguist–linguist-i-cally, you're demeaning me." She wobbled again, but regained her balance before he could help.

"They're nicknames," he said. "Pet names. I'm not trying to demean you. But you seem, well, you are slim, and you're regal and haughty like a princess, and uh, you have beautiful red hair. The names fit." He took a swig from the bottle.

Pet names? Nobody had ever had a pet name for her. She'd been called "Mac" by her friends, but that was a variation of her name, not a pet name. His names for her were new and different.

"Well, okay. But it's embarrasshing." Dammit, she couldn't stop slurring.

"I'm sorry. I'll call you by your name from now on. Mackenzie." He said her name so softly she had to lean in to hear him. He certainly didn't get loud or obnoxious when drinking.

"Thank you." There was a long, charged silence.

"You're evading my question," he said.

"What?"

"My question. You bragged that you could guess what I used to do."

Gazing at him again, she tried to clear her head. She took in the half-smile. Bushy eyebrows. A high forehead, thinning hair, and strong jaw.

"Hmm. I don't know. I think you helped people. I think you went to a good college and are from the East somewhere. Probably had money."

He sat back, and she snatched the bottle from him.

"Aha," she said triumphantly.

"Why do you think that? Why would you think I helped people? And the other stuff?"

Mackenzie smiled. Obviously, she'd been right. "Because you have kind eyes. Old eyes. I don't mean you're old," she amended. "Old-soul eyes. Knowing eyes. Like you've seen a lot. And you've obviously gone to college. Your vocabulary and sentence structure tell me that. Your inflection and pronunciation tell me you're from the east coast. Probably Mash... Massachusetts or Maryland. There's some southern influence there, too, in your vowels. The way you draw words out, and the rhythm underneath. You've lived in the South, or maybe your parents were from the South." She drank and wiped her mouth with her sleeve. It occurred to her she must look like Frankenstein's Bride. She took her hat off and finger-combed her hair.

He stared at her, and she stared back. She broke it first, looking down. When he didn't say anything, she continued, "Why? Am I right? What were you? I'm a linguist, remember? You have to tell me now. Them's the rules."

He took the bottle back and held it up in front of him, gazing into what was left of the amber liquid.

"Okay, you're right," he said in a quiet voice. "I did help people. I'm an M.D. A doctor of internal medicine. I went to med school and worked in upstate New York, but I grew up in North Carolina. In Charleston, actually." He stared into the fire.

"Ha," she cackled. He didn't react. "I'm right," she said. "But why did you quit? Why aren't you doctoring?" She regretted asking the moment the words landed. The question hung between them like a balloon waiting to be popped.

"Some things, uh, happened, and I left five years ago. Bought the houseboat and moved to the lake."

She didn't want to ask, but she seemed to have no control over her words. "What happened? Did something bad happen?"

He turned toward her. She couldn't read his expression, but he was smiling slightly, so she eased up a bit, waiting for him to answer.

"Yes, something bad, but something good, too. In the end."

"Huh?"

"Well, I was married, and I discovered the hard way that my wife was having an affair with another doctor at the hospital. Someone I had gone to med school with. Someone we had both gone to med school with, actually. My best friend. So I decided they deserved each other, and I deserved another life. And here I am."

"You just left? Quit?"

"Yes. Been living on the houseboat for almost six years. Living like a king. But that first year was, well, a blur."

Mackenzie didn't say anything. He handed her the bottle, but she pushed it back. He took a long pull.

"W-wow," she stammered, "I didn't expect that. I mean, the doctor part. Or the other part, really." Lame. She was so lame.

He stuck a toe in the ashes, pushing a log farther into the fire. The flames reared up, before dying down. "Yeah, well, that part was easy. The rest of it was hard."

Images flooded into her mind. His immaculate hands. His knowledge of cactus treatment, and the scientific names for it all. The secret cove for the houseboat. He'd hidden away in the canyons. It explained a lot, and she felt a kinship with him that warmed her more than the fire. She'd always hidden herself away in plain sight, like him.

"I knew you helped people," she said. "I would have thought a lawyer, though."

"Why a lawyer?"

In for a penny. "Uh, because you're smart, but argumentative. Always have to be right. Obsessed with ethics. Kinda have a god complex."

Instead of a sharp retort, his voice was soft. "You know, I don't always have to be right. But for some reason, I've always got to be right when you're around. With you, I mean."

Suddenly, his arrogance seemed endearing. "Yeah, I know. You push my buttons, too." She giggled and took the bottle back. Tequila was so much better than she remembered. "It's like I'm your sister." She drank, watching him. "You have a sister?"

He didn't answer. She gazed down at the red and gray embers. The fire was fading. She was dizzy and closed her eyes for a moment.

He broke the silence. "What about you, Sl—er, Mackenzie? Why are you really here?"

The dreaded question, but this time he had asked differently. She'd better watch her words. Her tongue couldn't be trusted. "Oh. It's a long story. And a secret."

"You don't have to tell me, if you don't want to."

She shook her head. Oops, dizzy again. "It's not that," she replied. "It's, well, I don't think you'll believe me."

"Try me."

Mackenzie sucked her bottom lip. It felt numb and fat. Maybe she would give him a summary and see where it went. "Well, a friend of mine found an ancient map."

Before she knew it, she was telling him everything. She knew it was convoluted and made no sense, but he listened. Every few minutes or so, he'd um-humm, or ask a question. She told him about the codex and the Aztecs and about Rainbow Bridge. She told him everything. Well, not quite everything. She didn't tell him that Charlie and she had been together.

Finally, after what seemed like hours but was probably only minutes, she ran out of story. He passed the tequila to her, but she declined. She was queasy, and the world was swaying more than it should. He took one long drink, emptying the bottle, and spun it around at their feet, like spin-the-bottle. It ended up pointing to the space between them. They fell against each other, laughing, fit to burst.

"Y'see why I couldn't tell you? Y'see why I couldn't tell anyone?"

"It's quite a story," he agreed. "A few details are a bit fuzzy to me. Might be the tequila, though."

She nodded and closed her eyes, letting sleep take her, once again leaning against him.

She was in a deep feather bed—except it wasn't stuffed with feathers, but paper. Crumpled paper that crackled every time she shifted. She could smell the ink pressed onto the pages, along with the musty scent of dirty water. She was rowing through the sea of paper, pushing a heavy oar, ripping the bed apart. Above, someone tossed more and more paper down, drowning her.

Mackenzie woke up, and it took several seconds to remember she was in a cave, sleeping on the ground. That she had been dreaming.

She was curled up on her right side. Sullivan was on his side behind her, spooning, but not quite touching, her. His large arm rested on her waist. She knew she had been holding onto that arm in her sleep, probably pulling it close, and blushed.

Her head ached and throbbed. Slowly, she shifted away, his arm still on her. The moon had forced its way in, and she blinked. Bright light streamed in like a beacon.

She eyed the offending arm, and the assorted clumps of dirt causing the hairs to stand up. She extended a finger to smooth them, but quickly retracted her hand. What the hell was she doing? Barely breathing, she gently returned his arm to him, stiffening when his breath caught for a second. After a guttural snort, he resumed breathing evenly again, and she relaxed.

Rolling away, she stretched her legs and passed a hand over her eyes. Had someone taken a pick axe to her brain? She remembered the tequila and fragments of the conversation. She closed her eyes.

It was cold. Mackenzie pushed her legs back under the clothing, moving closer to him. She dragged part of a jacket over her. Just then, a loud crunching sound bounced off the walls. She jumped. There was a creature in the cave with them.

Stifling a cry, she leaned on one elbow, trying to see the back wall. Sullivan was still sleeping. The rustling continued, and she flinched each time she heard it. Should she wake him? Or ignore it? Were they in danger? Thoughts of animals eating their remaining food played in her head, and she poked him on the shoulder. He mumbled incoherently, but didn't wake.

"Sulley," she whispered. Nothing. "Sulley." Mackenzie grabbed his shoulder and shook him vigorously.

"What? Wha? Oh, it's... Christ. What's wrong?" He sat up, peering this way and that like a disoriented mole.

"There's something in our food. Something's getting into the food."

He ran his hand through his hair, causing it to stick up in ridges, and in the moonlight, she could see his scowl. "Nothing's getting to our food. Go back to sleep."

"I heard it. I heard something. Probably a, a, rodent." Her voice cracked, and she cleared her throat.

He sighed, leaning back with his arms under his head. "I'm sure you heard something. But don't worry about the food. It's a cave, for God's sake. Was it on the ground? Or on the ceiling?"

"Ceiling? What could—"

"Bats. Cave, remember?"

Gulping, she squinted at the ceiling but saw only black. She heard the crackling again. On the ground. Her head was splitting.

"Okay, not bats," he said. "Rats."

"Rats? Do you mean you're sorry it's not bats, you know, like, 'rats, I've got a run in my stocking.' "

He raised his eyebrows at her.

"Or rats, like vermin in the sewers? Oh, my God, you, you mean *rats*." She sprang up.

"Sit down. You'll scare them. They won't bother us. They're after food, not us."

Mackenzie remained standing, arms crossed over her chest. "You told me they weren't getting into our food."

"That's right. They're not."

"What? Why not?"

"Because we ate it all. There's nothing left."

Oh. For an instant, she was drowning again, like in her dream. They were in a cave, with rats or bats. Probably both. They had no food and were alone in some canyon in the vastness of Lake Powell, separated from the rest of the group. No one knew where they were. *They* didn't even know where they were. Tears slid down her cheeks.

He stood up next to her. "What's wrong now, uh, Mackenzie." He hesitated. "Ok if I call you 'Mac?' "

She nodded, but she couldn't stop crying. He was only a few inches away, and it was obvious he didn't know what to do. Stand there? Hold onto her? Shake her?

Deciding for him, she melted against his broad chest.

He responded immediately, wrapping his arms around her. She held onto him, and they stood there a long moment, breathing in sync. The rats and bats and the wilderness faded, and her headache eased a bit. She stiffened. What the hell was she doing? He probably felt sorry for her. Embarrassed, she dropped her arms and leaned back.

"Hey," he murmured. "Don't worry, I'm here." He reached for her again.

She shook her head, pushing him away, but he inhaled deeply and held on to her.

She remembered the warmth of his body. His smile. The way he smelled. Those little hairs on his arms. His gentle hands. She gave up.

He crooked a finger under her chin, tilting her face up to his.

He didn't stand there, or hold her, or even smile. He kissed her.

CHAPTER 13

in each other's arms. The first kiss was soft and questioning, the second hard and searching. Mackenzie answered it eagerly, forgetting her doubts.

He ran a hand down her back, and she held onto him, pulling him closer. Then he let go, and for a moment she was uncertain again. Before she could say anything, he took her face in his hands and kissed her deeply, urgently.

She felt his desire, and her body answered. How well they fit together, she thought, and then she thought no more. Time slowed down, elastic, folding back on itself like a piece of pulled taffy.

They explored each other, seeking the hidden places. She wanted him to touch her everywhere and guided his hands as he fumbled with her clothing. She helped him with his clothes, tossing them on the blankets. For a moment in the dimness, they stood there, fragile and vulnerable, heedless of the cold. She pulled him to her.

"Mackenzie," he whispered, gazing into her eyes. "Oh, my God. Mackenzie."

They sank to the pile of clothes. She ran her hands through his hair, feeling its strange, wiry texture, as he lowered her to her back. Lying there, stretched out full length, he covered her completely, hip to hip, thigh to thigh. Cupping her breasts, he squeezed them gently and moved, searching. She lifted herself up to him, and they found each other.

She knew it was morning even before opening her eyes: The sun was soft and warm on her face, and she heard birds calling to each other. She forced herself to keep her eyes closed, feeling his warm body next to her. She nestled in that secret space in the crook of his shoulder. Evidently, in her sleep she had flung her arm over him, and his hand rested possessively on it. This time, she allowed herself to stroke the fine hair that covered his arm. Burying her head deeper in his chest, she inhaled, taking him in.

As she snuggled, his chest hair tickled her nose, and she sneezed. He woke with a start, trying to free himself, and she retrieved her arm. What should she say? Last night had been wonderful, but she was self-conscious. Maybe he would be sorry about what they had done. Maybe he would just pretend it hadn't happened. She looked away.

But he pulled her to him and enclosed her in a great bear hug. "Going somewhere?"

"Uh, no. I was just—"

"Moving in closer," he finished, nuzzling her cheek.

Mackenzie took a deep breath, resting in his arms. He deftly pulled her on top of him, holding her close, and she felt all of him beneath her. He was already hard. The awkwardness vanished and they rolled to their sides.

Unlike last night, they took their time this morning, probing and laughing and touching each other. His skin, where tanned, was much darker than hers; on those spots the sun hadn't reached, he was as fair as her.

Watching his hands trace the swells and angles of her body, she let herself go. Caressing each other, they fell into an intoxicating rhythm, a dance, that included the other and then didn't.

Later, she asked, "Shouldn't we get up?" Her nose was inches from his. They were laying next to each other, under a mountain of clothes, watching the steam rise off the cave entrance. He didn't answer, but kissed her again.

It was the shifting wind that separated them, finally. A long gust rifled the expended fire, sending ashes flying, and a chill through her.

Sullivan pushed himself up. "You're right. We've got to get going." He rose, searching for his clothes, and she studied him appraisingly, delighting in the angular planes of his body.

"So ... how old are you?" she asked, extracting her own clothes. Her heart pitched, and she regretted her words. She hoped she wasn't being too forward.

"Older than you."

She glanced up and saw a crooked smile on his face.

"Too personal?"

"No. How old do you think I am?"

"Hmmm. I'd guess, well ..." She caught herself, knowing that any guess would be insulting. She shook her head and said instead, "Well, I'm thirty-four."

"Thirty-four? That old?"

"Yes, that old. So come on, what about you?"

"Well, I'm more than ten years older than you. Is that good enough?"

She considered. "That works for me. For now. I'll find out anyway, you know."

Their clothes were cold and stiff, and she started shivering again. After dressing, she wrapped herself in a blanket and walked to the cave entrance. Below her, canyon walls were stacked against each other, like a curvy row of dominoes. Mist floated among them, sometimes completely covering them.

Mackenzie turned back to see his eyes on her. "How the hell did we get up here?"

He answered, "Not very easily. I had to drag you up. Literally."

She turned again, sniffing the air. Wet rock smelled inviting, she decided. Musty and clean at the same time. Like Sullivan. She realized that she was enjoying their predicament. She was no longer afraid. She was happy.

He came up behind her, enfolding her. "You have to court a canyon: listen to its secrets, embrace its dark side. The canyons will change you if you let them." He paused. "Someday I'm going to really show them to you, teach you to climb," he said. "The right way."

Someday echoed in her thoughts, prominent and meaningful. She covered his arms with hers and rested against him.

They stood there for several minutes, taking in the vista. He's thinking about someday, she thought. And smiled.

Her good mood ended abruptly. It turned out they had to climb up, not down, from the cave.

He tied knots in the rope, with a loop at the end, and went first, taking the rope end with him. She followed, looping the rope around one hand, clutching the rock with the other. No way he could keep her from falling. They'd both fall to their deaths, she was sure.

But they didn't. Once on the ridge, she collapsed. He sat down behind her and rubbed her shoulders.

"You're doing great. You just climbed a 5.5 route. You're incredible."

She was out of breath and squeezed his hand while he massaged her shoulder. "Yeah, with you hauling me up it."

They started off, circling a craggy bluff, staying high. After an hour or so, they came to a flat mound of slickrock. He let his pack slip to the ground on a dry spot.

"Where do you think they are?" She dropped her pack near his. They were trying to find the rest of the group.

"Oh, Sam took them to high ground, I'm sure." He wound the rope into a snug bundle, with loops on either side, clipping it onto his backpack.

"I can take the rope," she offered.

"Thanks. I'd rather carry it. No offense."

"None taken." He wanted to keep it so he could bail her out, she thought, this time without anger. Once again, she resolved to be as independent as possible. She asked if he knew where they were going.

"Heading back toward the waterfall. I'm hoping they're above and beyond it. Close to where we were. Mike said he'd been up there before. I know Sam has." He was striding ahead of her. She had to jog to keep up with him.

Winded, she pulled on his arm. "Sorry, I've got to rest for a moment. I don't seem to have any energy."

He studied her. "We've been going for a while with little food. Let's sit down." A tiny gray lizard did pushups on the rock nearby, before darting off. "Why don't you stay here for a bit? I'll scout ahead."

"Nothing doing. I don't want to be left alone. I can keep up." She hesitated. "But, can we rest a little longer?"

"Sure. Let's rest." He pulled her to him roughly and kissed her, his hands running down her back.

Desire welled up in her, obliterating her thoughts. She arched against him. He drew in an uneven breath as she traced her finger down his chest to his abdomen. The ease with which they touched each other implied an intimacy she'd never felt before. He grazed her breasts with his nails, and she shivered. She wanted to bring him closer, to lie in the sun, naked. She longed to touch him with a question, and have him answer her deeply, with his body.

But now wasn't the time for that, and she broke away. He met her eyes and sighed, taking her hands in his and bringing them to his lips.

After a long moment, she gently reclaimed her hands. "What's over there?"

"On the other side of the ridge? Canyons that lead to the river."

"I thought the river was the other way."

He shook his head. "No. Well, yes. Remember? We took one branch of the river to Iceberg. The other branch is south of us. We're in between them, like an island."

"Oh. Right."

Like on Charlie's map. The thought of Charlie made her heart skid in her chest. She'd forgotten all about him.

"Come on. Enough resting." He rose, and she struggled with her backpack, suddenly clumsy. He led the way, slowing down for her. They walked, side by side, for a few minutes in silence. She'd think about Charlie later. He took her hand, and she let him, smiling to herself.

She tugged him to a stop, tilting her head up to him. "How far is it?" It was a ploy to rest again, and she didn't care if he knew.

"Well, it's maybe three miles total. We've probably gone a mile and a half. If they're on the ridge, we ought to see them soon." He shifted his weight from foot to foot.

She nodded, forcing herself to continue.

Ten minutes later, they appeared. She spotted a speck of color in the distance. A flash of bright pink moving in the distance. "Look, I think that's them," she cried.

They met halfway. Lucy immediately embraced Mackenzie, holding her prisoner, like they'd been long-lost best friends. It was awkward. "I'm so glad to see you. Where were you when it started raining?"

Mackenzie stepped back. She was sure she gave off the distinct perfume of sex and desire. She made herself describe the ordeal, leaving out most of what happened in the cave. Sullivan was a few feet off, talking to Sam, glancing over at her every few moments.

"I can't believe you guys survived."

"Well, Sulley did most of it," she said. "I would have died out there on my own."

Lucy raised a dark eyebrow. "Sulley? I've never heard you call him that."

Mackenzie bent down to tie a shoe lace, hoping Lucy wouldn't see her blushing. She waited a beat. "Oh, I'm sure I have. Maybe you weren't around." She looked up, shielding her eyes and face with her hand as she scanned the surroundings.

"Maybe so. Anyway, you're back. Mike made us climb up past the waterfall, fast, you know. With our backpacks. It didn't rain that hard until we got to the top, thank God. We sort of laid low in a little cave, waiting for it to end."

"Good thinking. Sullivan was sure you'd climbed to high ground." She pronounced his name clearly, for Lucy's benefit. "Glad it's over, and the sun's out again."

"And that we're back together, too," Lucy said. "I was worried. And I'm sure you're relieved you're not alone with Sullivan. That must have been weird."

Mackenzie didn't reply.

"I guess this is as good a place as any to have lunch." Sam set his backpack down. They had been hiking for almost an hour, and the sun was high in the sky. He crouched by a low overhanging rock that provided a bit of shade.

"I'm certainly happy to be dry," Sandy said. "This damned desert."

Mackenzie edged around him and asked Sam if she could help.

"No," he replied without looking at her. "Got it covered. We're having sandwiches today."

"Well, if you're sure." She was puzzled by his coldness, but figured it had been a rough day and night for him, too.

She was restless and didn't know what to do with herself. She kept sneaking looks at Sullivan, but he was all business. Apparently, they were to act like nothing had happened. She knew her expression would give her away, so she decided to ignore him. It was the safest way.

She sat down next to Mike. "What do we do now? Do we have to climb back down to where we camped?"

He cracked his knuckles, one at a time. "Well, we could. That's where the kayaks are. Or, we could continue down the way you and Sullivan went and cross Gray Mesa. We might be able to head down to the river there. That'd put an end to the trip, though. Guess it depends on Vic and Sulley."

Mackenzie was silent. She had to sway them to head back toward Iceberg Canyon. Back to where she and Sullivan had ventured. The cave had to be just beyond. And Charlie with it?

She blinked. Charlie. She was here to find Charlie. Thinking of him was like probing an aching tooth. It might pass the time, but the pain didn't go away.

She glanced over at Sullivan. What really happened in that cave? Was she making too much of it? Maybe it was one of those bonding-flings two people experience during extreme events. She took a huge breath and pressed a hand to her chest, remembering the night before. Her heart felt like a hand-grenade: one small click, and it would explode.

They ate sandwiches, clustered in small groups. She and Mike sat together, eating in silence. After finishing, Mike leaned back, his eyes closed.

Mackenzie waited a few moments, going over things in her head. She coughed lightly, and he looked up. "Uh, Mike, do you have a map?"

He pulled a rather worn map from his backpack. He spread it out on the ground in front of them, using four rocks in the corners to keep it in place.

"We're here." He pointed at the map with his forefinger. "This is Iceberg. You and Sulley headed that way, to the left."

She leaned closer. She had to get them back to the left fork of Iceberg. The cave in Charlie's map looked like it was in a canyon close to where she and Sullivan had spent the night.

"This is a canyon?"

"Yes. Looks like it hooks around and runs into this canyon that feeds into the river. So one long canyon. Maybe."

"If you wanted to get to, say, that canyon," she pointed to the canyon marked in Charlie's map, "couldn't you take a shortcut?"

He shook his head. "No. See these lines on the map? They mark changes in elevation. When they're this close together, it means it's steep. This is a high, rocky ridge that you can't get through. It's full of little side canyons. If you crossed there, you'd get stranded pretty quick. No, the only way to that canyon—and the river—would be through a canyon itself. And you'd have to make sure you picked the right canyon. One that you could actually get through."

"Hmm. It looks so close, though." She leaned in.

"Well, the lines show thirty-foot differences in height. It's deceptive. If a cliff was twenty-five feet high, it wouldn't even show on the map. See right here?" He pointed to the ridge between Iceberg Canyon and the gooseneck and patiently repeated, "See how those lines are almost on top of each other, running around the ridge? It means it's a high cliff. No, you have to find a pass through it or follow a canyon."

She pondered the map for a moment. She wished she could check Charlie's map again, but her notebook was in her tent.

Her notebook. She remembered she'd left the notebook out, under her sleeping bag, when she and Sulley had set out to explore the left fork. She hadn't taken it with them when they'd left. Where was it now?

"Uh, Mike, who gathered everything when I was gone? When the storm came? Did you leave the tents and other stuff. You know, my tent and sleeping bag, and..."

"Hmm. I think Lucy got your things. Or maybe Jennifer. We were hauling ass at that point, trying to get it together before the weather hit. Not sure."

Bounding to her feet, she said, "Thanks. I think I'm going to find my stuff."

He nodded, folding the map back.

"Looking for this?" Jennifer came up behind Mackenzie, spooking her. Shit. The blonde woman had her notebook tucked under an arm.

"That's mine," Mackenzie said. "My notebook."

"Yes, I can see that. Very interesting."

She lunged for it, but Jennifer turned, twisting out of the way.

"No, not yet. Not until I share it with the rest. We're a team, remember?"

"No," Mackenzie replied loudly. Mike glanced up. Sullivan, Sam, and Lucy broke from their conversation and turned toward the two women. Sandy and Henry were a few feet away. They had viewed the exchange and were avidly watching.

"Give it back," Mackenzie said through clenched teeth. "It's not yours."

Jennifer glared at her, eyes narrowed.

"What's going on?" Sandy asked.

Jennifer faced the group and held the notebook up. "This. When I was packing up Mackenzie's things I found it. You know, when I was helping during the rainstorm."

Lucy opened her mouth slightly, ready to interrupt. Mackenzie frowned at her, cautioning.

"When I was gathering everything up," Jennifer continued, "To help her, this, uh, fell out. Her notebook."

"Yes." Mackenzie agreed. "It's my notebook. It's private."

"I know. I'm so sorry, but I couldn't help but see what was in it." Jennifer looked at the group, grinning.

Mackenzie took a breath. "Jennifer."

"No, don't you say anything. I'm telling them." She turned toward Sullivan. "You see, Mackenzie has a map. A treasure map." She opened the notebook to the photocopy of the map.

"A treasure map? You mean like in gold and jewels?" Sandy stared at her.

"Whatever it is, it's probably private," Lucy said. "We should respect her privacy."

Nobody said anything. Jennifer said, "An Aztec treasure map."

Mackenzie felt hot and woozy. She'd been keeping things to herself for too long. Sullivan knew now, so why not the rest? "Yes." Her voice was flat.

Laughter erupted in little spurts, here and there, from the group. Henry nudged Sandy, who winked. Even Mike had a half-smile on his face. She rushed Jennifer one more time but was slapped away.

Sandy scoffed, "You've got to be kidding. You're on a treasure hunt?" He looked at Sullivan. "She's got a treasure map, Sulley."

Sullivan remained silent.

"Mac," Lucy said, "Just ignore them."

Dammit. Lucy might be right, but she was tired of keeping the secret. It had been wearing on her, riding on her shoulders like an uncomfortable backpack. The problem was, she didn't know how to explain without sounding like a nutcase. She snuck a glance at Sullivan. His expression was neutral, but when she caught his eye, he flashed his eyebrows at her.

She spoke the words before she realized she'd made a decision. "Yes, it's a map." She paused. How much should she tell? To make it sound real? "It's really a codex that includes an Aztec map. It shows the way to a cave that, uh, Montezuma used. When the Spanish came, he hid important things in it. Some think he hid gold." Her words died, and she was suddenly aware of how foolish it sounded.

For a long moment, no one said anything. She watched an ant crawl onto the toe of her boot. It was like she was standing in front of a class again, paralyzed. She couldn't look up.

"Come on, let's hear it," Vic said. "I'm sure there's an excellent story to tell. I for one want to hear about Montezuma. I'm sure you've done your research."

She glanced up at him, but couldn't gauge his expression. He wasn't smiling, but his words were sincere, not sarcastic, and he looked genuinely interested.

Sullivan stepped in, taking the notebook from Jennifer before she could react. He handed it to Mackenzie, who latched onto it, hiding it behind her back.

"Okay, Mac, tell them what you told me."

"You knew about this," Lucy said to Sullivan. "You knew she was after treasure."

He shook his head. "I found out when we were trapped in the canyon. But I believe her. You need to listen." He looked around the group. "Mac," he said. The tone of his voice when he said her name spurred her on.

Jennifer looked at him silently, one hand on her hip.

Pressing her lips together, Mackenzie let a breath escape. "Okay, I need to start at the beginning. So it might take a few minutes." Someone groaned. "A few weeks ago, I received a phone call from a friend..."

Half an hour later, her throat felt like chalk. She had talked without a break the entire time. When anyone attempted to interrupt her, Sullivan had silenced them with his eyes. He was a few feet from her, arms crossed over his chest, legs wide. Ready for battle.

She worried about Sullivan and purposefully left the particulars about Charlie vague. She couldn't remember how much she had told him in the cave. He occasionally caught her eye when she explained some of the details. Her version must have been mixed-up. He'd had more to drink than she had. The fact that he had supported her, had believed her improbable, tequila-infused explanation, encouraged her.

As she related the details of the story, letting them look at her notebook, the attitude of the group subtly shifted. One by one, each of their expressions changed from doubt to eagerness. Sandy seemed to be the most eager, leaning toward her, nodding at her when she slowed down.

"Here are the photocopies of the map Charlie found." She took the notebook from Vic and knelt, placing it on the ground. They moved in closer, and she flipped it so they could read it right side up.

Turning the plastic-enclosed pages, she expanded on what she had deciphered. When she got to the map Charlie had sketched of Rainbow Bridge, Sullivan said, "That's why you were out there that night."

"Out where?" Lucy cocked her head.

"I found her exploring in the middle of the night, back at Rainbow Bridge."

Lucy stroked her chin, a puzzled expression on her face. "Was that when you hurt your ankle?"

Mackenzie frowned at Sullivan. "Didn't I mention that? I can't remember, with all the teq—"

He cleared his throat, obliterating the last word. "I'm sure you did. With all the excitement of the storm, I probably forgot."

"Yes. Well, anyway, that's right. I did explore around there." She looked up. "Oh, I almost forgot. I took photos of the wall. They're in my camera." She frowned again. "I'll get them later."

Vic asked in a quiet voice, "So all the stuff about the glyphs pointing to Rainbow Bridge. That was made up?"

Oh, no. She'd forgotten about that part. She took her time answering, choosing her words.

"No it wasn't made up. That's the ironic part. I do think the glyphs are related to the map. It was only because I was thinking of Charlie's drawing of Rainbow Bridge that I came up with it. See?" She pointed to it in the notebook.

"How do you know this Charlie person?" Jennifer asked.

There was no point in hiding it any longer. If she was going to induce them to help her find the treasure, she'd have to give them more incentive. She had no choice. She had to suck them in, appeal to their sense of the heroic. She would talk to Sullivan later, smooth it over if she needed to. She sat down, stretching out the time, choosing her words carefully.

"He was a friend of mine," she said. "A very close friend. He's missing. That's the real reason I joined the group. I wanted to find him. I think he might be somewhere near the cave."

CHAPTER 14

Mackenzie avoided looking at Sullivan. "But we're not together now," she added, hastily. "It wasn't that serious, and I haven't seen him in over a year. Then a couple weeks ago I got a call from him, asking me to go with him to find the map."

"And the gold," Jennifer added.

"Well, yes, that too. But there's more." She gazed at Sullivan. His baseball cap was pulled down, obscuring his eyes, and his mouth was a thin, straight line. His arms were still crossed over his chest.

"I told him I couldn't go. It was during finals and..." She stopped. Too much information would just drag it down. "Uh, so he told me he was going to put a team together without me. Find it with them. I guess that's what he did." She shut the notebook. "And then I saw on the news that a man was missing in Utah. Presumed dead. It was Charlie."

Lucy was across from Mackenzie, on her knees. "But he wasn't dead? How did you get the photos?"

"I didn't get photos. I got files. Charlie mailed a memory card with them to me. With the drawing. It must have been before he went missing." She stood up. "He wanted me to go to Rainbow Bridge, and especially to Painted Rock."

"Why do you think he's near the cave? Maybe he *is* dead. Has he contacted you?" Lucy stood, brushing off her knees.

"He left me a clue on the drawing he sketched." Mackenzie opened to the page in the notebook. "See. Right here." She pointed to the symbol next to the label for Painted Rock. "When Charlie and I were in school together, we shared our notes, and we came up with a kind of shorthand. We had symbols for 'need more info,' and 'redundant,' and one for 'not too sure about this citation.' She paused. "And this one, for 'see below.' "

"See below?" Mike asked.

"Yes, *vide infra*. It's noted by *v.i.*," Henry interjected, "In scholarly circles. It means, 'see the following.' "

"Right. Our symbol was literally the phonetic characters for 'vee' and 'i.' No one else knew about it. So I knew Charlie had left more info for me at Painted Rock."

"You came all this way to find him based on your little shared symbol." Sullivan lifted a brow.

"Yes." Her words sounded harsh, but she continued. She would talk to him later. "I was mostly interested in the codex. If it's authentic, it's an unbelievable find, not only for linguistics, but for history. Worth a fortune." Mackenzie looked up at him. "And then I found out he was missing."

"What did you find at Painted Rock?" Sam asked.

"Oh, right. Well, you remember when I was taking photos?"

He shook his head. "Nope."

"I think you were napping." She shook out her legs, assessing the group. Sandy leaned in, rubbing his hands together. Jennifer was unreadable. Vic was smiling, thank God. Henry yawned, revealing silver fillings. Mike didn't meet her eyes. Lucy was frowning, and Sam was very still, focused on her.

This is like opening Pandora's Box, she thought ruefully. What's going to happen if we do find Charlie and the gold? She didn't know them well, even Sulley and Vic. She didn't care for Jennifer or Sandy. Lucy was her only ally, but even she was acting strange. Mike seemed sincere, but he was young and idealistic. Henry was just a pain in the ass. She wasn't sure she could trust any of them. She missed Hillary.

"So what did you find?" Sandy broke the silence.

"When I went back that night, I checked the ground beneath the painted panel," she said. "There was a small boulder that had been moved. Under it, I found a message. A piece of paper with the words, "Follow the map. I'm heading there." She paused. "It was signed CP. For Charlie Peterson."

For almost an hour, the group fired questions at her. She sat back down on the ground, arms wrapped around her knees. A slight breeze lifted strands around her face, and she absently ran her hands through her bangs, trying to keep them out of her eyes. Her head ached, her throat burned, and she was hungry.

Sullivan didn't say much or ask any questions. Shit. She had to get him alone, talk to him.

But memories of Charlie flooded back to her as she answered questions. How did this get so complicated? She came here for Charlie, she reminded herself. To find him and show him she could change, that she could be what he wanted. Charlie trusted her. He had proved that.

Sullivan simply happened. Anyway, he was acting like it meant nothing to him. He didn't even want the group to know what happened between them in the cave. It was probably just a fling to him. Just sex. She laid her head on her arms, hiding her face.

"You okay?" Vic asked.

Mackenzie sighed, a wan smile on her face. "Fine. Just tired."

"What do we do now?" Mike asked.

"Well, I vote we try to find Charlie," Lucy said. "He could be in trouble, or hurt. We're not too far from the cave, are we?" She glanced at Sullivan.

"I'd have to see the map again."

"Isn't it up to Vic?" Mike looked at Vic and Sulley in turn. "It's his expedition, after all."

"I think finding someone lost in the canyon is a little bit more important than the expedition," Lucy said, smiling at Vic.

Vic rubbed the back of his neck. "Lucy's right. The glyphs can wait. Besides, we may find something much more valuable. Anyway, as Mac mentioned, the glyphs might be related to the cave."

Sullivan was studying the map, his nose less than a foot from the photocopy. Mackenzie moved toward him, and he stiffened. She backed off a bit.

"Can we get there?" Her voice was low. She knew the answer already, but she wanted to engage him somehow. "I mean, from here? Can we get through?"

He replied without looking up from the map, "I think so. We're here, on this ridge. We'd have to go back the way we came today, and go a ways farther." He tapped a finger on the map.

Mike edged in closer, followed by Lucy and Sandy.

Sullivan said, "I believe this curved canyon leads right into the canyon you want. We'll have to go a different way than how Mackenzie and I went, because we don't want to cross the river. If I'm right, the Aztec cave is in this side canyon, here, that branches off. At least, it could be there."

"Are we all decided?" Vic asked. "We're going to find Charlie? And the gold?"

"Not me," Sam answered.

He was sitting on a flat rock, a few feet from the others, leaning on one hand. His hair was pulled back into a braid, emphasizing the sharp planes of his face. His eyes looked more gray than blue in the light.

Mackenzie's head shot up. "What? You don't want to go?" Of all of them, she had wanted Sam to back her up and to be interested in the map and the gold. It belonged to his people, after all. Didn't it? She felt drained suddenly, her arms tired.

He smiled crookedly, but his voice was serious when he spoke. "It's not that. I just think someone needs to go back for the kayaks and the food."

Food? Oh. She swallowed. "Is the rest of the food back at Iceberg?"

"Nope. Some of it is, along with the supplies. We got a lot of it up here, in those packs." Sam motioned with his head toward two bulky green packs. "But not all."

"We should be okay, right?" They would need at least three days worth, she calculated. Those backpacks could hold enough food for all eight of them.

"Well, there's plenty there, if you're careful. It won't be steak and eggs," he said, "But I think you've got enough for—"

"Three days," she finished.

"Yeah. Maybe four. You'll have to be smart about it, though. There's some good water in that first canyon. So that's not a worry."

Sullivan rubbed the back of his neck. "Yeah. But I need you with me, Sam. Too much could go wrong. I don't think it'll take us three days. Two most likely. One for the first canyon, and one for the second. We can leave the kayaks and food till then." His voice was low, his words measured.

"What about after?" Sandy kneaded his hands. They looked pink and mottled. "We've got to get out of there and back, too."

"Well, that's another reason I'm leaving." Sam said. "I'll take the kayaks around, meet you at the mouth of the cave canyon, where it meets the San Juan arm. I'll bring food and water."

Sullivan raised an eyebrow. "We can send you out later, Sam."

"Sure, but I think it would be best this way. For everyone."

He paused, scanning the group, ending with Mackenzie. "There are too many of us. You'll travel faster with less people. Besides, this way I'll know where you are. Right now, no one knows our location."

A gentle murmur drifted through the group.

"Okay," Sullivan said. "If you're set on this, I guess you're the best one to go back."

She endeavored to read Sam. "You'll be okay? By yourself?"

"You bet. Don't worry about me. I'll be fine." He turned, heading for the overhang where they'd left their gear.

She waited to see if anyone else had anything to add. Waited for someone to argue with him. After a few moments, she realized it was settled. She asked, "So? When are we leaving?"

"Not till morning, Sullivan said. "First we have to head back toward Iceberg, send Sam off. Find a place to eat and camp." He gazed at her. "That okay with you?" His voice had a slight edge to it.

He's mocking me, Mackenzie thought. "Fine with me," she said, matching his tone. "Let's get going." She turned, fighting back tears. She was exhausted and emotional, with a short fuse. High maintenance? Well, so be it. Anyone would be oversensitive after what she had been through. She heaved her backpack onto one shoulder and walked over to Sam. "I wish you weren't going, Sam. We'll miss you. I'll miss you."

He nodded, his gaze steady and level, but didn't say anything.

"I guess it's good that you'll know where we are, and that you'll be there for us." She wanted to hug him; instead, she extended her hand.

He covered it with his. A faint smile softened his face. "Be careful, Mac. Things aren't always what they seem in the canyons."

CHAPTER 15

THEY SET OUT SINGLE FILE THE NEXT MORNING, SHUFFLING along like a disjointed caterpillar. A breeze whispered at them as they hiked through slickrock. The view was spectacular in the low light, the colors of the canyons vivid.

Sam stayed with them for a few minutes. They stopped, and he shook each of the men's hands, wishing them luck. He briefly hugged Jennifer and Lucy. With her, it felt like he held on for a moment too long. Or maybe she did. She found herself wanting to comfort him for something she couldn't understand. Comfort herself. She was sure the group hadn't picked up on the subtle difference between hugs, but she turned away from them anyway to avoid questions.

After he left, they plodded along, weaving their way through the ridge. She was third in line, behind Sullivan and Vic. She missed Sam even more than she had thought she would. He had been the steadying force in the group. She kept her eyes on the ground, pushing her feelings aside. She had to look ahead: They were on their way to the canyon.

Another hour passed, and she jogged up to Vic. The group had spread out, was no longer quite so connected. Sullivan was far enough to be out of earshot.

"Are we going the right way? I'm so lost."

He pointed to the left. "Well, this might be a trail of sorts. See those three rocks piled on top of each other? They're called cairns. Somebody's been here before us and placed them."

"I know what cairns are," she told him. "I just haven't noticed any before now. They kind of blend in with the rocks."

"Yeah, but once you've seen one, it's somehow easier to spot the rest." He paused, slowing down a bit. "Are you doing okay, Mac? You seem sad or depressed or something."

She told him she was just anxious and thanked him. But of course, he was right. She *was* sad and depressed.

As they hiked, she noticed cairns everywhere. It was like a scavenger hunt, and she needed the diversion: A blister under her little toe stung with every step, and her ankle ached.

The ridge rose, becoming more rocky and uneven. The drop on the right fell away sharply. On the left, fifty feet below them, slickrock mounds rose, layered with varying shades of copper, rose, and ocher.

When the path narrowed to ten feet across, Sullivan halted. "We'll head down here to the right. Some of the rocks on the cliff face are loose in places. Be careful and give the person in front of you plenty of room." He disappeared down a sharp vee created by two boulders.

Vic cast her a tentative smile. "Here goes nothing." He leaned over the edge, examining the drop, before turning back. "It's not that bad. Just take your time. I'll be there at the bottom waiting."

She watched him downclimb. For most of the way, the rock seemed solid, with razor-blade edges and corners, but toward the bottom it ended in a pile of scree. His "not that bad" looked terrifying.

Cinching her backpack tighter, she glanced back at the group that was clustered in a semicircle behind her. Mike stood near Jennifer. Henry and Sandy were conversing in low tones, heads tilted toward each other.

Lucy stood behind her fidgeting with her backpack straps.

"Okay, time to go," Mackenzie said.

Lucy nodded. "I'm sure it'll be fine. I'll be right behind you."

Mackenzie took a deep breath, returning the nod. Now that Sam was gone, Lucy and Vic were her only allies, and she couldn't afford to lose another friend.

The drop from the top of the ridge looked almost vertical. The rocks were covered with fine sand that she hoped wasn't slippery. Facing the cliff, she took her time, placing her feet carefully before descending.

After a few moments, she rested and gazed around her. Below, Sullivan and Vic were making their way to what looked like a dry creek bed farther down that hadn't been visible from the top of the ridge. Sullivan got there first and stood looking west, a hand shading his eyes.

Focus on the climbing, she told herself. Focus on the climbing.

About fifteen feet from the bottom, she reached broken bits of loose rock and boulders that covered the slope. Instead of backing down it, she decided to glissade. It looked manageable, so she tested a rock, weighting it with her right foot. It held for a split second, before giving way. Both feet went out from under her, and she lost her balance. She landed hard on her left hip.

"Shit," she yelled, "Rock!" Her voice was drowned out by the noise of stones and earth tumbling down below her. She slid, feet first, down the scree slope. "Look out! Rocks!"

The slope shallowed out at the bottom, and she gradually slowed. Sullivan and Vic ran to her, one on each side. Her backpack had taken the brunt of the slide, but her thigh and elbow were bleeding.

"Mackenzie. God, are you okay?" Sullivan knelt, an arm around her. "Can you sit up?"

She willed herself up, leaning into him. He brushed her hair off her face. Vic looked at them, eyes narrowed, and cleared his throat.

Sullivan glanced up. "Help me get her to that rock over there." He avoided the other man's eyes.

"Okay, Mac," Vic said. "Let's see if you can stand." His voice was calm and encouraging. The two men lifted her, and she stood between them on her right leg. She dropped her backpack to the ground.

"Let me take a look," Sullivan said. Angling her body to rest on her uninjured hip, she lowered herself down on the rock.

He pushed the leg of her shorts up a bit. "Looks nasty. We'll have to clean it, and get you an Ibuprofen. I'll get my kit."

By the time Lucy reached them, Sullivan had expertly cleaned and bandaged her scrapes. They stung like hell, and looked worse, but he assured her they'd heal cleanly. She pulled on a long-sleeved t-shirt to cover her elbow, and tugged her shorts down, but she couldn't quite hide her thigh.

"Please don't say anything," she implored them. "I don't want the group to know."

"Embarrassed?" Sullivan asked, softly.

"No. Well, maybe a little. I just don't want it to be a big deal. I'm fine now. We'd better keep moving, don't you think?"

He nodded. "Yes. We should." He held her gaze, his eyes soft, and she looked away first. He was so close. Her breath caught in her chest, and she fought the physical need to touch him. Her thoughts were thick, like cold honey.

Mackenzie walked over to Vic, who was perched a few feet up the slope, warning each of the group about the loose rock, advising them to slide down on their butts. Even Henry made it down without incident.

She must have too much on her mind. She was getting clumsy. Taking a deep breath, she forced herself to concentrate.

Sullivan called out from a few yards away. "This is it." He gestured behind him. "This is the beginning of the canyon." He was standing in front of a wide creek bed.

"It doesn't look like much," Sandy said. "You sure this is a slot canyon?"

"Don't worry, you'll be in the slot soon."

They continued down the path. The canyon walls bulged and twisted, growing closer. Shadows deepened as they descended, and several times they had to negotiate drops of ten feet or more. At one point, Sullivan lowered each of them on a knotted rope, down a fifteen-foot overhanging chute that couldn't be downclimbed. He then rappelled, leaving the rope behind. The rope was the only way back up the sheer face. If they had to retrace their steps, they had to leave it there.

The largest obstacle was a massive boulder wedged between the canyon walls. It hung, suspended, a foot or so above the canyon floor. It reminded her that a rock that size had at some point broken off the wall and fallen. Passing it required either climbing over, boosted by Sullivan, and jumping down on the other side—or going under it. She chose the latter, wriggling under the boulder on her back first. Everyone else climbed over, hopping down.

After a brief lunch of protein bars, they resumed hiking. Sullivan rounded a bend and halted. The canyon walls were fifteen feet apart here, but the path ended. A hole about three feet wide split the path. It looked like a spiral drain in the rock.

"We'll have to rappel here." He peered down at the break in the earth.

"Rappel?" Henry raised his eyebrows. "Down that?"

"Yes. It's not far, but it might be a bit cumbersome. Not too dangerous." He scanned the group. "This would be a good time to rest, as I've got to set up the rappel. Mike, we'll have to use your rope."

"Does the canyon get deeper after we rappel?" Sandy asked.

Sullivan replied, "Sometimes these slot canyons can drop to hundreds of feet below the surface, but sometimes they level out. We'll have to take it one step at a time."

Retreating, Sandy flopped down next to Henry. "I don't know," he said plaintively. "I don't like this at all. There has to be another way."

"Buck up, Sandy." Henry clapped him on the back. "We're committed, you see. Think of the gold."

"If there is any. Maybe it's not there, and we're risking our lives for nothing."

"I seem to recall that you were very eager to search for it."

"Yeah, but that was before we got ourselves into this canyon. Don't you think there's another way? I mean, this can't be the only way to get there."

"I suppose there could be an alternate route," Henry said. "However, I don't believe we have a choice. Not unless we returned the way we came. I, for one, doubt that I could climb the rope we left."

"Oh, I don't think it would be that bad. I'm not great in tight places, but I'm a hell of a rope climber. But there's no way the group would turn around." Sandy pressed the heels of his hands against his eyes. "You're right. It seems like we have no choice."

"Sandy, I need your help, too," Sullivan called out. "Here, flake the rope out, like this, so it's not all knotted up." He demonstrated, while Sandy rose to join him, arms crossed.

"What are we going to do about harnesses?" Mike asked. "They're back with Sam."

"Shit." Sullivan let out a breath. "We've got one harness. Mine. We can either send it back up each time, or—"

"Or teach them how to self-rappel," Mike looped the end of the rope around a deep saddle in a rock at the edge of the drop and raised an eyebrow. He finished securing the rope and tugged on it. "It'll take a long time to get a group like this down. And we'll have to leave the rope again." He looked up at Sullivan, who towered over him. "Just in case."

"Right. Really don't want to leave another rope, but if we turn back, we'll need it." Sullivan produced a harness from his backpack. "I'll go down. You stay up top, okay?"

Sandy fed the rope out into a pile. "You're leaving the rope? Don't we need it?"

"We'll pick it up on the way back. For now, make sure there aren't any knots or twists, okay?"

After a moment, Sullivan returned to the task at hand, whistling as he stepped into his harness. Mackenzie remembered how cheerful he had been when they were stranded in the cave. Obviously, he liked these situations. He's having fun, she thought. This is an adventure for him.

When he had all his gear on, he looked like a soldier dressed for battle. Carabiners and slings hung from loops on the harness and clinked as he moved. He ducked as Mike placed a knotted sling with various types of climbing gear over his head, like a sash. Next, he slipped the rope through his harness and rappelling device.

Lucy sat down next to Mackenzie. "Don't know how they expect us to get through this. It seems like too much to me."

"Well, it's not that bad. It's actually more like figuring out a puzzle. When it's tight, it's like an obstacle course. Sometimes you have to stem across the walls. You know, with your hands on one side and feet on the other. Or prop your back against one wall and your feet on the other," she replied. "You've got to inch your way along."

"And you know this because?" Lucy asked.

Damn. She'd have to be more careful. "Oh," she said, keeping her voice emotionless, "when Sullivan and I were in the rain storm, we had to do some of that to get to the cave." She reached into her backpack to hide her expression and busied herself digging around for a moment. "Uh, could you help me loosen my backpack straps?"

Although she wanted to appear calm to Lucy, the thought of rappelling down the wormhole caused Mackenzie's pulse to skitter about. Images of climbing in the rainstorm returned, merging into each other like a kaleidoscope playing in her head. She volunteered to go first—to stave off her rising fear.

Mike held the harness out, a mystifying tangle of loops and belts, and she stepped into it. He adjusted the loops around her legs, and she winced. Raising his eyebrows when he saw her scraped thigh, he said quietly, "You know, you got to tighten that loop all the way. I'm going to put my handkerchief between it and you. Might help."

"Thanks," she whispered. "That does help."

He nodded and straightened. "This belt's going to be way too big for you. You could slip right out. So I'm going to tie you in with a sling, too. Okay?" He trussed her up and passed the rope through the harness and rappelling device. "All set."

"Now, to begin with," he said sternly. "Always keep hold of the rope in your right hand, and jerk down hard if you want to brake. You don't have to hold on with your left."

She grinned, releasing her left-handed death-grip on the rope.

He continued. "Your right hand is your brake hand. Okay. Now this is the tricky part. You have to face me, and push your butt out over the edge. Yeah. A little more. Now let some rope out, but slowly. Keep your feet high—as high as you can."

She let a few inches out, keeping her feet on the rock, and she eased below the edge. "How much more do I let out?"

"Try to get your feet as high as you can. Trust it. Right. You're doing great. Now, inch your feet down the rock and let the rope out at the same time."

Easing a few more inches of rope out, she paused. Her feet were almost above her head, but she felt strangely secure. She remembered how she had stemmed through the abyss in the canyon with Sullivan. You had to move to stay balanced. She let a bit more out and shuffled her feet. It was a different type of movement, but the principle was similar.

"Perfect. You're a natural. Keep doing that. It's going to be uneven at places, and you might have to improvise—but don't let go with your right hand."

Down she went, foot by foot. The tunnel curled, the walls shiny and smooth, with bands of color. The interior of a nautilus sea shell would probably look the same. A few feet down it narrowed, and she pressed her back against one wall for a second, shifting her weight. She peered down but couldn't see anything. The tunnel continued to curve, narrowing. She let more rope out, dropping slowly, as it widened again.

Suddenly, the wall before her ended. Her feet were right at the edge, and she was perched, butt hanging over space. She grabbed the rope with her left hand.

"Mike? What do I do now?" She fought the urge to look down. She couldn't see anyone above her.

"Keep your feet high," she heard. "As high as you can." But it wasn't Mike's voice, it was Sullivan's. She had forgotten he was already at the bottom.

"O-kaay. What's next?" She still didn't look down.

"Don't worry, the rope will hold you. Let go with your left hand. You just need one hand. Good. Now ease back with your brake hand—the right one—and let yourself down slowly. Keep your feet up if you can, like you're sitting in a chair. Slowly. That's right, a few feet more. Try to stay level."

She let the rope feed through the rappel device and lowered herself in spurts. With one small move she swung free. The wall in front of her was concave. She spun slightly and hazarded a glance down, seeing Sullivan below her, maybe twenty feet down.

"Good, Mackenzie. Just relax."

She fumed, "Relax? Are you kidding? I'm hanging on this skinny rope with my ass hanging out in mid-air. Don't tell me to relax."

He grinned. "Yeah, and—"

"Don't say it." She glared down at him.

"Okay, understood. But keep lowering yourself. Come on, you're almost there. That's great. I'm right here. I'll catch you."

She eased back with her brake hand. I have to trust him, she thought, and let herself go.

An hour later they were all down, huddled in a group. They were in a dark, narrow alcove. The canyon walls ahead were taller, narrowing until they were less than a yard apart at the top. They marched on, no one talking. A few feet farther on, a gray, wind-sculpted branch of driftwood was wedged horizontally twenty feet above their heads. It could only mean that water had risen at one time to that height.

She shuddered, remembering the flash flood in the canyon with Sullivan. She glanced at him. He seemed confident now, almost breezy, pointing out water marks that had stained the walls a deeper color below the driftwood.

"We'd better get going." He addressed the group bunched behind him. "It took too long to rappel down here. The good news is, I think we're pretty close. Maybe an hour or two from the side canyon. If I'm reading it right."

She scanned the dusty, bedraggled group. The rappel had been hard for Henry, easier for most of the others. He mopped his head with a handkerchief. Sandy stood near him, leaning against the sloping wall of rock.

The dynamics of the group had changed. The two weaker links in the group, Sandy and Henry, had bonded, forming one strong interdependent entity. Mike had stepped up. He was now Sullivan's second in command. Vic, although as seasoned as Mike, hung back, remaining with Mackenzie and the others, lending support when needed. Surprisingly, Jennifer wasn't clinging to Sulley anymore; she had gravitated toward Vic. Lucy still shadowed Mackenzie.

Even out here, she thought, everyone falls into their roles. As she ruminated, she realized she was on a quest, an actual quest, to rescue Charlie. It was possible that he had discovered a pre-Columbian codex of legendary value. And they were hunting for Aztec gold.

Mackenzie shook her head, trying to take it all in. Thoughts of Charlie suddenly swamped her, and her stomach clamped down. She should feel happy, eager even, to find him: This was what she had wanted. The purpose of the trip was to find him, and she had persuaded everyone to help her. So why was she dreading it?

Sullivan broke the silence. "We're going to have to stay close, now. Help each other out. We can always go back, but it would be difficult. We left the ropes there as our escape route. Right now, climbing back out the way we came is still possible. As we get deeper into the canyon, however, things could change. We don't know what we'll find. So we have to keep the pace up, keep our eyes open, and support each other. Make decisions as a team."

He scanned the group. "I think of it this way. When traveling through a canyon, you've got to respect it. It's not about you in the canyon. It's about the synergy between you and the rock."

They set off at a rapid pace. She went first, this time to gain some space. She wished Lucy would give her a bit more room.

At one point, they had to cross over a murky pothole filled with slimy, foul-smelling water. It was impossible to avoid breathing in the stench as they stemmed over the pothole. The water was about ten or twelve feet below them, but she couldn't estimate its depth. She didn't want to think about anyone falling, or what was in that water.

Vic and Jennifer crossed with no problem. Jennifer whined the entire time, but actually proved very adept at crossing. Henry had difficulty from the beginning. He was obviously tired, but after a few false starts, he made it.

Only Sandy remained on the other side, reluctant to stem. "Isn't there another way?" He twisted his hands together, knuckles white.

The pothole was four feet across at its widest, filled with what looked like moldy, stinking coffee sludge. The walls around it sloped up sharply. Something floating off to the side. A small dead rodent?

Sandy chunked a small stone into the pool, breaking up some of the scum on the surface. "Maybe it's not that deep. It's not that wide at the bottom. I bet I can straddle it there, down where it meets the walls."

"For God's sake, Sandy, just stem the damned thing." Henry said. "The girls bested it, for heaven's sake."

"You shouldn't straddle it," Mackenzie warned. "It's safer to stem."

Sandy had already squatted and was sliding toward the pothole, his backpack under him. He progressed slowly, using his feet as brakes, his hands to balance.

Mackenzie bit her lip. Maybe he'd be able to do it after all.

A few feet above the water, however, the walls became more vertical and fine dust made the surface slippery. His feet no longer held, and his speed increased. Spreading his legs, he tried to stop his momentum, but his shoes found no purchase, and with a loud cry he slid into the pothole. He submerged, his arms flailing about above him, his backpack floating free.

A long second later he surfaced, spluttering and coughing. "Shit. Help me. Help! I can't touch the bottom. Fuck!"

Mackenzie cast about for something to hold out to him. She tugged her belt off first, then her t-shirt. It was no time for modesty. Looping the shoulder strap of the tank top through the belt buckle, she tied a makeshift knot. Vic sprang to life and flattened himself on the ground, pushing Lucy and Henry out of the way.

"Here. Hand it to me. Mac, hold onto my belt. Henry and Lucy, hold onto her." Vic took charge, and she was relieved to have help.

He called down to the thrashing man below. "Sandy, stop fighting. Make your way over here. I'm going to lower this down to you."

Sandy obeyed, and Vic stretched over the edge. Mackenzie leaned away from the hole, grasping Vic's belt, hoping her knot would hold and the fabric wouldn't tear. Lucy's arms were around her waist, and Henry in turn held onto her, forming a human chain. They couldn't see what was happening.

"What the hell happened?" The voice startled her, but she didn't look up. It was Sullivan, she knew. He and Mike must have finally discovered the group wasn't behind them and returned.

Wriggling backward, Vic continued to haul Sandy up, and she and her helpers inched back with him.

"Okay, okay. Grab onto that rock there," Vic said. "Good. I'm letting go now. You okay?"

Sandy didn't respond, but his head rose above the edge, gray hair plastered to his head, a bit of green slime on his forehead and in one ear. He smelled like a sewer. Vic pulled him up.

Mackenzie wrinkled her nose, hoping the smell wouldn't linger, and released the belt. Lucy and Henry let go of her. Vic swiped at dust on his knees, and she followed suit.

Sullivan raised his eyebrows at her, and she realized she was down to her bra. Crossing her hands over her chest, she said, "Sandy didn't want to stem. Apparently, he wanted to swim."

Lucy, standing next to her, erupted into laughter. Sandy glared at her, as he took off his t-shirt. Lucy ignored him, saying, "Yeah, he didn't want to do it the 'girls' way. You know, the dry way."

Vic laughed too, saying, "There's a reason they call them keeper potholes."

She laughed, looking around.

Mike smiled but was suddenly efficient, digging into his backpack, tugging out a dry t-shirt. "I don't have spare shorts, Sandy, but this will help some." He held up the shirt, and Sandy grabbed it greedily.

"Look, I don't mind rescuing you," Vic said, "But next time, could you choose a cleaner pool? This one stinks." He winked at Mackenzie.

"I don't see how this is funny," Sandy retorted in a muffled voice, pulling the dry t-shirt over his head. He coughed and spluttered.

"You're right, Sandy," Sullivan said, no longer smiling. "It's not funny. There's no harm in trying new techniques, but it's better to try them out in safer places. Keeper potholes are dangerous. Any idiot can see that."

Sandy muttered something under his breath and turned his pockets inside out. Mackenzie expected him to find a dead rat and was relieved when he didn't. He emptied his backpack, which was now full of greenish-brown clothing.

Sullivan motioned to Mackenzie with his head. "Still undressed, I see." He studied her, a half-smile on his face. She felt his eyes taking in her body, and she wanted to hold him, be with him.

Flushing, she hiked up her shorts with one hand. She must be losing weight. Without the belt, they hung several inches below her waist. Her scrapes were exposed, too, although no one seemed to notice. Vic, ever the gentleman, returned her the shirt and belt. She threaded the belt through the loops, tightening it, then appraised the shirt. It was muddy and wet. Digging through her backpack, she produced another long-sleeved, only marginally dirty, t-shirt. "This will do until the next rescue," she said, grinning.

After Sandy had wrung out his clothes, wiped off his backpack, and repacked, they continued, falling into a rhythm of sorts. Sullivan and Mike were much faster and scouted ahead, while Mackenzie, Lucy, Vic, and Jennifer formed a foursome. Henry, as usual, lagged behind them, quite a way back, and Sandy brought up the rear.

An hour later, they entered a deep alcove. High above them, the walls almost met, forming an atrium at the ceiling. A shaft of dusty sunlight pierced the darkness, illuminating the canyon floor like a spotlight. It smelled heavily of ammonia. Much better than Sandy, she mused.

Sullivan and Mike sat down against the right side of the grotto, backpacks in front of them.

"We'll eat lunch here," Sullivan announced. "Don't sit in the guano."

"Guano?" Jennifer scanned the niche. "Bat shit?"

"Yes. It won't hurt you, but it smells terrible."

Jennifer sat down gingerly, eyes wide. She pulled her knees to her chest and peered at the ceiling above her.

Mackenzie slid to the ground to inspect her legs. Bruised and scratched, they didn't look like they were hers. She pulled her shorts down to hide the bandage, which looked almost as dirty as her skin.

Sullivan tossed everyone bars. "We've got some bagels and salami, but let's all have a bar first." He held up the promised treats. "Make sure you drink water. You can still get dehydrated, even if you're not in the sun."

A few minutes later Henry joined them, and Sullivan asked, "Henry, where's your buddy?"

"Sandy? I assume he'll be along shortly. I haven't seen him for some time now. Nursing his pride, possibly. Perhaps that swim tired him out."

"How long since you saw him?" Mike rose to his feet

Henry shook his head, lifted a shoulder. "Not quite sure. It's been awhile, however. Time is so deceptive down here."

Mike glanced at Sullivan. "I'll round him up. He can't be too far back."

No one spoke for a while. Despite her aching ankle and sore muscles, Mackenzie felt energized. It couldn't be much longer. She grabbed the notebook from her backpack and scooted to the far wall of the cavern. She unfolded the photo of the map, spreading it on the ground.

"I'd love to take another look at that," Vic said, "But I can't move."

"Yeah, me either." Lucy was on her back. "I'm not sure I'll be able to get up ever again. You all may have to carry me. Or leave me." She raised her arms above her, stretching her fingers. "I'd be happy to stay here. With the gold, of course."

Jennifer had apparently recovered from her scare. She stretched her long legs, which looked remarkably unscathed. "Yeah, about that. Let's say we find this fabled Aztec gold. And it's a lot. What happens then? I mean, it's ours to keep, right? Don't we just split it up and haul it out?"

"It depends," Vic said.

"What do you mean?" Jennifer bit a ripped and dirty fingernail, and Mackenzie smiled to herself, looking at her own nails. At least their nails looked the same.

"Well, it's complicated," Vic said. "Back when Montezuma hid the gold, this area was claimed by the Spaniards. When the U.S. purchased the land, it belonged to them. Then, some time after that, according to state law, it belonged to Utah. Of course, then the government dammed the river and formed Lake Powell. They took it over, and it became a national recreation area. But, really, if you think about it, the Indians should be the rightful owners of something during Montezuma's reign. Of course, there aren't many Aztec descendants left." He took a breath. "Then again, the Navajo were in the region, too, so they might have something to say about it. Spain could make a case, since they considered everyone, including the Aztecs, Spanish property back then." He paused, smiling. "Does that help?"

Nobody answered. A few moments later, Henry said, "Actually, it should be covered by the Archaeological Resources Protection Act, I imagine."

"Lucy, you should know this, right? It's your field, after all," Jennifer said.

"Uh," Lucy said, biting off part of a bar. "I'm not really up on the details."

"Well, Henry's right, it is probably covered under that," Vic said grudgingly. "That means the gold would most likely go to the federal government, and we would all be imprisoned for taking it."

"Whoa," said Sullivan. "That's not good."

"Right," Vic continued. "But there's a hitch. Or a loophole, if you will. You see, a case could be made if the gold is found on a religious site, or is 'grave goods.' You know, if there's a grave or something nearby, it would all go to the Indian tribe most closely related to the buried individual. So, to the Navajo Nation, or the descendants of the Aztecs."

Henry interjected, "But that generally becomes nasty. I believe I've heard of cases where foreign governments get involved." He raised his eyebrows and looked around the chamber, grinning. "So Mexico and Spain could theoretically step in, then. The only ones who really don't have a chance are the poor buggers who find it. Us."

"So, we can't just take it?" Jennifer asked.

"Well, not legally," Vic replied. "Usually, the finders don't tell anyone, and then it doesn't matter who really should get it. Of course, then they have to sell it on the black market. Just like in the movies."

Mackenzie listened but didn't comment. She wasn't worried about the gold at the moment; she was more worried about finding the cave. The map wasn't detailed. She hoped they weren't lost. A lump formed in her throat, and she swallowed hard.

Sullivan wandered over toward her. She inhaled his scent, and memories of their shared night in the cave returned. Funny how smells could bring back memories. She turned to the map, letting her hair hide her face. "You know," she said in a low voice, "we could turn back. I mean, it's not too late."

"You don't want to keep going?"

She didn't answer. She didn't want to tell him how conflicted she felt about searching for Charlie.

He looked at her for a long moment. He cleared his throat and stood. "I think we're near the end, folks. We can always go back the way we came. We still have a choice."

Suddenly, Mike's voice boomed out, cutting him off. "No, I'm afraid we don't."

He walked to the center of the cave, letting the light spill across his shoulders. "We have no choice. We can't go back."

"What? Is this a joke, Mike? If it is, I'm not laughing." Sullivan narrowed his eyes.

Mike removed his cap and slicked his hair back. He shook his head. "No joke. It seems our friend Sandy has stranded us. I went back to where we left the last rope. Where it was supposed to be. It's gone." He twisted the cap in front of him with both hands, looking up.

"Gone? How can it be gone?" Vic was standing now, too, and had edged closer.

"Well, I think he turned back somewhere along the way. Maybe right after the pothole. He probably climbed back up, taking the rope with him. Can't see it being anything else."

"Shit." Sullivan stared with glazed eyes at the wall behind Mike.

"Can't we climb up without the rope?" She asked.

"Nope. Even an experienced climber couldn't climb that without equipment. Remember? You need a rope. A long one. One that's anchored from above."

She remembered the steep walls and the end of the rappel, where they had all hung freely on the rope.

Mike was right; they were stranded.

CHAPTER 16

 seemed prophetic. Everyone gathered around Sullivan, talking at once.

"I can't believe he did this." Jennifer exclaimed.

Lucy stared at her. "I can. It makes sense he chickened out. What I can't believe is that he took the rope. I mean, if he wanted to turn back, I'm sure one of us—maybe all of us—would have gone with him. Taking the rope, cutting off our only way back, that's, that's evil." She paced in the small space, turning decisively each time she reached a wall, like a bull thwarted by a bullfighter.

"Maybe he didn't know." Vic spoke in a flat monotone.

"He knew," Sullivan replied. "He must have had more grit in him than I realized. Climbing the rope would have been tough."

"The signs were all there," Henry said. "I knew he didn't want to continue."

"He told you?" Mackenzie asked.

"Not in so many words. He was just so dreadfully negative most of the time. I didn't take him seriously. He whined about everything."

Henry's words were like a slap. Mackenzie realized she was unaccountably angrier at Henry than Sandy and bit back her words, forcing herself to stay quiet. Henry might be a pain in the ass, but at least he didn't leave them alone in the middle of nowhere.

Mike crouched over his backpack. "I think we ought to see how much food is left. See if we have anything useful."

Sullivan nodded, kneeling beside him. "Yes, let's all throw everything on the ground here. Channel our anger toward devising a plan, rather than berating Sandy. What's done is done." Everyone tossed their backpacks into the chamber.

While Sullivan, Vic, and Mike inventoried the contents of the packs, she studied the topo map. The canyon was a thin line, too narrow for detail. It seemed inconceivable that such a forbidding place, deep and treacherous, looked so benign on a map. She traced its curves but couldn't picture the twists and turns they had followed. She huffed with frustration.

Lucy plopped down next to her. "What do you think?"

"Not sure. I have no idea how fast we've been moving. With all the stops, I'm betting we're not as far along as we should be." She checked her watch. "It's already three-thirty. We have less than six hours before dark." Panic filled her, and she took a deep breath. "We have to keep on. We have to get through it. I want to get to the end before dark."

"Me, too," replied Lucy. "We've got to get to the cave."

Sullivan stood up. "It looks like we've got enough food for several days, as long as we ration it, so no worries there. We also have three first-aid kits, several headlamps, some matches, and other odds and ends. We've divided everything into equal shares, so no one is carrying too much. Or too little." He looked over at Jennifer. "Well, except for you, Jennifer, as I see you only have your camera case."

Mackenzie focused on Jennifer, realizing that she had almost forgotten about her.

The tall blonde smiled lazily at Sullivan, tilting her head. "I know. I don't know how that happened."

"Doesn't look like you have any pockets in those shorts, either." Mackenzie felt a flash of irritation as she watched Sullivan's eyes travel up and down Jennifer's smooth legs.

"No, I guess not," Jennifer replied. "I wish I could help but—"

"You're in luck." He smiled. "You can take my pack. It'll be easier for me to scout ahead without the extra weight. It won't be too much, will it?"

Surprised, she recovered gracefully. "Oh, no, it'll be fine. Thanks so much, Sulley. I'd love to carry your pack."

Damn it. Somehow Jennifer had turned it around again, Mackenzie thought, rubbing a toe in the dust. She had skipped from helpless female directly to sainthood. Even with chipped nails.

They started out again. The canyon beyond their cozy alcove changed abruptly, and they faced a slim, dark tunnel barely eighteen inches tall, that slanted 45 degrees. The only way to get through was to either shinny along on their backs or do mini-pushups on their stomachs. Dragging their backpacks after them. Neither option sounded good. Mackenzie's back was scratched up, her arms were tired, her abs sore.

Sullivan, Mike, and Henry went first. They all scraped along on their backs, dragging their packs along beside them. Choosing to do pushups seemed like the lesser of the two evils, but she wondered about her decision.

"It's not that far," Sullivan called out. "Maybe a hundred yards or so."

After the first dozen pushups, Mackenzie rested. The rock ceiling above her was only six inches from her head. She felt like the filling in a gigantic rock sandwich and felt a twinge of claustrophobia. Ignoring her fears, she pressed on, catching Henry after a few minutes. He was struggling, breathing hard.

"It won't be for too much longer," she told him. "I think we're halfway there." A lie.

"Right. Oomph. Hardly a comfortable position. Oh, my back. Shall be glad to get through this. Umph. Why did I ever agree to—eech."

She sighed. Henry had taken on Sandy's role, becoming the whiner of the group. There always had to be one, even in a group this size. There were only six of them now. What was Sam doing? If he'd come with them, he would have stayed back with Sandy. Been patient with him. But if Sandy hadn't left them, she realized, they might have voted to go back. Now they had to get to the end of the canyon, and with luck, find Charlie.

The passage was shorter than she had thought. After Henry exited, she took Mike's hand and leaped down to the canyon floor, which was almost five feet below. Ahead, the canyon widened slightly, promising easy and rapid passage, and she grew impatient to continue. She scanned the walls around her, waiting for the others. Vic emerged a few minutes later, relaying that Lucy and Jennifer were moving slowly.

Mackenzie singled out Sullivan, who was leaning against a wall a few yards ahead. She massaged one of her triceps. "I'm going to check out the canyon," she told him. "See what's up ahead."

"Mac, please don't. Won't you wait a bit?"

She hesitated at the mildness of his tone, and her heart beat faster. He was asking, not telling. Wavering, she said, "Okay. But, look, we must be close." She gestured down canyon. The walls gradually widened and the floor seemed to level out. She couldn't see much, because it turned, but she was sure they were almost there.

He smiled, his eyes crinkling. She grinned back at him, feeling loopy.

"I wouldn't count on it being the end," he said. "The canyons have a way of deceiving you. Just when you think you're there, another twist pops up."

She nodded. "Yeah. Kind of like life, I think."

He started to say something, but hesitated. She felt someone tap her on the shoulder and she jumped.

Mike was right behind her. "Hey," he said. "Something happening?"

"Nope," Sullivan replied. "Are the girls through yet?"

"Almost. Want me to go on ahead?"

Sullivan shook his head. "No, you stay with the others. Let them rest a while. Mackenzie and I will check it out." When Mike raised his eyebrows, Sullivan added, "She wants to. I can't let her go alone." He shrugged his shoulders.

"We-ell, that's probably a good idea, I suppose. I want to keep an eye on the rest of them anyway, to make sure everyone's holding up. It's probably best if we split up."

"Yeah. Stay here till we get back. It won't be too long. They need someone to take charge and keep them in line. Keep them here, resting. We'll be back soon."

She stood there, stunned. What the hell? First Sullivan said 'no,' and now he was acting like he had to babysit her again. Like he was forced to go with her. Her anger grew. She had to talk to him alone, and this might be her only chance. Slinging her pack over one shoulder, she started off. Sullivan followed, keeping a few yards between them. She turned a sharp corner, where the canyon goosenecked back on itself, and waited for him.

He almost ran over her when rounded the sharp turn. She started to speak, but he cut her off.

"Come on," he ordered. He jogged past her.

"What? Wait for me."

He didn't stop.

"Sullivan, I'm not going a step farther." He was already beyond another bend in the canyon. No way, she thought. No way she was going to let him keep running off ahead of her. She rubbed her neck, leaning against a wall.

He appeared again. "Keep up," he said, grabbing her wrist.

"Wait. I want to talk to you."

He propelled her along with him, and after rounding a sharp promontory, dragged her to a halt and released her. She massaged her wrist, opening her mouth to finish. She didn't have the chance. Without preamble, he placed his hands on her shoulders. Tracing her chin with a finger, he tilted her face up. "What was it you wanted to say?" Before she could reply, he kissed her, enfolding her in his arms.

For a long moment they stood there, arms around each other. Even though she was angry, she craved him. She could taste him and feel his need for her. She pressed herself closer, feeling his strong, angular body. Suddenly, she pushed him away. "No. We have to talk."

"I don't want to talk," he said huskily, tucking a strand of her hair behind her ear. "I don't want to talk at all."

"But I do. I want to know what's going on with us."

He blinked. "What do you mean?"

"You know what I mean. I have to know. What happened in the storm? Was that something? Anything?"

"It was something. You know it was." He let his arms fall.

"I don't understand. Why is it a big secret? Are you ashamed?" She paused. "I can't read you at all." Folding her arms deliberately in front of her chest, she gazed up at him.

"Ashamed? Is that really what you think?" He closed his eyes for a moment. "Mac, don't you get it? Do I have to spell it out? No matter how much I want you—and God knows I want you—I can't give in. We're out here on the ragged edge of nowhere, in more danger than you realize. I can't let my feelings get in the way of leading the group. They're my responsibility. You're my responsibility."

He uncrossed her arms, placing first one, and then the other, around his waist. "It's been hell. I can't think about anything but you. All I want to think about is this." He cupped her face in his hands, kissing her again, lightly. "And this." He slid his hands to her breasts, and she fought back a groan. Then his arms were around her waist, and he pulled her closer.

Shit. She hadn't considered his overarching sense of responsibility. Or that he could have feelings he didn't show. What an idiot she was. He tightened his grip on her and she pressed her hips to his, tingling from his touch, pressing against his hardness.

He pulled away this time, and she closed her eyes, dizzy.

"We can't do this," he said. "We have to go."

"I'm sorry. I wasn't thinking." She stepped back.

"We'll talk later," he said, running a finger gently over her lips. "We'll talk all about being together after we get out of here. But right now we need to get going. I promise. I've got some things I want to talk to you about, too. Charlie, for one."

She stiffened, but he once again wrapped her in his arms, holding her tightly until she relaxed. "But not now. It's not a big deal. Trust me."

She didn't respond.

They continued to scout the canyon, hand in hand, until it narrowed. Neither spoke, and she found the silence comforting. They walked slowly until they were forced to go single file.

He led. Her eyes lingered on his wide shoulders and strong legs, the determined way he attacked each obstacle. Try as she might, she couldn't, however, remember much of their conversation the night they spent in the cave. He was divorced. A doctor. The rest was fuzzy, and she yearned to question him, to uncover everything about him. Why Lake Powell? Why not practice medicine in another place? How long had he been married? Where was his ex-wife?

He stopped, and she bumped into him. He turned, his expression dark, and her heart clamped down.

"We're not at the end of the canyon. Take a look."

He didn't move out of the way for her. Instead, he put his arm around her shoulders and drew her up beside him. Beyond them a vast canyon wall shone golden in the late afternoon sun. They were standing opposite it, a few feet from the edge of a cliff. Between them and the other canyon wall was a deep abyss.

She didn't say anything. The most she could manage was breathing in and out.

He asked, "You okay?" He didn't wait for an answer. "Stay here. I'm going to check it out."

"No. It's, it's too dangerous."

He deliberately guided her away before walking back to the edge.

"Sulley. Please. What does it look like?"

He turned. "It drops. We're on an overhang of some sort, I'd guess. I can't see the wall below us." His voice was toneless and flat.

"And?"

"And nothing. It's maybe a hundred feet to the bottom. Or more. It's like this path ends in the middle of the canyon wall."

"Oh." Tears formed, and she let them slide down her cheeks unchecked. They were trapped, deep in a canyon that may not have been traversed in decades. Who knows how long it had been since someone had gone as far as they had?

She studied the steep walls that rose hundreds of feet on either side of them. There was no way to scale them, rope or no rope.

"We have to go back," she said. "We'll have to try to climb out somewhere else. There has to be a way to climb out. There has to be."

He turned to her. Before he could answer, she continued, "We'll climb out, or someone will find us. Sam will find us. Sam knows where we are. He'll find us."

He brushed a tear off her nose. "Let's go back to the others. We need to tell them."

She didn't move. "That's not an answer."

"What do you want me to say? That Sam will figure out that we're stranded? That he'll, what, simply know where we are?" His voice was rough, like the sandstone that surrounded them. "We're on our own.

We're deep in the wilderness. Sam has a general idea of where we are, but that won't help much. Once he sees we're not coming back, which could could take days, he'll have to get help. They'll search, but I doubt they'll find us. All we can do is wait it out, and we don't have enough food to wait it out." He sucked in a deep, uneven breath.

She recognized fear, not anger, in his eyes. A strange calm floated down on her, like a blanket. Her words were quiet, measured. "We'll figure it out." She met his eyes, wishing she could give him her tranquility.

He gazed back at her and dropped his shoulders. He looked tired and defeated. "Yeah, sure. But not tonight. Tonight we need to rest up, and back with the others is about as good a place as we'll find."

The next morning she woke with a start. Every inch of her body was stiff, and she rose slowly, like an arthritic dog. Lucy and Jennifer still slept, with Jennifer's head crooked on Lucy's shoulder. Two mismatched dolls. She wanted to straighten them, to prop Jennifer up, but resisted.

Vic and Sulley were a few yards away, deep in conversation. Henry stood off to the side a bit, head cocked, listening but not participating. She couldn't see Mike.

Her neck crackled as she rolled it to relieve her tight muscles. She could feel every muscle in her body. There were almost 800, she remembered. And now each one of them was complaining.

Sullivan glanced up, and for one unguarded moment they connected. She smiled, disguising it with a yawn, hoping no one had noticed. She understood his motivation, now. He was right: It was best to keep their relationship secret.

She walked over to Henry. "Where's Mike?"

"I assume he's gone back to check on our exit route. I'm not sure, however, as I've not been awake long."

Nodding, she asked, "Have you checked out the cliff?"

"No. And I'm not sure that would be the best use of our time." He lifted his chin. "As soon as everyone has risen, I intend to lobby that we leave immediately."

"Really? And go where? Return to where Sandy left?"

"Yes." His tone was clipped. "Do you have an alternate plan?"

The stress of being lost and uncertain deep in the earth was eroding each of them. Their resolve was being eaten away, like a crow on carrion. Even under the best of circumstances Henry was annoying; now she found him almost unbearable.

"No, but—" She stopped. She had no idea what to say.

CHAPTER 17

of her own abyss of exhaustion, fear, and dread. Her emotions threatened to swamp her. She had an overpowering need to hide, to sort things out alone, but she couldn't get away from the group.

After a breakfast of bars, Mike, Sullivan, and Vic checked out the cliff. They had looped their belts together, forming a rope of sorts, and Sullivan had added a short length of cording scavenged from his pack's drawstring. He was going to explore. That makeshift rope, she thought, couldn't hold a baby, much less a man. She forced back the bile rising in her throat.

He glanced over, like he was checking with her. He wasn't asking permission, but having her join him in the decision. There was a hint of a smile, with a softening around his eyes and a faint uplift of his brows. For a moment, before the others could notice, they connected again. She nodded, and he turned.

Henry had wandered away. She sank to the ground. Her vulnerability caught her off guard. She wouldn't cry, she told herself. She would stay strong. She needed to stay strong.

Moments later, she heard Sullivan call out. "A ledge. There's a ledge maybe 10 feet below us. It looks like there might be a niche or cave or something, too."

The men talked among themselves, trying to figure out what to do. She didn't want to be part of it.

Finding a groove beneath the sand, she traced it absently with a finger. The coolness of the sand was comforting, reliable. In the desert, sand was the constant, changing but always there. She let her eyes glaze, pushing grains around. Forcing her mind to calmness, she shut her eyes. And frowned. The indentation her fingers traced was regular, more than it should have been if simply a crack in the path. Opening her eyes, she bent down, whisking sand away.

"What are you doing?" Lucy squatted next to her in the narrow path.

Mackenzie didn't answer, concentrating on her discovery. She had cleared sand from a flat section of solid rock, and several carved symbols were visible.

Lucy knelt and she brushed sand from the rock. The pair cleared a space in the path, uncovering a carved circle with seven symbols inside.

They stared at each other.

"These are Aztec," Mackenzie whispered. She stood and pulled her friend up.

Lucy wiped sand from her knees. "Can you read them? Do you know what they mean?"

"I don't know. Maybe." She studied the canyon floor. She pushed aside tangled hair that obscured part of her face. A circle about eighteen inches in diameter had been carved into the rock, with symbols inside.

"Hey," Lucy said. "There's one of Vic's glyphs."

A circle, bisected by a long line was definitely there. "Okay. That's Rainbow Bridge, if my theory is right. It doesn't seem like it has anything to do with the others. Unless it's orienting us to it somehow."

"This has to be good news. Let's tell everyone." Lucy's voice rose.

"Wait. Let's think about it first." Mackenzie sat back down, pulling Lucy down next to her.

Lucy opened her mouth, ready to object, but Mackenzie held up a finger. "Whoever made these symbols was down here, too, in this canyon."

"Well, right. Sure. Someone had to be here to make it."

"No, really, Lucy. Think about it. Someone a long time ago was right where we are. They thought it was important enough to take the time to carve out the rock in this particular place."

"It's got to be a map," Lucy exclaimed. "What else could it be? But I don't get it. We're at a dead end." She stared at the group at the edge of the cliff.

"Let me think a bit." Mackenzie traced the symbols with the tip of her index finger, prying out sand. "Nahuatl, or Aztec, writing isn't read in any particular order. Glyphs are generally arranged to represent a scene to tell a story. Hmm. There's the Rainbow Bridge one. I think this other one means 'above, or upon the edge or end.' This one could mean 'place abundant with, uh, something.' Don't know what it's abundant with. Treasure, maybe? Or food and water. Anything. The one on the left there means 'in the mountain.' And, this one. Oh, wow."

"What?"

"I think this symbol means a great ruler. Montezuma, in fact."

Lucy leaned in. "What about those two. Can you read them?"

"That one may be a warrior, or servant. He's carrying something. It might be one of Montezuma's runners. And there's this one." She pointed to the glyph in the center of the circle: It was the face of a scowling animal, with three parallel, vertical lines above it. Below it were two parallel horizontal wavy lines. Mackenzie had seen the same symbol on the rock panel by Rainbow Bridge.

"What do those squiggly lines mean?"

"Well, they usually mean water. In this case, though, it's different. See, it's connected to the other symbol. I bet it means Cortés. See how he looks like a monkey or something? He would have looked very odd to the Aztecs, with his Caucasian skin. The pointy chin probably means he had a beard. Which he did, in fact. Hmm. Maybe the three lines are masts of his ship. And the wavy lines—"

"Are the ocean," Lucy finished.

Mackenzie put a warning finger to her lips. "Yes. Well, let's piece this all together. Some things we know from history. Obviously, Montezuma came first with his treasure. Cortés followed. Montezuma's warriors carried the treasure to a secret place, presumably Aztlan. Maybe Vic's glyphs were part of the map to that secret place, and the cave near Rainbow Bridge held the actual history. The final glyph, the one that means 'at the edge or end,' may point to where Sullivan is. If I'm correct, we're not at a dead end. I think there's a tunnel that leads to the cave with the treasure."

The pair sat in silence for a moment. Lucy stared at the symbols, tense and eager. "Unbelievable. Without this panel, most people would turn back. Or die." She glanced at the group. "I can't stand it. Let's show the others." She ran off, not waiting for an answer.

Mackenzie sank down, letting the cool sand trickle through her fingers to the path. If she were right, they would find more than Aztec treasure. They would also find Charlie. Instead of elation and anticipation, she felt disconnected—like she was on the outside, watching, not participating.

"Might as well get on with it," she said aloud, and stood.

Lucy rushed past Henry and jammed herself into the trio of men standing at the edge. "We found something," she said, interrupting them. "Mac found some symbols carved in the stone. An Aztec panel that's like a map. Come see."

"A map?" Henry asked. "Another map? You're joking, surely."

The group gathered around Mackenzie and Lucy, crowding them. Mackenzie quickly explained her theory about the meaning of the symbols.

"I say we check the ledge out," Sullivan said. "We've got to keep moving. Mike, how do you feel about going first? If it seems okay, we'll follow. If it doesn't, we'll pull you up."

Mike removed his hat, wiping sweat with the back of his hand. "Sounds good."

Several minutes passed. The ledge wasn't that far in terms of distance, but the exposure was daunting. If the belt-rope combination didn't hold, Mike would fall several hundred feet to his death. She thought about his upcoming wedding and fought back tears. They knew what they were doing. Mike would be fine. She repeated the mantra to comfort herself.

And he was fine.

Sullivan called out to them when Mike reached the ledge. "He's there. He made it, easy. He says there are good hand- and footholds on the rock. Depressions in the rock that are pretty deep."

She squeezed her way through the group until she was beside Sullivan.

"Mike," Sullivan shouted down at the man. "What do you see?"

There was no reply, but suddenly the rope hung free. Sullivan flattened himself, head hanging over the edge. He held onto the rope, letting it swing over the edge. Silence filled the canyon, and she realized she was holding her breath. She let it out slowly.

No one moved. After a few minutes, Sullivan rolled over, and sat up. "What we do now," he said, "is wait."

It wasn't easy. Several minutes passed before they heard anything. She felt herself rising above them, in her mind, like a balloon. Like Sullivan said, they were on the edge, but they were together. Not quite the team he expected, but a group nonetheless. An unbidden, but not unwelcome, fondness for them swept over her—even for Jennifer. Who knew what her life was really like, what problems she had faced?

"It's a tunnel," Mike called up. "Send someone down."

"Does it open up?" Sullivan asked. "Can we get out through it?"

"Not sure. It's dark and seems tall. But there's a breeze coming from somewhere."

Sullivan glanced up, and Vic grinned. "Yep, I want to go next."

"It's actually not too bad," Mike called up. "There are big pockets to hold onto, and a few good bumps for your feet. It's solid. I think you could even free solo it."

"Some other time," Sullivan replied. "How large is it? Think we'd all fit?"

"Sure. You thinking of sending everyone?"

Sullivan paused, turning to the group, eyebrows raised. Each of them responded with a nod. She wanted to stand next to him, support him, share in his decision. Later, she hoped. Later.

"I'm sending Vic and then you all. I'll follow. No worries, right?"

"Right," Mike said. "Easy as pie."

"You're going last, Sulley?" Vic frowned. "Oh, that's right—the last one down won't have a rope. You *are* going to free solo it, aren't you?"

Sullivan rubbed the stubble on his jaw. "No, not likely. I'll throw the end of the rope down. You boys can hang onto me from there. If I fall, I'll swing a bit, but I think it'll hold. Let's hope we don't have to test it."

The climb to the ledge was amazingly uneventful. Mike's promise of holds was accurate, and even Henry was able to navigate the cliff down to it.

Mackenzie marveled at how experienced they had all become.

The cave was dark and cold. Fresh air brazenly announced its presence, and she raised her nose like a deer sniffing for water. "There's air coming from somewhere, Mike. But where? I don't see any light."

"Dunno. We'll have to explore."

"Okay." Sullivan faced the others. "Let's see if we can find a way out of here."

It was so dark Mackenzie couldn't see her hand in front of her. She calmed herself by thinking of the fresh air up ahead. The men with headlamps switched them on, and patches of light bounced around the walls like fireflies. She focused on shuffling her feet with small, tentative steps, making certain the tunnel floor remained firm below her. Occasionally, cobwebs clung to her face and hair. Ignore them, she told herself. They're not spiderwebs. Spiders and whatever were the least of their worries.

"Hold up, everyone. Wait." Sullivan's voice rang out sharply.

"What?" Vic asked. "What's happened?"

"I want everyone to chill." Sullivan enunciated each word. The teacher, talking to rapt students. He trained his light on the left wall. A skeleton was propped against the wall.

She tugged on Vic's sleeve. "Who is it? Um, is it recent?"

He leaned in, shining his headlamp on the skeleton. "Nope. I'd say he, or she, has been here quite a while. Maybe even centuries. Nothing to be afraid of." He put his arm around her shoulders and eased her forward.

"This is so Indiana Jones," she whispered.

He laughed. "Yes, but this is real." He turned away, casting the skeleton into darkness, illuminating the path ahead. "Hey," he called out. "Be careful, it looks like—stop!"

Sullivan froze. "Vic?"

Vic knelt down, surveying the path. "It's like I thought. Not exactly a booby-trap, but there's a deep trough cut into the path here. Covered by stones. Stay to the edges and we'll be fine." His tone was low and comforting. "I know it's scary. But we've got to keep going."

Sullivan said, "Right. We'll take it easy. Vic, why don't you lead? Mike and I will follow behind you. Everyone else line up in pairs and stay alert, ready to stop. This might have been it in terms of hazards, but we don't want to take any chances. If we go slowly, we'll be all right. "

No one answered. In a quiet voice Mackenzie said, "Okay. I'm all for slow."

It started small but gained momentum. The entire group laughed like she'd told the best joke ever. She laughed, too, knowing that her comment wasn't funny. It was simply a release, a catharsis. They enjoyed it for a few seconds, allowing it to die naturally. The three warriors, as she now thought of them, led the way, creeping through the blackness.

CHAPTER 18

A few minutes later, it opened onto a huge cavern. They were blinded by brilliant sunlight that swept in on the opposite side. Mackenzie shaded her eyes, letting them adjust to the brightness. Her heart jackhammered in her chest.

The cavern was circular, with a domed ceiling that seemed at least twenty or so feet tall. A cathedral of sorts. Around the circumference were several deep, evenly spaced alcoves. It looked like a glove with fingers. She counted seven alcoves in all.

Everyone split up. Lucy and Henry set off alone, each checking out an alcove.

Vic, Mike, and Sullivan huddled together, murmuring. They stood near one of the outer walls of the cave. Vic looked up and gestured to her. "Mackenzie. Over here."

He intercepted her before she had taken two steps. "It's all right. Nothing to worry about."

She cocked her head. "What do you mean?"

He stepped aside, and she gasped.

A backpack rested against the wall. She saw a rough pallet of clothes first, and then dirty blonde hair. Charlie lay there, looking thin and fragile. And unconscious.

She stood there for a moment, taking it in. Not believing what she saw. "It's Charlie. Is he all right?" she asked finally, in a tight voice.

"Yeah," Sullivan said. "His breathing is normal, and he doesn't seem to have sustained any injuries. I'd guess he hasn't been unconscious for long. We need to get some water in him. Pronto."

Just then Jennifer squawked loudly, holding onto the tunnel opening for support. She'd been the last to enter the cave.

Mackenzie exhaled. She flicked a glance at Jennifer and turned back to Charlie. A moment later she whipped her head around, staring at the tunnel opening that Jennifer leaned on. The arched entrance was bordered by carved symbols.

They had to mean something. She squinted but couldn't read them. She would look at them afterward.

Sullivan dribbled water into Charlie's mouth. The unconscious man groaned but didn't wake up. "That's a good sign," Sullivan said. "That's a really good sign."

She turned to him. "Thank you. Oh, thank you. I can't believe he's alive."

He thrust the water bottle into her hand. "Here. Give him a little every few minutes or so." Standing, he zipped his backpack.

She gazed up at him. She couldn't sort her emotions. Seeing Charlie unhinged her, but all she could think about was Sullivan. What he was thinking? Feeling?

Placing a hand under Charlie's neck, tipping his head back, she dripped a teaspoonful of water into his mouth. Glancing up, she caught Sullivan's eye, but he lowered his gaze quickly.

She concentrated on Charlie, ignoring the feelings that threatened to overtake her. She was tattering, coming apart, like old, weakened fabric.

Mike and Sulley walked to the edge of the cave, staring down. Vic walked back to Jennifer, peering at the symbols on the sides of the tunnel opening. For several minutes he gently brushed dust and cobwebs away like he was bathing an infant. He called to the two men by the mouth of the cave. "What do you see?"

"Plenty of sky," Sullivan replied, "And a sheer drop. It must be at least a couple hundred feet down. Maybe five hundred. The river is below, too. It curves around the cliff we're on. I think we're finally through the canyon. Just a couple hundred feet too high."

"Is there anything on the other side?" Vic had pulled out a small notebook from his shirt pocket and was sketching the symbols.

"Yeah, another canyon wall really far away," Mike said. "A little bit lower than this one."

Sullivan dropped to his knees and flopped on his belly. "Oomph. Don't think we can climb down this cliff. No ledges or tunnels here. It's slick as glass."

She glanced up, and a pang of fear shot through her as Sullivan inched closer to the edge.

A tiny movement in her patient made her look away. Charlie's fingers jerked. She grasped his hand, massaging it.

"Charlie? Charlie, can you hear me?"

Sullivan and Mike rose. They motioned to Vic.

She repeated his name again. His eyelashes fluttered. She squeezed his hand harder.

"Ouch," he croaked, barely audible. "My hand."

She released it. "Charlie, it's me, Mackenzie."

He opened his eyes. "Mac. I knew you'd find me." He blinked several times. "And you brought friends."

She laughed and gazed up at Sullivan, wanting to share her relief.

But he wouldn't meet her eyes. Instead, he said, "I'm sure you've got quite a story to tell. I'm Sullivan, by the way. This is Vic and Mike."

"Hey."

Vic took her by the arm. "Come on. Why don't we sit down for a while. I want to ask you about the symbols at the tunnel."

Mackenzie nodded, dumbly. Her legs threatened to betray her. Her thoughts were slow and elusive, and she wondered if she might be in shock.

Henry poked his head out from an alcove, scrunching his eyes at the light. He said to everyone, "It's unquestionably Aztec gold. Coins, figurines, plateware, and the like. There are piles of it in each of the niches. Rather large piles."

She had forgotten that he and Lucy had been exploring. The news that he'd found gold seemed surreal. She should be ecstatic, she knew, but she couldn't quite comprehend it.

Taking out a handkerchief, stained orange-brown from the slickrock, Henry cleaned his glasses. "Not only that, but I believe there's another tunnel in one of them."

Vic raised his eyebrows. "Where?"

"Third one on the right. There are seven, you know. Seven caves, seven stockpiles of gold. And we are seven." Henry looked over at Charlie, seeing him for the first time. If he was surprised, he didn't show it. "Not including, of course, the invalid. I assume this is Charlie?"

She nodded.

"Speaking of seven," Sullivan said, "Where's Lucy?"

On cue, Lucy appeared from an alcove across from them. "Here. I was exploring the alcoves, checking them out." She, too, viewed the man on the cave floor for the first time. And spun on her heel.

Charlie's eyes went wide, and he tried to get up. Sullivan knelt again. "Hang on there, champ. Slow down."

Charlie shook his head and stared at Mackenzie. "No, no." He pushed Sullivan's hands away. "Let go of me. I know that voice. I'd recognize it anywhere."

Mackenzie glanced around. "Charlie, what voice? What do you mean?"

"I know what he means." Lucy turned around, unsmiling. She held a small gun. "I know exactly what he means."

Charlie's expression was grim. "Yes, I'm sure you do," he said. "Jordan."

"Jordan? What do you mean? This is Lucy." Mackenzie gaped at her friend. What was going on?

Charlie shook his head. "Well, she's dyed her hair, but it's definitely Jordan."

She pointed the gun at him. "Yes, Charlie, it's me. Never thought I'd see you again. I should have killed you myself when I had the chance." She waved the gun at the group. "Okay, everybody, please sit down in the middle of the floor there."

Nobody moved.

Jordan shoved Henry, saying, "You first, grandpa. Down. Now."

Henry sat down heavily. "What do you think you're doing, whoever you are? You can't keep all of us down."

Her laugh was brittle, almost hysterical. Not the laugh Mackenzie had become accustomed to. The laugh scared her more than the gun. Who was this person she thought she knew?

"Of course I can keep you down. Mackenzie, come here." Lucy pulled some plastic zip ties from her cargo pants pocket and tossed them at her. "Fasten these around each of their hands, in back, please. Tight. Ankles, too. I'll be watching."

Sullivan turned his back to Mackenzie, crossing his wrists. "Do as she says."

Fumbling with the zip ties, Mackenzie placed them around his wrists and pulled them taut. She did the same for the rest. She turned to Jordan. "If you're not Lucy, who are you?"

Jordan motioned for her to sit next to Sullivan. "Turn around and cross your wrists." She placed the gun on the ground next to her as she squatted to cuff Mackenzie.

Charlie propped himself on one elbow. "She's the one I was working with, Mac. The one I was running from. She's the reason I disappeared."

The world closed in around her. What the hell was happening? How could Lucy—now Jordan—have fooled her? Lucy had always been so, so normal. She was stunned.

"Yes, like Charlie said, my name's Jordan Bannock, not Lucy. I'm not a historian. Well, not in the true sense of the word, anyway. No, I guess you could call me an opportunist. After meeting Charlie, and realizing his research was brilliant, my husband Ted and I partnered with him."

Charlie mumbled something. Mackenzie wanted him to say something, but he was lying down again, eyes closed. She worried that he needed water.

"Ah, what a godsend Charlie was," Jordan continued. "You see, Ted and I first met with the descendant of Louisa Wetherill. Oh, wait. You probably don't know about her, either." She winked at Mackenzie. "Mac, why don't you fill the group in on the whole thing. And please don't leave anything out." She switched the gun to her right hand, wiping her left hand on her pant leg.

Mackenzie dutifully, if reluctantly, filled in the blanks for the rest of them, describing Louisa Wetherill's journals, adding more detail when Jordan prompted. When the story reached her meeting at the marina with Sullivan, she paused. Her throat felt chalky, and she couldn't swallow.

"You know the rest. I essentially forced my way into the expedition, hoping to find Charlie." Mackenzie coughed, unable to cover her mouth.

"We've been over that," Vic said. "You were a welcome addition. You've been invaluable."

"What?" Jennifer's voice sounded loud in the enclosed space. "Look at what she did. We're here, trapped. And it's all her fault." She hiccuped the word, 'fault.'

"Shut up. I'd say that it worked out just fine," Jordan said, grinning. "And it'll be good to be free of you, bitch."

Jennifer glanced at each of the group, silently urging them to defend her, but no one said anything.

Jordan laughed again. "Okay, I need a few minutes, guys. I'm going to explore one of the alcoves a bit more. Henry says there's a tunnel. I think I'll see for myself." She walked around them, checking the zip ties. "Be back in a jif."

As soon as Jordan left, Mackenzie shifted toward Sullivan. She started to say something, but he shook his head.

A faint rustling noise disrupted the silence. Next to Sullivan, in front of them both, Vic was twisting and writhing.

"What are you doing?" Sullivan whispered.

"Getting to my knife. It's strapped to my right ankle."

Sullivan gestured with his head. "Maybe Henry can help you."

Vic rolled onto his left side, and Henry wormed his way toward Vic's ankle.

"It's difficult working behind my back," Henry said.

"You're almost there, Henry," Sullivan cajoled. "A little more to the left and higher. That's it."

A noise issued from the alcove. Everyone waited, but Jordan didn't return.

Sullivan whispered, "Okay, another inch. Yes, you're there."

Henry pulled the knife from the sheath on Mike's ankle. Mackenzie held her breath, praying he wouldn't drop it.

"Now cut Vic's ties," Sullivan instructed. "Then he'll free you. But be quiet, for God's sake."

Henry and Vic edged closer to each other, back to back. After several tries, Henry finally got the knife in place.

"When I give the word, bring it down." Vic extended his wrists. "I'll pull my hands up."

Henry obliged, but the knife lodged in the plastic.

"Not so hard, Vic. Let me try it on my own." Henry struggled with the knife.

Mike shushed him "Quiet. She'll hear you." He scuttled closer to Vic and Henry.

After several tries, Henry found the sweet spot and bore down on it. The zip tie split neatly.

"Thanks." Vic rubbed his wrists. He cut Henry's ties and turned to say something to Sullivan.

He didn't get the chance. Jordan emerged, blinking.

Vic quickly crossed his wrists behind him, keeping his ankles still. Henry apparently couldn't move.

Jordan studied the group, her eyes slits, and walked toward them.

Shit. She had to do something. Mackenzie said loudly, "You're a good actress, Lu—I mean, Jordan. I thought you were my friend. I really bought it."

Jordan stopped, and Mackenzie stared back at her. Henry placed both wrists behind him.

"Oh, it was so easy, honey. You're so transparent. So needy. All I had to do was smile and ask questions and we were best buddies. Besides, I'd researched you enough."

"What do you mean?"

"Now, who do you think rifled your office?"

Mackenzie stared at her. "No. That was you?"

Jordan nodded. "Yeah. Well, my husband."

"So, how'd you arrange it?" Mackenzie asked. "I mean, how did you get on the expedition?"

"It wasn't difficult. After I found out the museum was sending someone named Lucy Fields, I, uh, took her place."

"And the real Lucy?"

"Don't worry about her." She waved the gun slowly over the group. "I doubt anyone will find her. It'll be quite awhile before that Lucy Fields pops up. If ever."

Mackenzie felt sick. Distracting Jordan had made it worse.

Holding the gun on them, Jordan scanned the cave, her brows furrowed. She walked swiftly toward Charlie and went down on one knee, still facing the group. Dumping the contents of his backpack, she turned it upside down, shaking it. She pocketed several items, including his granola bars. "This'll do, I think, for a while."

"You're going to leave us here?" Jennifer's voice was high and thin.

"Yup. Guess I'll make a few trips back and forth for more gold. Want to get enough. Or can you ever get enough?" She chuckled. "After things settle down, Ted and I will come back to get it all. Of course, you won't know that though." She paused, studying the upturned faces. "Because you'll be dead."

CHAPTER 19

JORDAN CHECKED THE GUN, MAKING SURE THE SAFETY WAS OFF. "Be right back. Ya'll be good, now." She slung the backpack over her shoulder and disappeared into the first alcove on the left.

Vic waited a beat before uncrossing his hands. He whispered, "Henry, stay put, okay?"

Henry nodded. "Of course."

"What's your plan?" Sullivan asked quietly.

"I'm going to surprise her at the alcove, take her from behind." Not waiting for an answer, Vic darted to the right of the alcove.

"Set us free first," Mike said. "We'll have a better chance if there are more of us."

"No time," Vic whispered. "Besides, if she gets the best of me, she won't think you all were in it. It's got to be me alone." He stood with knife ready, an eager expression on his face.

Minutes seemed to last for hours. The plastic zip ties chafed Mackenzie's wrists with every movement. Next to her, Sullivan strained against his.

She whispered to him, "Don't you have a knife?"

"Not on me. I put it in my pack earlier."

Suddenly something flashed by, and she flinched. Something shiny—a gold necklace—landed on the cave floor, and for a long moment Mackenzie couldn't figure out where it had come from. By the time she did, it was too late.

Jordan sprang from the opening, gun in hand, and rushed Vic. Although distracted by the golden projectile, he evaded her, striking her gun arm. The gun clattered to the ground.

Jordan stepped back, adopting a fighter's stance. "Vic. You should have known I could see you from there." She pivoted, ready to go for the gun, but he was faster and kicked it away.

He squared off. "This is a knife. You think I'm afraid to use it?"

Without warning, Jordan spun, launching herself toward the gun.

"Oh, no, you don't." He lunged at her, knocking her away with his shoulder.

Rolling, he ended on his side, knife in hand, the gun several feet from him. He reached for it with his free hand, but she got there first. She stomped on his hand with the heel of her boot. He let out a cry, and turned over to his back, dropping the knife. In an instant, she bent down to retrieve it.

While her eyes were focused on it, Vic drove his foot into her stomach, and she sat back, eyes and mouth wide. He grabbed the knife, then the gun, before standing up. Training the gun on her, he tucked the knife into his belt.

"It's all over, whoever you are." His back was toward the cave's mouth. Jordan was on the ground a yard or so away. "Stand up and raise your hands," he commanded.

Gasping for air, she held up a hand, palm forward. She see-sawed to her feet, doubled over to catch her breath. Without warning, she pushed off, flinging herself at him.

She hit him solidly in the chest with her shoulder, and he reeled from the impact. Once again the gun fell, to the cave floor. Vic held onto her, and she struggled against him. Locked in each other's arms, they gyrated like two lovers in a grisly dance. Then, she squirmed and head-butted him, connecting with his nose.

Blood coursed down his face. Reflexively, he loosened his hold on her. She pushed away, but he caught her wrist, pulling her to him again. The movement threw him off balance, and he stepped back. There was nothing there. With a cry, Vic hurtled backward over the cliff edge, taking Jordan with him.

"Oh, my God," Jennifer cried. "Oh, my God."

Mackenzie couldn't speak. She sat there with her mouth open. What had just happened? It couldn't be real. She wanted to cover her ears to block out the screams, but her hands were still tied behind her. Instead, she closed her eyes, trying to shut off the images in her brain. It didn't help.

After a few moments, the cave was eerily quiet. Her thoughts were so loud in her head that she was sure the others could hear them. Vic was gone. He was dead, and he had died trying to save the group. Her stalwart companion, the best of them, was gone. And Lucy, or the woman she'd thought of as Lucy, was dead, too. She forced herself to take air in and expel it. Curiously, her tears wouldn't come.

Sullivan was the first to say something. "All right, everyone. Let's get out of these ties before anything else." He jerked his head at Henry, urging him to stand.

The older man got to his feet, one hand on his chest, and padded unsteadily toward the cave wall. He removed his glasses.

"There's a knife in my pack, Henry," Sullivan urged. "In the outside pocket. You can use that."

But the older man didn't move. His eyes were glazed, and he stared vacuously in the direction of the wall above the group.

"Come on, Henry. We're waiting," Mike said.

Blinking rapidly, Henry scanned the group. "Yes. I know. You're all waiting."

Mackenzie frowned, puzzled. What the hell was he saying? Almost at the same time, Henry moved, and she relaxed. Obviously, he was in shock. They all needed to process the incident. He was older and slower than the rest and likely needed more time.

But he didn't move toward Sullivan's backpack. Instead, he stepped forward and booted Mike, who was on his side on the ground.

"What are you doing, old man?" Jennifer screeched.

"What am I doing?" He squatted slowly, picking up the gun. "What am I doing? I should think it's obvious what I'm doing."

CHAPTER 20

"YOU CAN'T BE SERIOUS," MACKENZIE CRIED.

"Oh but I am, Ms. Campbell. Very serious. Now, I'd like you all to stay just as you were."

"You won't get away with this," Sullivan said in a low voice.

"What's that? You're in an unusual position to be threatening me, I should say." He aimed the weapon at Sullivan. "Now, do shut up."

Henry pointed the gun at each of them in turn. "Don't think I can't handle this. I am a crack shot. Grew up with a gun in my hand. Trap shooting and all that. Not this, uh, Glock, however. Damned thing's plastic. But at this range, I cannot miss." To emphasize his statement, he ejected the clip, checked it, rammed it back into place.

"Now, Sullivan, I am going to retrieve your backpack. And find the one Lucy, er, Jordan, so kindly loaded for me." He caught sight of Charlie, whose eyes were closed. Mackenzie didn't know if he was sleeping, pretending, or worse. Henry sidled over and nudged him with his foot. Charlie didn't move or react.

"I'm afraid your friend Charlie is no help at all, Ms. Campbell." Henry smiled at her. "I rather think he's unconscious."

She blinked. She had to put Charlie out of her mind. Her first objective had to be to free them.

Henry cocked his head. "I must warn you that trying to escape would be wasted. I shall be gone for a moment only, and I won't be as naïve as our unfortunate friend. It was so considerate of her to thin the ranks."

His vapid stare was an affront, and she desperately tried to quell her anger.

Henry turned Sullivan's backpack upside down, dumping the contents. "Thank you for mentioning your knife, Sullivan." He retrieved the item and turned away from them.

Mackenzie brought her knees up to her chest. Rocking to avoid falling on her side, she felt something cut into her right hip. Nail clippers. Nail clippers in her back pocket. Surely they could cut through the zip ties?

She twisted until she could maneuver them out. Sullivan raised his eyebrows but didn't say anything. She matched his expression.

Behind her back, she fumbled with the nail clippers. Suddenly, Henry stood and faced the group. She went rigid.

"Henry," Sullivan said quickly. "Why the about-face? I would have thought a man of your stature would be above this."

"Well, that's an interesting question. You see, as I told Ms. Campbell near the beginning of this expedition, I am approaching retirement. Nearly thirty years spent researching. I am quite tired of academia, and between you and me, research does not pay."

"You planned this from the start, as a way to fund your retirement?"

"Oh, no. Had no idea. But one must improvise. The opportunity was simply too tasty." He tittered.

Mackenzie realized she had never heard him laugh like that. She almost had the nail clippers in place, and fervently hoped they were strong enough to cut the ties. And that she was coordinated enough to use them.

"When Jordan and Vic, ah, decided to remove themselves," Henry continued, "Everything fell into place. I simply waited for the right moment. And now, it's time to pillage and plunder. Please remember that I'll be listening for the smallest sounds." He backed up until he was at the entrance to the second alcove.

The moment Henry disappeared, Mackenzie told Sullivan about the nail clippers. Without speaking, they both began rocking until they were back to back. She faced the alcove and watched for Henry, trying to find Sullivan's wrist. Closing her eyes, she visualized cutting the tie; it was thicker than she had realized, and she couldn't get the right angle. After several attempts, her hands were so sweaty she could barely hang onto the clippers. Finally, she found the right leverage and snipped Sullivan's zip tie.

After cutting her restraints, Sullivan whispered into her ear, "Stay here. I'm going after him."

"No deal," she said, rubbing her wrists. "I'm helping. Two against one is better odds." She rose to one knee. "What's the plan?"

He exhaled. "Plan? I haven't got a plan. I guess at the very least we need to ambush him."

She scanned what remained of the group. Mike was sitting up again. Jennifer had rolled around so she faced them. Charlie was still unconscious. "Shouldn't we free them, too?"

Suddenly there was a loud crash, and they heard Henry's muffled swearing. Sullivan got to his feet. "We don't have time. Come on, let's get into that other alcove. Hurry."

They ran past Charlie and Mike and Jennifer, into the blackness.

Henry dragged the heavy backpack out and looked around suspiciously. "Bloody hell," he muttered. He released the backpack strap and edged back into the alcove behind him, drawing the gun from his belt. He trained the weapon first at Jennifer, then Mike. Holding it straight out in front of him, he stepped out again and rotated, pausing at each alcove.

Mackenzie held her breath when he pointed at their hiding place, sure he could see them. Sullivan was directly across from her, on the other side of the opening. Okay, she thought. We wait. But for what? How in the world are we going to surprise him now?

"Mr. Sullivan," Henry boomed, "or should I say Dr. Sullivan? Come out now, and I won't hurt your friends here. You, too, Ms. Campbell. Let's be reasonable, shall we? I don't care one way or the other, as I have a full clip. Indeed, I have ten bullets. More than I require."

Sullivan slipped to one knee in the darkness and scooped up some dirt.

Henry turned toward Jennifer and Mike. "Tell me where they are, Mike. Or I shoot Jennifer." He edged along the perimeter of the cave.

"Please, oh, please, don't shoot me," she whined.

"We don't know where they are," Mike said. "They're probably gone by now."

"Oh, yes, they developed wings and flew away. Like your compadres, Vic and Jordan." Henry continued to turn slowly.

Mackenzie tensed. In a moment Henry's back would be toward them. Sullivan motioned for her to kneel, and she did so, her legs trembling.

"I will shoot your friends, Sullivan. And your friend, Ms. Campbell. I am a competent marksman, I promise you. I will end them."

Suddenly, Sullivan whistled shrilly, and Henry spun around. As he did, Sullivan threw dirt into the man's eyes while diving for the ground. Mackenzie wasn't sure if she should stay or follow him out.

Henry tore his glasses off with his free hand, firing blindly into the alcove. Jennifer shrieked, and Mackenzie covered her head with her hands. The bullet struck the wall behind her with a sickening thud. Bracing herself for the worst, she looked up. It had missed her by a foot.

Sullivan grasped Henry's gun arm, trying for the Glock. Without warning, Henry went limp, sinking to the ground. Surprised, Sullivan lost his balance, and Henry pulled the younger man over him, flipping him. Springing up, Henry slammed the butt of the gun into Sullivan's head.

Mackenzie watched in horror as Sullivan sank to the ground. Without thinking, she charged, knocking Henry over. He dropped to his knees, and she climbed onto his back, trying to choke him. Again Henry went slack, but she was ready for him. She let go and rolled away.

But it took too long to get to her feet. Henry beat her to the gun and deftly pointed it at her. "All right. Don't move," he panted. He waved the gun at Jennifer and Mike, his attention on them for a long second.

It was enough. Mackenzie tackled him, and he fell backward, still holding onto the gun. He pulled the trigger, shooting up at the cave's ceiling. An ominous rumble resulted, and dust and small clods of damp earth rained down on them.

She glanced up automatically. When she looked back, Henry was on his elbows, leveling the weapon at her. He was less than a yard away.

"The next one's for you, my dear. I am too old to play this game. I assure you that from this distance, even with my vision, I will not miss."

She raised her hands. "Okay. Don't shoot me. I won't do anything, I promise."

He got to one knee. "Now, please hand me my spectacles. Yes, over there. And clean them as well."

She moved toward the glasses, facing him. "I think they're broken." Stooping down, she picked them up. "I'm not sure I can—"

Crack. She jumped and watched as Henry, in slow motion, crumpled to his knees, landing in a heap on the ground. Sullivan stood behind him, weaving slightly. He grinned.

"Sulley," she gasped. "You're all right."

"Well, not exactly all right," he said. "But I'm standing. How about you? You okay?"

She knew her knees were torn up, and her face raw. Her entire body ached. "I feel like I've been hit by a truck, but I'm good."

"Yeah, well, you look good to me."

She smiled. "How's your head?"

He turned his head. The right side of his head and neck were covered in blood. She put a hand to her stomach, nauseated.

"It's nothing. Head wounds bleed a lot." He looked at the other two on the ground.

Jennifer whimpered, a hysterical note in her voice. "Untie me now, please."

"Sure thing, Jen." He knelt down next to her on one knee. Mackenzie saw Henry lift his head. She screamed, just as the older man rolled to his back, aiming at Sullivan.

It wasn't like slow motion; it was more like they were moving through water. Sullivan pivoted, throwing himself to the right. A shot rang out, and he fell to the ground with a thud.

Mackenzie heard herself screaming, "No!" again and again. Ignoring Henry, she ran to Sullivan. She pulled back, hand to her mouth, as the blood stain under him slowly darkened the cave floor.

CHAPTER 21

Mackenzie dropped to her knees and placed her ear on Sullivan's chest. She couldn't tell if she heard her heartbeat or his. She scanned the cave wildly, looking for something to staunch the wound, but nothing was close. She pulled her over shirt off and wadded it up, pressing it against the hole in his shoulder.

Henry, who had retrieved his broken spectacles, crept over to her, gun arm by his side. With one eye closed, he regarded her through cracked glass. "Campbell, it's all over. Please take your place with the others."

"No," she snapped. "Shut up." She leaned closer to Sullivan and heard a soft groan. Holding her face near his, she felt his warm breath.

"He's alive," she whispered. "He's alive." She stroked his jaw, and he opened his eyes.

He groaned. "Mac. You okay?"

She laughed, and tears slid down her face, landing on his chest.

"I've been hit," he said. "That son of a bitch shot me in the shoulder."

She nodded. "Yes. And that son of a bitch is right behind you, holding a gun."

Much to her surprise, Henry allowed her to help Sullivan. She half-carried him to the wall near Charlie. The bullet had passed completely through his shoulder. It would be painful, but it wasn't serious, he assured her. Under his direction, she cleaned and bandaged him and made a sling from one of his shirts. She also cleaned his head wound, but had nothing to bandage it with. He told her it would be fine.

Henry also let her tend to Charlie, who had been unconscious for most of the excitement. He was deathly pale, his skin almost translucent.

Great, she thought. She had two patients. And no idea what to do.

She implored Henry to free the other two, but he declined, saying they'd have to wait. An odd smile played on his lips, but he agreed to let her give Jennifer and Mike water.

While she attended to them, Henry dragged Jordan's full backpack next to the one he had filled. He had clearly decided that without Sullivan she was no threat.

She glanced over. Sullivan and Charlie appeared to be sleeping. Jennifer and Mike looked drained as well, and both stooped forward, heads on their chests.

She, too, was exhausted. Her eyes kept closing on her, and she found herself jerking awake, her vision blurred. She rubbed her eyes, watching Henry. His back was to her as he adjusted the overstuffed backpacks full of gold.

She wanted to stay quiet, hoping he would continue to allow her to remain zip-tie-free. But when she saw the backpacks, she couldn't contain herself. "You're going to carry both of those?"

"Yes. I may have to leave a few items behind, but I'll take quite a bit, don't you fear. I'll return for the rest."

Mackenzie cleared her throat. "Henry, I have no interest in the gold. Nobody here does. You're welcome to it all. We just want to get out of here alive."

"Ah. Very generous of you. However, it doesn't change my plan. You're an intelligent woman. I'm confident you realize that I can't allow you to follow me out of the tunnel. You might jeopardize my escape. You'll simply have to stay."

"What?"

"Oh, yes. Much easier than killing you all, don't you think? It would be a shame to waste bullets, you know."

"Henry, there's no way you can make it on your own. You'll get lost. You don't have enough food. Who knows if the tunnel really leads out?"

"Why thank you, Ms. Campbell. You're certainly right. I don't have any food. Or water." He crossed to the pile of backpacks. "However, as you kindly reminded me, everything I need is in these."

She was dumbstruck. What a dolt she was.

He dumped out the backpacks and, choosing one, filled it with their remaining food and water. "I guess I may have to wear a third backpack, but I'll manage."

He hesitated for a few seconds. Then, looking directly at her, he kicked the remaining backpacks over the edge.

Shit. She tried to calm herself. Yes, he had gotten rid of their backpacks and taken their food and water. But she was still free.

She knew that although he had said he wouldn't kill them, he could easily change his mind. She couldn't let that happen.

Jennifer was wide awake, now. "Oh, no," she cieed, "Not my camera bag." With her streaked mascara and tear-stained face, she looked like a Goth Barbie.

Henry turned to face her. "Stop being maudlin, Jennifer, or I may gag you."

Closing her eyes, Mackenzie focused on forming a plan. She had to compartmentalize, block out everything else. She took stock.

Sullivan and Charlie were too weak to help. Jennifer was a liability. But Mike ... .

Henry fidgeted with the contents of a backpack, ignoring the group.

Mackenzie glanced at Mike and caught his eye. Crossing her wrists in front of her, she silently asked him if he could get out of the zip ties. He lifted his eyebrows, mouthing, "No."

Her shoulders sagged. She couldn't risk tossing him the nail clippers.

Maybe there was another way. She swiveled so she could study the tunnel opening. The Aztecs believed there should be one way in and a separate way out. They were a militaristic empire, constantly battling neighboring peoples, and they were usually the aggressor. They were famous for their hidden rooms, secret exits, and false exits to lure the unsuspecting. Hollywood had capitalized on this theme, and the film portrayals were grossly inaccurate, but there was a smidgen of truth behind it all.

Mackenzie was certain they had come through the designated entrance. But had Henry found the true exit, or had he found a false one intended for enemies? Her knowledge might be a bargaining chip.

"Henry," she said. "Could I talk to you for a moment?"

"What is it?"

She kept her voice calm, hoping it sounded sincere. "I just wondered, you know, if you were positive the tunnel you found was the true way out." She didn't know how to word it without giving away too much. "I mean, it might be a trap."

He laughed. "My dear. Your intentions are so obvious. It's the bona fide exit. Although I'm not an expert in Mesoamerican languages like you, I am able to piece some words together. And I definitely know the glyph for 'exit.' "

"It could be a red herring," she argued. "I'd have to see the surrounding symbols myself to make sure."

"Right. Well, I'm afraid that's not going to happen. But you have reminded me of something." He pulled the gun from his pocket, checking it. His eyes on her, he pulled some string from his pocket. "I think it's time I tied you up again."

Dammit, not only had she had provoked Henry, now she had gotten herself tied up. Her throat constricted. She glanced at Sullivan and Charlie, but they hadn't moved. She felt alone and powerless.

Suddenly, irrationally, she missed her tiny apartment and dull routine. Since she had received Charlie's letter, things had been changing and unfamiliar at lightning speed.

Henry placed the small backpack of essentials on his chest. He donned the other two backpacks, which he had strapped together to form one oversized pack. He faltered under the weight of the load, taking a step to right himself, and pulled the shoulder straps tight.

"Adieu, everyone. Till we meet again." He grinned. "Well, actually, it's goodbye. I doubt very much you'll be conscious, much less alive, when I return."

She tried one more time. "Henry, I'm not trying to trick you."

He held up his hand, palm forward. "Enough."

As he disappeared into the alcove, Mike asked in a hushed tone, "What were you doing?"

"I was trying to buy some time. I thought that if I could get a look at the tunnel, I'd have a chance to do something. Stall him somehow."

"Yeah, well, I guess that could have worked. But look at us now. We're dead."

"Oh, why did we have to follow you?" Jennifer's wail was more of a moan. "It's all your fault."

Mackenzie exhaled. She couldn't let Jennifer rattle her. "Let's think of a way out of here. We can't change what's taken place." She looked over at Sullivan, wanting to rush to him, but that had to wait.

"How did you break your zip ties before?" Mike struggled with his own ties.

"Oh, my God, I forgot." Henry had tied up her wrists in front of her, not behind her back. She withdrew the nail clippers from her pocket. "With these."

"Well, d'ya think you could clip us free?" His voice was gentle, not harsh.

"Me first," Jennifer cried. "It's been harder for me."

"Harder for you?" Mike snorted. "Jennifer, what's wrong with you? What the hell are you talking about? Think it's been harder on you than Sullivan? Or Vic?"

Mackenzie hacked at the string that bound her wrists, letting them argue.

Jennifer pleaded, "My wrists are raw. I'll probably have scars. And emotional scars. I'm not used to this kind of treatment."

He choked out, "And we are? Sorry, sweetie. Be glad you're alive. Henry could've killed us. The way you were complaining, I was afraid you were driving him to it."

"Well, it's fine for you to say. You're a man."

"Oh, you noticed? I thought you only had eyes for Sullivan. Don't think we didn't know what you were doing."

Before Jennifer could answer, Mackenzie cackled. "Aha. I'm free."

She was kneeling behind Mike, ready to cut the tie, when she heard it. A loud, low rumbling, almost like thunder. She stood up, forgetting about him.

The earthen ceiling shuddered above them, and cracks began to form. Small bits of rock pelted them, and the rumbling continued. Mackenzie covered her head with her arms, trying to include Mike as well.

How ironic. They'd come all this way to be killed by the cave itself.

The noise rose to a crescendo, and they waited. Finally, some minutes later, they heard a loud wrenching sound. Then nothing. Mackenzie sneezed. Fine dust poured out of the tunnel Henry had just entered.

"It caved in," Mike whispered. "I think Henry's tunnel collapsed."

She nodded slowly. "I know. It was too easy, too simple. The Aztecs were sneaky. They lived in dangerous times, and they made sure they couldn't be followed, except by friends." She released the pair from their zip ties.

"So there could be another way out?" Mike backed away from the tunnel. The air was heavy, thick with dust

"Yeah. But it's also possible they built several fake ways out."

"Shit," he said. "Could you tell by reading?" Mike rubbed a wrist on his shorts, leaving a smear of blood.

"Maybe." She wiped her nose with her sleeve.

"What about Henry? He bragged that he could read the symbols."

"Well, I know he could make out a few simple words. But it's a tough language. Some combined glyphs have one meaning on the surface and another hidden meaning."

He scowled. "Then how can anyone ever read them?"

"Uh, it's difficult, but not impossible. Context sometimes helps. And knowledge of who was writing, or communicating. Who the intended audience was. Mostly it's just plain luck."

"I hope for our sakes, Mac, that you can understand all those glyphs. And that there's another way out."

"What's going on? All what glyphs? What happened?" Sullivan's voice was hoarse.

"Sulley. Thank God, you're awake. How do you feel?" Mackenzie picked her way through the rubble toward him.

"Uh, The shock is wearing off and it hurts like hell. What happened?" He sat up, then immediately laid back down. "Wow. Headache."

"You need to rest." She knelt in front of him. "You missed a lot. You might not believe what's happened. Are you up for it?"

"Of course I am." He coughed and shifted awkwardly.

While she daubed at his head wound, which had begun bleeding again, she filled in the missing details. He listened, wincing occasionally. When she reached the part where Henry had been crushed by the tunnel, she paused. He didn't comment.

"Now, I think we have to move on," she said. "Try to figure a way out of here. We don't have much time. I mean, without food and water."

"Oh, I wouldn't worry about that." Charlie's voice rose ghostlike.

She turned, startled. "How long have you been awake, Charlie?"

"Since the tunnel cave-in. I thought I'd let you talk for a while."

"Thanks," she said dryly. "Now, what do you mean we don't have to worry about food and water?"

"Well, we have some. A little bit, anyway. I stashed a bag of it over there, in that depression in the wall." He pointed toward the general direction of Jennifer. She immediately scurried to it and turned her back to them.

"Wait for us," Mike told her.

"I just want to see what's in there first. I'll share."

He started to walk toward her, but Mackenzie grabbed his pant leg. "Let her be," she whispered. "Maybe she'll be less of a pain if she has something to do. Something to be in charge of."

"Yeah," he muttered, "sure. But she'd better not push it."

Mackenzie turned back to Charlie. "That was good thinking. Why did you hide food?"

"Well, I didn't plan it. That's where I left it when I made it in here. I sort of forgot about it. Looking back, I should've kept it nearby."

"You think?" Sullivan asked.

"I wasn't feeling well," Charlie protested.

She glared at Sullivan. "Forget it. It worked out fine in the end."

Jennifer was as good as her word. After she had pawed through the contents of the bag, she doled out stale granola bars and a bag of what looked like mixed nuts. "What's this?" she asked.

"GORP. You know, Good Old Raisins and Peanuts. Mine's a custom mix, with granola and coconut and M&Ms."

She sniffed the bag and took a handful before tossing it toward Sullivan. It fell next to him.

Charlie said, "Check the side pocket. There should be a bag of GORP Without Pretense." He grinned. "It's just M&Ms. I ate everything else, saving them for last."

They ate in silence. Mackenzie studied the symbols on the border of the entrance tunnel, but it was slow going. "Well, my best interpretation of these glyphs is they're a warning. Sort of like, 'Woe to all who enter here.' "

She reached for the water and took a long draw. "There's mention of Montezuma, and of the gold, as well as of Cortés and Quetzalcoatl. Most of them are fairly easy to figure out with the context. One, though, is puzzling. It's the symbol for bat combined with the one for 'way through.' Now, bats guided the dead to the underworld, and the Aztecs elevated death, you know. There were all sorts of rituals and stories with bats prominent in them. Bats were important. So, having a bat glyph connected to one for the way through is kind of redundant. They wouldn't have done that." She drifted off, frowning.

"Could bat mean anything else?" Mike asked.

"What? Oh, sure. It has a few other meanings when paired with certain symbols. It's also the symbol for the fourth month of the Aztec calendar." She swallowed. "And for human sacrifice."

CHAPTER 22

"YOU DON'T THINK THEY SACRIFICED, UH, HUMANS HERE, DO YOU?" Jennifer was standing, her arms crossed tightly over her chest in front of her.

"I don't think so," Mackenzie said, thoughtfully. "We'd see more signs. Like an altar, tools, that sort of thing. If they were sacrificing, there'd be a record of it somewhere in the cave. And skeletons. So far, I haven't found anything to indicate that this was a sacrificial site."

"Well, we got that going for us," Charlie said.

"Yeah. For all it's worth. I'm more worried that we'll be crushed if there's a cave-in." She stared up at the top of the cave.

"All the more reason to figure it out sooner, rather than later," Charlie replied. "I doubt it'll cave in. I bet they rigged it so just the fake tunnel would collapse."

"What about the fourth month thing?" Sullivan asked. "Could that be important?"

She bit her bottom lip. "Maybe. I wish I knew how." Turning back to the stone glyphs, she squatted. "Hold on, I think I've got something. There's something here that I think means caves. Plural. Each one has been named for an animal, I think. Or a tribal name, I suppose. But one of the caves has a bat."

"Well, maybe we're in the bat cave," Charlie smirked.

She rolled her eyes at him, and his face went blank.

Mike said, "Much as I hate to admit it, what Charlie said makes sense. Right?"

"I don't know," Sullivan said. "How can we be sure?"

Her voice rose. "I need more context, because the symbol for cave is a tricky one. It could also mean womb, or a reptilian earth monster whose open mouth led to the underworld. Or even creation. Caves were considered living things by most Mesoamerican cultures."

He shrugged. "Are we in one of the seven caves, then? Or are they calling the alcoves caves?"

"I don't know yet. I'll have to decipher more symbols to see if I can put things into context."

"So, this doesn't help." Jennifer placed her hands on her hips.

"I'm not certain. There is another weird thing, though. Remember that the Aztecs claimed they came from a place called Aztlan? And that Montezuma declared that he'd found it? Well, the word 'Aztlan' is usually transcribed as 'place of the herons.' But the strict translation is literally 'place of the winged things.' Knowing the Aztecs, they could have meant something deceptive by that. I mean, a bat is a winged thing, right?"

Nobody moved. She stared at them expectantly. "What if it does mean the alcoves? And this is a long shot, but what if the fourth month thing means the fourth alcove? That would be either this one," she said, standing in front of one opening, "Or, one-two-three-four—this same one. It's number four, either way."

The alcove faced the mouth of the cave. She stood, dusting off her shorts and clapping the dust off her hands. Sullivan and Charlie were now sitting up.

"I think Mike and I can handle this," Mackenzie said. "You two stay put. We're just going to scout it."

Charlie settled back against the wall.

Sullivan leaned forward. "I'm feeling better now. It's only a flesh wound. I'd like to go."

"No. Mike and I will go." She paused, continuing with a softer voice, "I can't have anything happening to you."

He remained motionless. Charlie looked first at Mackenzie and then at Sullivan. She caught a glimpse of his expression, but ignored it, and ducked into the alcove.

CHAPTER 23

Mike laughed. They sat on the floor in the fourth alcove. "Can you believe I said that? Only on this trip would mounds of gold be ho-hum."

Long and narrow, the alcove's slightly rounded walls were lined with mud bricks. Many were in good condition, but most were crumbling or loose. The floor was simply dirt.

He cast light at the ceiling. "Nothing above us, I'd say."

They felt their way along the walls, each taking a side. Although several bricks had fallen, and more came off in their hands, the walls behind the bricks revealed nothing. It was slow going.

She turned to the dirt floor next, sweeping her light back and forth, covering every inch of it. "Yeah, nothing on the ground, either. Let's check out the wall behind the gold."

They moved items: cups and bowls, bracelets and heavy necklaces, some larger pieces and a box of thin, gold coins. The pile was nearly four feet tall, and it took them the better part of an hour to move everything away from the back wall.

Starting on opposite sides, they traced their hands along the wall.

"What are we looking for?" Mike asked.

"Anything unusual or out of place. A loose brick. A small depression, or a crack. Even a hollow sound." She thumped the wall in several places. The bricks at the end were in better shape than those on the sides of the alcove, and unlike the side walls of the alcove, the end wall was straight, not bowed.

For more than twenty minutes the pair probed, pushing and prodding and knocking, but the wall kept its secrets, yielding nothing.

Mackenzie dropped to the ground, clicking her flashlight off. "Dammit, I was positive we would find something." She brushed the hair off her damp forehead.

He clicked his flashlight off, too, and sat next to her in the dark. "There has to be something. Let's try again."

She didn't answer. Her spent body railed at every movement, and her mind felt raw. Thoughts of Vic, Jordan, Charlie, and Sullivan threatened to engulf her.

Mike scooped some dirt from the ground and sifted it through his fingers. He brushed some of it away. Under the soft earth were bricks as well. He frowned, thinking. A moment later, he said, "Mac, I may have something."

"What?"

"Not sure. I'm going to check it out, okay?"

"Fine," she replied, perplexed. She was too zonked to argue, much less follow him.

When he returned, she was on her hands and knees on the floor, running her fingers through the dirt, examining the bricks he had found.

"So," Mike said. "I checked the floors of the other alcoves. None of them have bricked-in floors. Only this one."

"That's interesting. Look, I found a large stone right here."

They swept the earth away, exposing a flat stone about three feet wide and almost as long. Using their fingers, they carved out a trough around it, trying to find the bottom edge. It was about two inches thick.

He flung dirt to the side. "Here, help me clear away some more."

After several minutes, they were able to get their fingers under the stone.

"God, I hope there's more than insects beneath it," she said. "Can we even lift it?" She buried the end of her flashlight in the earth next to her. Mike did the same.

"All we can do is try." He squatted, his fingers under a corner.

She squatted beside him. "Okay, but take it slowly. Watch for bugs."

"With all we've been through, Mac, I can't believe you're worried about insects."

"Well, it's not just that," she replied, curtly. "I mean, it could still be a trap." She shoved her fingers under the stone. "Ready. Tell me when."

They wrenched the heavy stone free. Stale, dank air rose from the pit below them as they slid the stone over a few feet. The smell of ammonia was strong, and she coughed, her heartbeat ratcheted up.

"Mike, stay back from the edge. We're still not in the clear. You'd be amazed at the types of things the Aztecs did to protect themselves."

"No problem. Should we get the others?"

She laughed. "Right. Jennifer to watch and complain. Charlie, who shouldn't move. And Sullivan, who can barely move and would insist on helping."

"Uh, yeah, I wasn't thinking. Well, what's next?"

Shining light down into the depths revealed a crumbly wooden pole ladder leaning on a beam sticking out a foot or so from the wall. The hole was only fifteen feet or so deep, she guessed.

"I want to go," Mike said. "It seems safe enough to me. I'm not so crazy about that ladder, though. Anything we can use as rope?"

"We could string stuff together. Charlie might have some. But we would have to tell the others."

"I could go back and say it was for exploring the alcove. That's the truth, anyway. Maybe they're asleep, or maybe they won't be that curious."

"Well, we do need rope," she said, "But I'll go. I need a break. I'm fried from lifting the stone. I'll get us rope and bars and water, if we can spare them. Anything else we need?"

"No. Damn it, if only Jennifer wasn't so useless."

"Yeah, I think we'll have to pass on her. I wouldn't trust her to belay us or be able to help us out if we needed it."

"Are you sure about Charlie? He's rested and had food and water. He's probably recovered by now."

"No, I think he needs a little more time. He's lost a lot of weight and strength. We'll have to go it alone."

He grunted. "Okay. But I go first."

"Be my guest. Just wait for me. I'll be back soon." She kept the headlamp off, conserving its feeble beam. Moving over to the left wall, she used it as a guide, wondering what she'd say to the others to keep their curiosity at bay. She realized that Sullivan and Charlie had most likely been awake and sitting next to each other for several hours. They had to have talked. Shit. What was she was more afraid of: Charlie finding out about Sullivan, or Sullivan getting to know Charlie?

Mackenzie blinked as she entered the bigger cave, not used to the light, and sighed. The two men stopped talking when she entered and watched her poker-faced. They weren't smiling.

"Hey, Charlie, do you have any rope?" Ignoring the situation was all she could at the moment. Getting out had to take priority. She would sort things out later.

"Yeah," Charlie said. "Got a pull-cord in my pack. About twenty feet or so long, but not very strong. What for?"

She fumbled her answer. "Uh, well, Mike wants to check out the ceiling, so we're, I mean, he's going to rig something to keep him safe." Lame.

Sullivan's voice was cool and formal. "And how, exactly, are you going to do that?"

"Mike has a plan. I don't know the details." She mimicked his tone. "The rope, please."

Charlie handed it to her. It wasn't a traditional climbing rope; it was much thinner. He met her eyes, and she looked down, hoping he wouldn't see her tearing up. Her emotions were all over the place. She and Mike were trying to find a way out. They were doing their best. Charlie and Sullivan had no right to be so untrusting. She nodded at Charlie, glanced at Sullivan, and left, forgetting about the bars and water.

"What do you see down there?" She grasped the slim orange cord that tethered Mike. He had obviously reached the bottom, as it had gone slack in her hands. She relaxed her hold but didn't let go.

"It's another tunnel. Kind of tight, but not too bad. I'm going to go a little farther."

Oh, God. "Be careful," she called out. She let out more rope, trying to keep the tension tight but not taut.

Several minutes passed, and the rope went slack. Her heart kicked about in her chest. "Mike? You okay?" She shouldn't have let him go down first. Dammit, she should have gone. He was too young. He has his whole life ahead of him. His wedding.

"Hey, Mac. Guess what I found?"

She exhaled, and realized that she had been holding her shoulders up around her neck. Consciously lowering them, she said, "What? Tell me."

"I'm not sure you're going to like it. It's another cave, sorta like the other one, but smaller."

Another cave. Shit. She'd had enough of caves, and enough of canyons, for that matter. "What does it open out to?" It had to lead somewhere. It had to. They couldn't have used up all this time and energy without finding a way out. The silence lasted a beat too long.

"Nothing, he said. "It's like the other one. A sheer drop of about two hundred feet."

An hour later Mike and Mackenzie were sitting with the others, leaning against the wall.

"It's getting too dark to do anything," Mike said. "The tunnel and cave face the other way, not west like this one. East, I think."

"How big is this fucking cave?" Jennifer asked. "Alcoves and tunnels, and who knows what else. I'm so tired of caves."

No one said anything. Charlie and Sullivan were next to each other, and Mackenzie could feel the iciness between them. She couldn't tell if they were angry at her or at each other. Neither would talk to her unless it was to answer a question. Even then, the answer was a single syllable.

Jennifer sat next to Charlie. Sitting a bit apart, Mike had one knee up and was staring at nothing.

Sullivan rose, pushing off the wall with his good arm. He was unsteady on his feet, and she hoped he would come and sit by her, but he walked to the entrance of the fourth alcove.

"How much food do we have?" Jennifer asked.

"Six bars, two bags of GORP, and two full bottles of water," Sullivan replied, not turning.

"That's one bar for each of us, with one left over. And Charlie's candy GORP for all," she said.

"Yeah. Enough for dinner and breakfast, but that's it." Mike spoke the words that everyone was thinking.

"Oh," Jennifer said in a small voice. "I guess you're right."

"Well, I want to check it out." Mackenzie got to her feet. "We still have some fresh headlamps, right? No sense in waiting for morning."

"I'll go with you," Charlie said. "I'm doing better." He stood up, holding onto the wall for support.

"No, I'll go," said Sullivan. "She needs someone stronger."

"Stronger? You're half a man. How're you going to help with one arm?"

"Even with one arm I'm better than a punk kid like you."

"Okay, you two. Stop it." She realized she was using her mother's voice, not her own.

"Mac, you know you and I are a good team," Charlie replied. "After we get out of this, we can go back to how it was."

She blinked, eyes wide. *Go back? He thought they could just pretend nothing had happened?* She blurted out, "Go back to how it was? Are you kidding? Charlie, you dumped me and left. You didn't even tell me face to face. That was more than a year ago."

"That's all behind us now. You came after me, right? I made a mistake."

Sullivan snorted.

"I don't think this is any of your business, Sullivan, no matter what happened on the trip," Charlie said.

"Oh, I think it is," the older man replied. "I think Mackenzie needs someone a bit more, well, grown up."

"You mean old. And you don't know what you're talking about. You've known her, what, a couple weeks? I've known her for years. Intimately. I think I know what she needs."

"A lot happened on the trip, kid. You have no idea."

"I'm sure you think it happened. I doubt she does. Anyway, I'm here now."

They were standing toe to toe. Charlie was shorter than Sullivan, and much lighter, but he made up for it with aggressiveness. She watched them, wanting to intervene, but said nothing. She didn't know what to say.

"Yeah," Sullivan said. "You're here now. But don't forget you left her. I know all about it. She told me a lot of things. Unlike you, I was there for her." He jabbed a threatening finger at the younger man's chest.

Charlie flinched. "I made a mistake, dammit. I know better now. And don't you forget that she came after me. Besides, I'm here now. Right, Mac?"

She stared at them mutely for a moment. Why were they wasting precious time arguing? "Hold on. Please. This isn't the time to go into this. We need to think about getting out."

Both men stared at her, and she looked from Charlie to Sullivan.

"Tell him," Sullivan said, harshly. "Tell him, now."

"Or what? You've both been talking about me like I'm some prized possession, some toy to fight over like little boys. Like I'm not even here." She stood, arms akimbo. "Sullivan's right," she said. Before Sullivan could say anything, she held up her palm. "But Charlie's right, too." She watched him through slitted eyes. "I did come looking for you, and I did want us to get back together. But a lot has changed. I'm not sure—"

"Not sure?" Sullivan ejaculated.

"I'm not sure," she continued, glaring at him, "that I still feel the same way."

"But I love you, Mac. I know that now." Charlie held both arms up, inviting her to come closer.

She was flabbergasted. They were the words she had always wanted to hear. Her heart flip-flopped as she took in his surfer-boy good looks. He looked so vulnerable and pathetic. He was thin and dirty and weak, and so different from his former self. They had shared so much. She knew him, knew what he was like. And that was the problem. He could make her feel wonderful when he wanted to. But he wasn't steady, wasn't dependable.

Mackenzie glanced at Sullivan, who was holding his hurt arm with his good one. Standing ramrod straight. She remembered their night together, and she wanted to hold him, tell him it was all right. He was a man; Charlie was just a boy. She opened her mouth to say something, but stopped. Charlie had a point. How well did she know Sullivan? They'd only been together for a short while, and most of that time she had ardently disliked him. He certainly hadn't told her he loved her.

"I can't think about this now," she said wearily. "All I can think about is finding a way out of here. I don't care who comes with me, I just need someone."

In the end, they all went: Mike to keep Sullivan and Charlie from getting into it, and Jennifer because she didn't want to be left alone.

Mackenzie donned Sullivan's headlamp and let them lower her into the tunnel. She shivered, gazing at the darkness before her. She was cold, she told herself. She wasn't afraid.

"Okay," she called up to them, "I'm going in."

She put one foot in front of the other, trying to keep her body small and compact. Although the ceiling was seven feet or so, she crouched over, keeping her eyes peeled for traps. Mike may have not found anything, but maybe he had been lucky.

The tunnel curved to the right before snaking to the left. She counted the steps, and by the time she reached twenty, the tunnel opened up a bit. The odor was stronger here. Bat guano. The orange cord around her waist had grown taut. She tugged at it three times, in their prearranged code, telling them she was taking it off.

About six feet from where she stood, the cave ended, and she could see a dark wall with a star-studded navy blue sky beyond it. She let out a sigh. Tears welled up in her eyes, and she squeezed them back. No crying, she told herself. This has to be the exit cave. There were no traps or surprises. This had to be the way out.

She methodically explored the walls of the cave. It really was a bat cave. Piles of guano decorated all the crooks and crannies along the wall. She ignored it as much as she could, pinching her nose.

She started at the left side of the cave, working back to the tunnel she'd come from. For twenty minutes she worked, checking every square inch. She found nothing but guano and cobwebs. Occasionally, she came across what looked like bat bones and insect carcasses.

She rolled her neck and stretched her back again. She explored the other side. Nothing. Screwing her eyes shut for a moment, she reached her arms above her head. And there they were. At the very edge of the cave wall, maybe six feet up, was a row of carved glyphs. She held her breath.

Standing on her tip-toes, she faced the carvings, letting her headlamp illuminate them. There were three symbols covered with cobwebs. They were each about eight inches tall and close to the outer edge of the cave.

She was too short to get a good look at them. The headlamp threw odd shadows. She couldn't make them out. She needed to get closer.

"Shit," she said aloud. "Shit, shit, shit."

She stretched, trying to dust them off to get a better view. Suddenly, she heard a strange scraping sound and realized it was her. She was losing her balance. One of her feet was slipping, and she knew she was going over. "No. Not now. Not—"

CHAPTER 24

"I'VE GOT YOU." THE WORDS WERE FIRM, AND SHE FELT A STRONG HAND pulling her up, away from the edge. She gazed into Sullivan's eyes and almost collapsed with relief.

"You've got to help," he said, grimacing. "Remember, I've only got one good arm. And I'm old."

She laughed, pulling herself up into his chest, holding on. "Oh, my God. You scared me to death. You could have called out or something."

He gave her a lopsided smile. "I know. It's okay. And you're right. I should have called out. I wasn't thinking. I was trying to get through the tunnel. My balance is a bit off with this damned shoulder."

"You must be in pain, too. Why the hell did you come down here? You could have sent Mike."

"I wanted to come. You had been here a while. Since you didn't have the rope on, I had to see if you were, uh, okay."

"Oh." He had been worried about her. Her eyes filled with tears. "Sorry. I don't know why I'm crying. I seem to be crying all the time."

He wiped a tear off her nose. "You've been through quite a lot, Mac. You're entitled. You've been amazing. You've been strong and brave. And you stepped up to be the leader."

She gazed up at him, tears still rolling down her cheeks. "I have? I mean, I guess I have. This isn't like me. You should have known me before. I was timid and afraid and definitely not a leader. A mousey workaholic."

"Well, like I said, the canyons can change you. They will bring out the best—and worst—in you. You face your real self."

"Well, I'm certainly different. Not at all like the woman you met at the marina bar."

"Oh, I don't know. You were pretty feisty back then. A little pushy."

"Pushy? Really?" She smiled. "So which is it, strong and brave or pushy?"

He chuckled. "Two sides of the same coin."

"What coin?" Charlie stood at the tunnel entrance, shining his headlamp at them. "Did you find more treasure?"

Sullivan sighed. "No. Nothing like that."

Mackenzie wiped the last of the tears from her eyes and turned toward Charlie. "I did find something, though," she said. "Some glyphs. Over there. I can't make them out. I'm too short."

Charlie directed the light toward the cave wall she pointed at. He twisted his shoulders back and forth. "I bet I can decipher them. With your help." He walked over to her and, taking her hand, pulled her to him. "Excuse me, grandpa. We've got some work to do."

Sullivan snorted. "Right. Go for it, boy."

"Stop it, Charlie." She quickly reclaimed her hand.

He laughed and began whistling while he studied the panel.

Sullivan sat on the cave floor, saying nothing. She eased down next to him. "I never got a chance to say thank you," she whispered, "for saving my life. Again."

"It was nothing. My pleasure." He smiled down at her.

She flushed, glad it was dark.

"What are you whispering about?" Charlie's voice echoed off the walls. "Come over here. We need to finish this."

Mackenzie shrugged. She and Sullivan rose together. He kept his good arm around her waist, and she leaned into it. "Charlie, we need to figure out what they mean. It's getting late." She nodded toward the darkened sky.

"Okay." He pointed at the panel. "The first one's a combined symbol for 'above' and 'cave.' The second seems like it's for planting. Or digging a hole for something. The third one's the glyph for 'good' or 'right.'

"Hmm," she said. "The first set of symbols must mean 'above this cave.' The second, though is tricky."

"What's it for, again?" Sullivan asked, moving away. "I mean, tell me the whole meaning."

Charlie spoke slowly, in a monotone. "It's the symbol for planting. Not the word for what was planted, like the seed. That's a different symbol. It's for actually planting something. You know, like digging a hole."

Sullivan ignored the insult. "Digging a hole? Like digging a hole in the cave? Or in the floor? Or is it for the verb 'to dig?' "

"Stop." She thought back to something Sam had told her. "I've got an idea. I think it could be for a hole on the side of the mountain. You know, like Moki steps. They could be considered holes."

"Moki steps. You're right. It could mean that. You're brilliant." Sullivan flashed her a big smile.

"Moki steps?" Charlie asked. "Right. Yeah, I guess it could mean that. I had to climb some for awhile on the way to the cave."

"You did?" Mackenzie whirled around. "Why didn't you say anything?"

"It didn't matter before." He shrugged.

"It matters now," she said. "It has to be the way out. We have to climb some Moki steps."

They spent the rest of the night in the big cave. Mackenzie and Jennifer leaned against each other under some jackets to keep warm, while the men spread out.

When the first ray of the morning sun reached the cave, Sullivan was up. "I'm going down again. Who wants to come?"

Although no one answered, half an hour later they all gathered in there, in the newly christened bat cave.

"There. About a foot or eighteen inches up." Sullivan was on his back, leaning out of the cave opening, and Mackenzie and Charlie were holding onto his knees and ankles, trying to be a counterweight. He protected his injured shoulder, using his body only.

Charlie smiled at her, and her heart hiccuped. He really was good looking. His teeth were stunning against his tan, as were his blue eyes. Shit. She had to focus. "How far to the top?" she called out.

"Uh, I can't see all of it. There's an overhang. If it's the top, it's not more than thirty or forty feet from here."

Thirty or forty feet? That would mean twenty or so carved-out steps. She closed her eyes, feeling a bit faint.

"That's not so bad, Mac," Charlie said quietly.

"For you, maybe," she said. "And for Mike. Jennifer and I don't have any climbing experience. And Sullivan's hurt."

"But we have the orange cord. We can figure out a way to make it somewhat safe. Unless." He paused.

"Unless what?"

He didn't respond.

"Tell me," she ordered.

"Well, unless the steps have been worn down by wind and rain. It's hard to know."

She pressed her lips together, sorry she'd asked.

"Okay, I'm coming back," Sullivan said. "But keep holding on."

"I want to check it out, too," she said, when he was safe. "And I think Mike and Jennifer should see it." If they haven't killed each other first. Suddenly, the memory of Vic overwhelmed her. He should have been there. He shouldn't have died. She shook her head, trying to clear it.

"Okay, I think I can hold you." Sullivan removed his sling, rolling his shoulder. She got into position, leaning with her back to the abyss as far as she dared. He sat lightly on her legs, holding onto one of her hands. Tilting her head, she studied the rock surface, searching, and found them: small depressions leading diagonally up. The first one was to the left of the cave as she faced the wall, about a foot above the floor. It looked to be three or four inches in height. It was worn and appeared softened by time and weather. The wall curved at the top, so she couldn't see exactly where they ended. She wanted to lean farther back, to see more, but Sullivan wouldn't let her.

"Can you see them?"

"Yes. I counted, uh, eighteen steps. There might be a few more. It's kind of a jumble at the beginning."

"Great," he replied. "Come back, now. Please."

She allowed him to pull her back. Charlie scowled at her but said nothing.

"Steps," Jennifer said. "Like in stairways? Who made them?" She looked at Mike.

Mackenzie cut in before Mike. "No. They're not steps as we know them. They're holes carved into the rock, probably made by the Aztecs. They carved them so they could climb the sheer cliffs."

"Holes? Didn't they use ropes or ladders or something? I mean, they couldn't have just crawled up like Spiderman, right?"

"Nobody knows," Sullivan said. "Some think they used ropes. But I think they were raised to climb without ropes from childhood. There is a bit of a legend about them. Right, Mike?"

"Yup. They say that some of them are carved with a built-in security system. You see, they're really hand- and footholds, right? In Mesa Verde, they're spaced and angled so that you have to start them with the right, I mean, the correct, foot—or you end up in trouble. I'm not saying these are like that, but some of them were that way."

"And if you don't?" Jennifer asked.

"Well, if you mess up, you're out too far to go back."

"How can you tell which is which?" She frowned.

Sullivan said flatly, "You can't. Possibly, there were clues or indicators of some kind so the Aztecs could communicate to others which foot and hand to use. I've heard theories about that. Or they may have been so familiar with steps like these they just knew."

"Do you think we could climb them? I mean all of us?" Jennifer raised her brows.

"Maybe," he said. "They could also just peter out on the rock. Erosion does that. Even if there's no trick to choosing the right hand or foot. And going back is difficult at best. They're hell to climb back down. It's almost impossible."

"What about you?" Mackenzie gestured toward Sullivan's shoulder.

"Oh, I should be okay, as long as I keep three points on the rock."

Mackenzie dragged her fingers through the soft sand around her, unseeing. She felt nauseated.

"Well, we have to try, don't we?" Charlie addressed the group. "We don't have a choice."

They busied themselves with organizing and arranging, retrieving things from the main cave. It was a collective way of calming themselves.

"Hey, Mike, Could you help me for a minute?" Sullivan was sitting with his back to the cave opening. "I want to see the steps from another angle. Can you hang onto my belt? I'm going to lean out farther, if I can. Standing up."

"Should you be doing that? I mean with your shoulder and all."

Sullivan glared at him. "I'm fine. It's just a little sore."

Mike looked at Mackenzie, and she shrugged. "I'll help, too," she offered.

They arranged themselves on either side of the cave lip. Tossing her head, she flung a drop of sweat from her forehead.

Sullivan squatted, and Mackenzie and Mike took hold of his belt. He stood up slowly, leaning backward over the drop.

"I'm going to try one," he said.

"What," she choked out. "How?"

"I'm going to put my hand in one of them, to see how deep and slick they are. No worries." He edged farther over, and they tightened their hold on him.

"But, he's only got one arm," Jennifer said, to no one in particular.

Mackenzie sucked in air and concentrated on Sullivan.

"It feels pretty good," His voice sounded far away and odd. "Okay, I'm coming back. Oh, fuck."

Sullivan's feet went out from under him, and he landed on his butt on the sandy rock of the cave lip. Suddenly, he was on his back, most of his body hanging over the edge. Mackenzie and Mike hung on desperately to his belt. Time seemed to simultaneously slow down and speed up.

"Hang on," she croaked. Her hands were cramping from the unexpected weight.

Charlie squeezed in next to her. "Give me your arm," he said. Without waiting for a reply, he caught Sullivan's arm, and with a sharp tug, pulled him to safety.

"Oh, my God," Mackenzie said. "That was close." The words died in her throat. In the excitement, Charlie had grabbed the wrong arm. The injured arm. Sullivan's gash had reopened, and he lay there, moaning in pain, blood everywhere.

CHAPTER 25

She pressed down on the wound with both hands, trying to stop the bleeding.

Sullivan was ghostly pale.

"Uh, it'd be nice to hear a 'Thanks, Charlie, for saving his life.' " Charlie leaned against the wall above her.

"We're busy," she snapped. She closed her eyes. "But, yes, thank you."

"Well, he would have cracked his head open, at the very least," Charlie muttered. "I mean, if he didn't fall."

She looked up. "I said thank you. You did save his life, and you're right, it could have been much worse. But right now we have to take care of him, okay? He's still bleeding. Please, Charlie, please." Her voice broke at the end, like an adolescent boy's. Her hands were soaked, and she didn't know how much longer she could keep pressure on the wound. The flow seemed to be slowing down, but she hesitated to let up.

Charlie stuffed both hands in his pockets. "Yeah. I know, Mac. I'm a bit fried. Sorry. You're right of course."

Her right eye twitched. "No problem. We're all there. Can you come and put pressure on it? I'm losing strength."

He knelt beside her. Using his shirt, he placed both hands firmly on Sullivan's shoulder.

Mackenzie gazed down at Sullivan. What the hell was he thinking? She should have stopped him.

An hour later, she had finished bandaging Sullivan's arm with rags torn from their shirts. He was still unconscious, but his heartbeat was strong, and his coloring good. She turned to listen to the conversation going on around her.

"Well," Charlie said, "Having the rope doesn't help that much. I mean it can't save you from falling. It's not really meant to support a human being."

"What do you mean?" Jennifer stared at him. "It's a rope, for God's sake."

"I think what he means," Mike said, "Is that even if we tied ourselves to each other—"

"—When one of us falls, everyone does." Charlie ran his eyes over the solemn group in front of him.

"Can't we tie the rope to something?" Jennifer's voice was close to a squeak.

"Sure. You tell me what." Mike gestured to the small cave. "See anything?"

They automatically examined the cave. Although there were dozens of small ledges, there were no rocks they could tie the rope to.

Charlie continued, "Our best bet is to have one or two experienced climbers go first, carrying the rope. When we get to the top, we can send it down for the others."

Silence.

"Mac, don't you think that's the best course?" He was so eager for her approval, she thought. He was like a vulnerable puppy.

"Sullivan would know what to do," Jennifer said. "Why is he still out?"

"He lost a lot of blood," Mackenzie replied. "I assume that's it. I don't know. I'm not a doctor." She felt light-headed, and her damned eye kept twitching. She pressed it with the heel of her hand.

"Well, how much food do we have left?" Jennifer asked.

Charlie dug around in the backpack holding their food and water. "Not much. Five bars and a bag of Gorp. A bottle of water. That's it."

"We're going to starve," Mike said.

"No, we're not," Mackenzie replied quickly. "If we start thinking like that, we'll sabotage ourselves."

"Right," Charlie said. "I'm not saying we should be Pollyannas, but we do have to think positively." He winked at her and grinned.

"I'm not being a Pollyanna," she said. "It's merely the reality of the situation. We have to move forward, not backward, and we have to work together as a group."

Sullivan's words in the bat cave came back to her. She had somehow developed a leadership gene. What happened to the linguistics professor who was afraid to stand up in front of twenty kids? She wasn't the person she used to be, definitely not the person who fell in love with Charlie. She sighed. Maybe the new her would be better for him. Maybe they could make it work?

Her thoughts drifted to Sullivan, and once again she wished she knew if any part of her feelings for him were because of hardship. She wanted to believe it was real. He had changed, too, she thought. He wasn't the shut-down, arrogant bastard she had met at the marina. He was less guarded and open. At least for the last part of the trip.

She rubbed her forehead. A headache was beginning, and her eye throbbed. This was not the time to be thinking about this.

Mike cleared his throat, and she looked up. "I'm with Mac. We have to work as a team. Our food is almost gone, and more important, so is our water. We've got to get out of here. Even though we might not be able to use the rope, at least the first one in the group might get out safely and drop it down for the rest."

"I'm tired," Jennifer said. "I haven't slept well in days." She looked around, aggressively, daring a response. "None of us has. We'll be clumsy."

"That's true," Mike said. "We're tired and hungry. But our adrenaline will kick in, and it'll help. Believe me, I know."

Mackenzie took a deep breath. "We're exhausted, yes. But we can't wait." She voiced the words that had been gnawing at her. "Everyone needs to get out, but, uh, we need to figure out what to do with Sulley. He won't be able to climb."

There was no answer. She didn't think there would be.

Surprisingly, it was Charlie who spoke first. "We can't carry him," he said softly, "But we can come back for him. We will come back for him."

She placed a hand on Sullivan's arm. At that moment, she knew the decision was hers. That she would be the one to decide for Sullivan.

Her thoughts raced nonstop—layer upon layer of questions and possibilities, relentlessly piling up in her mind. How could she leave him here, alone and injured? If anything went wrong, he'd die in this cave.

She closed her eyes, and in the space of a few seconds it was settled. She would have to leave him. She couldn't let her emotions hold up everyone. It was the best decision, the only decision. They would make it out. And return for him.

She stood up. "All right. We can't waste any time."

Almost before her words were out, Charlie took over. "Now, before we get all excited, you need to know a few things about the steps. Well, not you, Mike. You seem like you know a lot. But Jennifer, you need to listen."

He repeated the history of the steps and how they were used for access to difficult-to-reach areas. "If we're lucky," Charlie informed them, "They won't be eroded. They'll be about two or three inches deep, and three or four inches tall and wide. Usually, the steps alternate between hand- and footholds. The handholds have a small lip, but the footholds don't."

Jennifer held out her boot. "Wow. I'm not going to fit."

"Well, you only need to get your toe in there, remember. Not your whole foot."

Charlie added, "Once you get started, always keep three points on the rock. Meaning, two hands and a foot, or two feet and a hand. It'll make sense when you're there."

Jennifer shook her head, looking bewildered. At that moment, with her wild eyes and dirty hair, she appeared fragile and waifish. Almost likable.

"If Sulley's right, we have eighteen steps or so, which means about thirty or forty feet of climbing," Mike said.

"What do you mean, if Sulley's right?" Sullivan spoke in a hoarse voice barely loud enough for the others to hear.

"Sulley. How do you feel?" Mackenzie clutched his hand, forgetting about the dirt and blood on hers.

He glanced down at his shoulder, wincing. "Did you bandage me again?"

She nodded. "Yeah. So don't look too closely. When we get out of here, you can have it redone."

He nodded, but the others remained silent for a long moment.

"About that," Charlie said. "Did you hear our plans? No? Okay, well, we're all going to climb out. Except you. You have to stay." He peered at Sullivan. "You okay with that?"

"Uh, no, actually I'm not," Sullivan said. "I think we all should go."

Mackenzie stared at him. "Wrong. You've lost a lot of blood, and you're in no condition to climb. We'll come back for you."

"I'm fine. Let me up. I'll show you." He pushed her away and sat up. "See?" He tried to stand but began to wobble and rock.

She rose and took his good arm, helping him to lie down again. He didn't protest.

"All right, then." She sat next to him. "You're staying."

He nodded. His face was pale, and he was sweating. "Okay. You win."

She grinned at him. "Finally, I get to tell you what to do."

He smiled weakly, wiping sweat from his forehead with the back of his hand. He reminded her of a little boy caught in a lie, and her heart swelled.

Charlie said quickly, "Okay. Let's get going. Mike, you go first. I'll go last. Jennifer, you and Mac will be sandwiched by us. We're going to take it slow. Leave some space between each other. You'll want to to catch up to Mike, but don't do it, Jennifer. Let him stay at least two holds ahead of you."

"I'll take the rope," Mike said. He looked at Sullivan. "We'll leave most of the water and food with you. What's left."

"You know what you're doing?" Sullivan regarded him through half-closed eyes.

"It's free soloing. Been doing that for years."

Charlie nodded, and Mike slung the rope over his shoulder.

"Here we go," Charlie said. "Let's do this."

Mackenzie moved to the edge and watched Mike get into position.

"How long was I out before you decided all this?" Sullivan asked.

She told him, abbreviating the conversation.

He shook his head. "So what did that last symbol mean?"

Mackenzie shook her head in frustration. He was distracting her. "Uh, we didn't get around to figuring it out. It didn't make sense. I mean, we know it has something to do with getting to the top." She paused. "You're wondering why they added another symbol?"

"Exactly," Sullivan said. "It's got to be important. They took the time to carve three symbols. I'm sure they didn't do it for fun. That third combined symbol has to mean something."

"You're right," she said thoughtfully. "It has to be a message of some kind." She looked at Mike, who was preparing to lean out to reach the first hold. "Mike, wait." Her voice echoed in the little cave. "Don't go, yet. Please."

The others froze like statues in various poses. Mike eased back into the cave.

"You can't go," she said, "until we figure out what the last symbol meant."

"I don't care what it means," Charlie said. "I don't think it matters. Tick tock."

"I know. But think. You know they wouldn't have written that third combined symbol for nothing. It's got to have something to do with the steps."

Mike and Jennifer sat down, too.

Mackenzie said, "Come on, let's at least try. All of us. The first symbol means above and cave. The second one is for a hole, a Moki step. The third symbol might mean something like 'right.' The right side? Or maybe the right way, as in correct? We have to put it together. It may mean the steps are the way to go, but I don't think so. That's too obvious, and the Aztecs were definitely not obvious. It must mean something else."

"But what else could it be?" Jennifer asked. "I mean, they're holes. Some for hands and some for feet, right?"

Mackenzie sat there, thinking, for several minutes. Something about Jennifer's words struck a chord somewhere. Suddenly, she gasped. "I've got it. I know what it means. Thanks to you, Jennifer." She grinned at the other woman, who looked perplexed.

Mackenzie smiled at Mike. "You're going to thank her for figuring it out."

"Come on," Charlie snapped. "Tell us."

"Well, like I said, Jennifer got it. Remember the legend about the steps?"

Charlie frowned. "Shit, Mac, this isn't a game."

Mike cut in. "Oh, yeah. I'd forgotten. There's more to it than steps. Is that what you mean? There's a specific beginning, and you have to use the correct hand and foot to start. It was like a final test, in case one of their enemies decided to follow them. You can get crossed and stuck if you're not careful."

"Yes," she said. "The third symbol has a double meaning. It's vague, so an outsider wouldn't get it. But it all makes sense now. The symbol's telling us to start with the right hand and the right foot."

"That's crazy," said Mike. "That means you have to commit from the start. Swing your whole body out there. Are you sure?"

"I'm not hundred percent positive, but it seems logical, from what I know of the Aztecs. They were such good climbers that throwing themselves out there from the first would be easy. Not so easy for outsiders. Enemies."

She stood up, rolling her neck, and walked over to the edge, leaning out behind Jennifer.

"Well, I'm not an Aztec," Jennifer said. "I liked it better before. Now there's too much pressure."

"You can do this," Mackenzie said quietly. "You know you can." She placed a hand on Jennifer's shoulder.

"I can go first. And take the rope." Charlie held out his hands.

Mike shook his head. "No. I'm fine. Just had to process for a bit. It's not like any climbing I've ever done." He settled the rope on his shoulder, tying one end to his belt.

Charlie chuckled. "It's an adventure, all right."

Mike ignored him. "Okay. Jennifer, watch what I'm doing. I'll guide you when I'm up there, too." He turned toward the wall. "So, right hand and right foot first."

He reached around the wall of the cave and stretched until he could place his right hand in the first hold. It was deep and had a big lip. Several feet beyond it, a few feet below the handhold, was another hold. It was nearly a yard from the cave wall, and he couldn't put his foot into it unless he swung out to it, which meant he would be hanging on the wall with only one hand. "Here goes nothing."

Straightening his shoulders, he let go, swinging around, and caught the other hold with his toe. It was angled away from the cave and deeper than it looked. He wedged his foot into it, clinging to the wall with his right hand.

"Fuck. What do I do now?" His voice was taut and high, like a wire stretched so thin it was about to snap. He was hanging on the wall, off balance, his left hand and foot dangling.

Charlie was right there. "Find the left handhold, Mike. That's it, reach for it. Easy, now. There. You got it. Now, relax. If you can't see the next foothold, scissor your left leg behind your right, using the wall. You'll be balanced and can take your time."

He grunted. "Okay. I'm okay. I see the left foothold. Looks easy after that. I hope." He placed his foot in it and perched on the cliff side like a beetle, butt out.

Jennifer's eyes were huge. "I can't do that," she cried. "I can't." She stared at Mackenzie.

Mackenzie lowered her voice. "Sure you can. You're tall and strong. Charlie will be right behind you. It's not very far. I know you can make it."

Moving behind Jennifer, he placed his arm around her and slowly walked her to the edge.

"No."

"Shh," Charlie said. "You saw what Mike did. Just do the same. Now that you know what he did, it'll be easier. Really."

She wiped a tear from her eye with the back of her hand. "Can you hold me while I start?"

"No, I'd throw your balance off. Trust yourself. Take it nice and slow, but keep moving. I'll be right behind you."

She nodded. She was as tall as Mike but with longer arms. She stretched for the first handhold and caught it easily. "It feels pretty secure. Oh, God. Here I go."

She lunged for the right foothold, swinging her body around, and jammed her foot into it. Wasting no time, she found the left handhold and pulled herself close to the cliff. "I've got it," she called out, not looking up. Her nose was pressed against the cliff face.

Mackenzie let out a breath. It had begun. Sitting at the edge was terrifying. She couldn't bear it if they fell. She didn't want to watch, but she couldn't look away.

Jennifer had both hands and feet in the holds but wasn't moving.

Charlie leaned out. "Great. Now, remember, always keep three points on the rock. If you can, move your foot first and then your hand. Right. Now keep doing that. You're a natural. Just stay focused."

Mackenzie looked at Sullivan. It was time. She wanted to say something poignant, something memorable and encouraging. She wanted to express all she felt for him in one pithy phrase. She was a linguist, dammit. Words were her tools.

She opened her mouth to speak, but he shook his head, smiling. He mouthed what she wanted to hear, "I know, I love you, too."

She stood there for an eternity—for a second. The world fell away, leaving only her purpose to climb the steps and save him.

Charlie had watched the interchange. He said gruffly, "Your turn, Mac. Ready?"

She ran her tongue over her lips and swallowed. "Ready."

When Mackenzie initially put her hand into the rough pocket, she faltered. Not as tall as Jennifer, she missed the foothold on her first try. For a long second she hung there by one hand, her arm twisting, her fingers locked. She couldn't look down, and she didn't want to look outward at the expanse of blue. She stared at the rock, seeing every crack and ledge and angle. Without thinking, she swung herself around, and planted her toe squarely in the hold.

She struggled to fill her lungs, which seemed smaller, somehow. Nonfunctional. She placed her hands and feet in the steps and allowed her eyes to scan the rock. The first eight steps were at an angle, requiring her to let go with her right hand and cross it over and above the left. Remembering that Sulley had told her feet were essential in climbing—for women, more important than arms at times—she hiked her left foot up to the next foothold. Her feet were secure now, and so she made herself relax. She began climbing, deliberately and cautiously.

As she moved, she forgot about Sullivan and Charlie. It became stone cold clear that she could die. She could plummet to the earth, whistling through the wind as she became one with it. Adrenaline flooded through her, and she switched into a higher gear. All she could do was focus on the Moki steps.

CHAPTER 26

IT WAS EARLY MORNING TWO DAYS LATER WHEN SHE rappelled down, stopping in front of the cave entrance. She let her thoughts drift back to the rescue. All four had made it out. It hadn't taken more than an hour to climb the steps. They were challenging, but reliable. And with each step she had moved against time, not with it, leaving Sullivan farther behind.

When the steps finally ran out, she wasn't at the top. The last few feet consisted of craggy rocks. She went rigid, but Mike had called down and dropped the rope for her. Grabbing it, she scrambled up to the top of the cliff and found herself on a wide mesa.

Miraculously, Sam was waiting for them there. He had guessed that if they weren't at the river, the only place they could be was above it. He had left the kayaks at the shore and climbed to the mesa. And called the sheriff's office, telling them his plan.

Even so, it still took a full day for the volunteer rescue team to arrive. The team checked for injuries and treated for shock before planning Sullivan's rescue.

Mackenzie had other plans. Once they assembled and laid out their gear, she gave them the news. She was going first. Of course, they argued, pleaded, and eventually attempted to order her. However,

Mike, Charlie, and Jennifer had sided with her, and they'd formed a solid wall of smelly, grimy, support. In the end the rescue team had given in. She'd go first but they would follow closely behind.

Now, though, hovering in the air in front of the cave, she hesitated. Sulley could be dead. It had been more than a day, and he was wounded. Maybe they'd been right. Maybe she shouldn't have been the one to find out. She clutched the rope. She could call out, and tug on the rope twice. They'd pull her back up.

No. Sometimes courage was simply ignoring those persistent voices in your head.

She hooked a toe into one of the steps and pulled herself closer. The cave was silent. He didn't call out to her, and she couldn't hear any movement at all.

Rappelling had been difficult enough, but figuring out how to disengage from the rope and stand on the rock was even harder. Her hands shook as she unclipped the carabiner and clung to the wall of the cave. She let the rope swing free.

"Sulley? Sulley, are you here?" She kept her voice low and inhaled, taking in damp air that reeked of guano and something else. It smelled dead. The cave smelled dead. She stood there, waiting for something, anything.

"Mac. Nice to see you." His voice was creaky, like that of a ninety-year-old man. She let out her breath all at once, and relief flowed through her. She moved cautiously into the cave and saw him on the ground near the back wall. He was tattered and thinner than she remembered, almost bony. Squatting, she saw that his eyes were sunken, his lips dry. The odor of stale blood and sweat mingled with other smells, and she had to swallow to keep from gagging.

"Why don't you come sit by me? I think I need some nursing." He waggled an eyebrow, and she laughed in spite of herself.

"Oh, you definitely need something, Dr. Sullivan. Or should I call you Cosmo?" She lowered herself to the ground next to him.

"Not Cosmo," he replied. "Unless I can call you Princess."

"Let's call a truce on names." She offered him a small sip of water from the bottle in her pack. He coughed.

She glanced at his crusty, bandaged shoulder, and then looked away. Did the smell mean his wound was infected? She couldn't tell. "How do you feel?"

"Good. Don't feel hungry, but that'll come. Water's good."

She gazed into his eyes, gauging his condition. He didn't look like he was in any condition to be lifted out.

"Back to the nursing, Mac. Maybe you could try a hug. See how it goes." With effort he pushed himself up until he was sitting upright.

She moved closer. "Like this?" She leaned against his good shoulder, and he flinched. She pulled back quickly.

"Uh, I guess we'll have to try something else. Apparently, my good shoulder is connected to the wounded one." He reached for her hand and brushed it with his lips.

She raised her hand to his face. "My lips are a lot cleaner, Sulley. And softer."

She leaned in and kissed him softly. He responded, his dry lips rough against hers. It didn't last more than a second. Afterward, she carefully placed her head in the hollow space under his good shoulder. They remained quiet for several minutes, at ease with each other. The rescue team would be there soon, she knew.

She wanted this moment to last. They were alone together, for the first time since the slot canyon. She fervently hoped his wound wasn't infected. And she wanted to be free of this damned cave and the canyons, free to start fresh.

He broke the silence. "What happened? How were you rescued?"

Mackenzie told him what had transpired, making it sound matter-of-fact. Easy. Her thoughts returned to Vic and the others, but only for an instant. There would be time to grieve. Time to sort out the unanswered questions that she was sure would come. Questions like, where was Sandy, now? What should they do about the gold? How should they go about retrieving the codex? Later, she told herself again, later. The biggest question had been answered, and she knew now she wanted to find the answers with Sullivan by her side.

She tilted her head up, her forehead grazing his stubbly jaw. She nuzzled his neck.

Sulley smiled. "Finally. I finally have you all to myself."

EPILOGUE

THE LOW GROWL OF THE HOUSEBOAT ENGINE WAS THE ONLY
sound that morning as they floated down the main channel of Lake
Powell. Mackenzie sat on the front deck, her legs crossed on the
railing. Behind her, Sullivan sat inside, guiding the boat. Every few
moments, she'd look back at him to point at something through the
captain's window, he would nod and smile.

After an hour, she wandered inside, where the air was significantly
cooler.

"Whew," she said. "I'm not sure if I'll ever get used to air
conditioning again." She wrapped her arms around her. "It's too
much like a cave."

"Most of the time I turn it off, but it's hotter than hell out there
today."

"Oh, I can handle it. It's the thought of a cave that makes me
queasy." She grinned. "I don't want to set foot in another cave for the
rest of my life."

He chuckled, gently turning the wheel.

She gazed at the lake, mesmerized. "This is odd. You've got to
admit it."

"What? Us on the lake in my houseboat? Weirder than all of the
other things that happened?"

"Well, it's hard to say." She slid into the matching chair next to his. Pulling both knees up, she placed her chin on them.

In the month since they were rescued, they had fallen into an easy routine. After an early breakfast, they floated lazily to a picturesque beach or canyon, swam in the lake, or explored the cliffs that bordered it. Sullivan knew the hidden places. Ruins that few people ever saw. Secret gardens in the soaring cliffs. They worked in the afternoon. At night, after dinner, they built a campfire or rested in the hot tub under a thicket of stars.

She said, breaking the silence, "You know, it's still hard to believe we all got out. Or, the five of us did." She looked down, thinking of Vic and Lucy and Henry.

He grunted, focused on steering.

"And how in the world," she asked, "Did Sam know where to find us? I thought he was going to wait down by the river."

"Apparently, he thought better of it. Said the map you showed him made him think. He knows these canyons better than anyone."

"It was quite a leap to recognize Gray Mesa as the mesa above the cave. I'm just glad he did. It's a big mesa. He could have missed us." She shivered.

He put the boat in neutral, letting it drift a bit. "But, he didn't."

The boat rocked gently, yielding to the water. After a few moments, he clicked the boat back in gear. "The really strange thing is what's going on with the gold."

They'd talked about this for hours on end. "I know," she said. "It's so damn complicated. The state of Utah, the federal government, and the Navajo Nation. They all have good claims. I'm surprised that Spain hasn't thrown a hat in the ring."

"You're not sorry we didn't take some with us, are you?" He raised an eyebrow.

"Nope," she replied. "I found myself a double treasure. You and the codex."

"Yeah, you did. And quit your job."

"Didn't quit. I'm just taking a leave of absence. While I write my paper."

"Right. While you hide out on my houseboat."

"I'm not hiding out." Mackenzie rolled her eyes. "Everyone important knows I'm here. Don't forget, my friend Hillary is coming out to visit in a week. You'll like her, Sulley."

"Don't change the subject. I still think you're holing up here."

"Well, maybe a little. But I need time. It's been all right with me here, hasn't it?"

"It's been all right. You know that. More than all right." His voice was husky.

He pointed to a little alcove with a narrow beach and generous overhang.

She nodded, and he turned the wheel. The sun was low, guilding the cliffs. The water glimmered in bright contrast. It was her favorite time of day. "I never thought we'd have any time together," she said. "I was sure we were going to die."

"I got to that place, too." He rubbed his shoulder unconsciously. "Thinking about you climbing the steps."

"I did all right. Those Aztecs knew what they were doing."

She uncoiled, stretching her legs, and stood behind him. "I was surprised at how well Jennifer climbed. Who knew?"

"I didn't tell you this," he said quietly, "But I almost went crazy when they lifted me out, leaving you behind in the cave."

"Really? I had no idea." During the rescue she had stayed behind, waiting for them to take care of him before letting them pull her up.

He hesitated. "Probably the injury. Clouding my mind."

She punched him on his good shoulder. "Have you heard from Sam?"

He shook his head. "No. And I just don't know what got into him. Maybe the stress was more than he realized."

"Maybe he needed to get away for a bit, to think."

"I guess," he replied. "I hope that's it. I'm not worried that he might get lost or anything, but it's never a good idea to go out into the canyons alone."

Mackenzie stared out the window. They were closing in on the little beach.

He caught her left hand, pulling her to him. She curled up against him. "You know, we haven't discussed this next month," he said.

"You mean when you go back to work?"

He snorted. "I have been working. Preparing. But, yes, when I go back to work." He'd taken a position as the head of the new Glen Canyon Medical Clinic.

"I guess it'll be tough. You being the only doctor at the Clinic. A lot of long hours and late nights. Especially till you hire a full-time nurse to help out. And there's winter."

"Don't even think about the winter. Winter in Lake Powell is unpredictable."

"You probably won't be that busy, though, right? Not too many people vacation here in the off season."

"Mac, you're avoiding the issue. You know what I want to talk about."

She took a deep breath. For the past weeks they'd been living in denial, not talking about the future. Or she had. Whenever he had broached it, she had evaded the topic, and he had grudgingly let it drop.

She had wanted to give herself—and them—time. Time to test their connection. Time together during normal, boring times. The in-between spaces in life that were so important.

They stopped at the little side canyon, and he slowed the engines, focusing on positioning the huge houseboat. She slipped out the side door to uncoil the rope and let down the fenders. When the water was shallow enough, he cut the engines completely and waded out to find a tree or rock to tie the boat up. Her job was to take up the slack and keep the rope taut. And back him up if anything went awry.

As Mackenzie watched him wade through the water, connected to her by the rope, she was overcome with the simplicity of it. She was making it too hard, too complicated. She had changed, and she would continue to change. That was guaranteed. But if she was with Sullivan, they'd change together. They weren't in a vacuum, she told herself, they were together. A man and a woman on either end of a rope.

He headed back to her. Nearing the side, he dived into the shallow water, shaking his head like a dog when he emerged.

She held out a hand when he reached the ladder.

"Okay," she said.

She pulled him up and wrapped her arms around his waist.

"I'll stay."

J. Reed Rich has worked in nonfiction publishing as an editor, production coordinator, book designer, and website manager. She canyoneers in her spare time with her husband and two dogs.

You may write to her at jamesonreedrich@gmail.com.

www.ingramcontent.com/pod-product-compliance
Lightning Source LLC
Chambersburg PA
CBHW031943130726
47905CB00002BA/480